grace river

Rebecca Hendry

LIBRARY AND ARCHIVES CANADA CATALOGUING IN PUBLICATION
Hendry, Rebecca, 1972–
Grace River / Rebecca Hendry.

ISBN 978-1-897142-37-0

I. Title.
PS8615.E539G73 2009   C813'.6   C2009-900982-X

LIBRARY OF CONGRESS CONTROL NUMBER: 2009920291

Editor: Lee Shedden
Cover image: Hal Bergman, istockphoto.com
Author photo: Lizette Fischer

Canada Council   Conseil des Arts   Canadian   Patrimoine
for the Arts   du Canada   Heritage   canadien

Brindle & Glass is pleased to acknowledge the financial support to its publishing program from the Government of Canada through the Book Publishing Industry Development Program (BPIDP) and the Canada Council for the Arts.

Brindle & Glass is committed to protecting the environment and to the responsible use of natural resources. This book is printed on 100% post-consumer recycled and ancient-forest-friendly paper. For more information, visit www.oldgrowthfree.com.

Brindle & Glass Publishing
www.brindleandglass.com

1 2 3 4 5 12 11 10 09

PRINTED AND BOUND IN CANADA

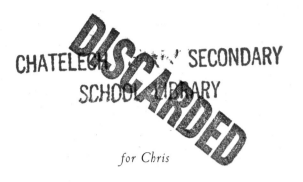
for Chris

The care of rivers is not a question
of rivers, but of the human heart.
—Tanaka Shozo

part one

Jessie

race River is like this: You're driving along the highway from Kelowna or maybe Osoyoos and everything is pretty flat except for the low hills that kind of bump along beside the road like little brown waves. For a couple of hours there's not much at all to see and then suddenly you turn a bend and there they are—the giant smokestacks of AXIS Smelting and its network of metal-sided buildings reaching out around the town like the arms of a protective parent. Then it's time to turn right, and when you do, you're on what will turn into the main street of town, which really is the only street worth mentioning. I mean, there are a few side streets, but the businesses on those are basically just the dusty old travel agency that's run by Patty Eldred, who I happen to know sells pot out of the storage room in the back, and the Chinese restaurant that I've never seen a person eat in since the rat foo yung story, and the discount clothing store that sells cheap underwear that loses the elastic in the waist so they wind up bunching up under your jeans and driving you crazy.

The main street is what the town has put all its high hopes into. The storefronts are redone with that heritage look everybody's so hot about these days and the hanging flowerpots, which makes it kind of feel like you live in a decent place with decent people, if you forget about the rat foo yung and the pot-selling just around the corner.

So it's 6:45 on a Tuesday morning and I'm in the Nick's Diner parking lot, right on time. Nick's is basically just off the highway, across from AXIS, which is great for business, but it isn't exactly part of the whole "beautification" project. It's about a block from where the town proper starts, and it's an ugly, squat, grey concrete building with a huge parking lot and then not much but dead earth until you hit Annemarie's flower shop. The town has talked about maybe putting in some condos or another hotel or something, but we already have a fancy hotel with a classy bar that most of the AXIS guys don't pay much attention to, plus a motel with little cabins on the way out of town, so who knows?

Soon I'll be stacking greasy dishes and trading insults with the guys, but for now I just sit and watch Daniel's *Playboy* air-freshener finish her dance from the bumps we hit on the gravel road. She's blonde and used to smell like summer peaches, but that's about the only thing she's got going for her. Her red lips have faded to pink and there's a white scar on her leg where the paper's been torn.

The reason I'm not hopping out of the truck and jogging in there with a big smile on my face is because I'm bone-tired. Lately I've been waking up in the night feeling like there's someone sitting on my chest, trying to press all the air out and leave me as flat and limp as an ironed-out dress. Last night I shook Daniel hard and told him to wake up, told him something was really wrong. He just lay there squinting at me in the dark and told me to go back to sleep.

Once, a few weeks ago, I even called the hospital. I know it sounds stupid, but Daniel was on night shift and sometimes when you're alone and it's dark and you're scared you lose control of your logical thinking. I was pretty sure I was having a heart attack or something, but they asked me if I had any pain and I had to say no. Not really. Not the kind you could put your finger on.

Anyway, last night after Daniel rolled over and kept on snoring, I went into the kitchen and made a grape jelly sandwich and sat at the table staring out into the blackness of the front yard. There wasn't much of a moon, but I could see the dark outline of Black Rock a mile or so toward town at the edge of Tom Bailey's hobby farm; it's hard not to notice the only thing that stands more than five storeys in all of Grace River, even if it is just a big old hunk of rock.

So I sat there and stared and ate and I didn't budge until that plastic owl clock that used to belong to Daniel's grandmother flicked over to five and started hooting at me. I guess I'll be drinking my fair share of Nick's battery-acid coffee today.

The diner is still pretty quiet, except for the yammering of the morning news from Vancouver on the wall-mounted TV in the corner. Nick's is a big, old-fashioned diner, the kind with the grill flush against the back wall and the long counter where folks sit and watch Nick cook their food.

I walk past the counter heading for the back storage room, and the smell of fresh coffee and slabs of grilled maple ham follow me like a familiar perfume. I breathe it all in, and it reminds me more of home than the farmhouse I live in with Daniel and our daughter, Lily, with the white lilac growing outside the kitchen door, the sweet rows of hyacinths blooming in their window boxes as we speak.

Jackson says, "Hey, Jess," as I go by, but the other guys are too engaged in some heated debate over a case of beer that went missing on Saturday night from the back of Bobby's truck up at Jade Lake. I grab a clean apron, put it over my uniform and tie it in back. We must be the only diner left in central BC where the waitresses still wear uniforms, but Nick likes the look of them. They remind him of those movies about teenagers in the 1950s, like *American Graffiti* and *Rebel Without a Cause*. Nick's big on old movies. He used to watch them when he was a kid in that country nobody around here can ever pronounce right.

"Jess, you picking those coffee beans yourself back there?" Bobby's gnawing on a toothpick when I return from the storage room, his plate painted with ketchup and yellow smears of egg. I pour his coffee and reach over to give him a swat on his red Anderson Trucking hat with my free hand and then move on down the counter and pour some for Mike.

"Jezzie—take the garbage out, will ya?" Nick yells. "Will ya" comes out more like "Vill ya," but Nick likes using Canadian slang, even though it sounds so funny coming from him. Also, you'd think with his wrinkles and grey hair and all that he's maybe hard of hearing too, but no, he's just loud.

"Do I have to do everything around here?" I say, but I'm only kidding. I peel the black bag from the can near the grill, and Nick gives me a little bump with his hip as he reaches up to the shelf for more bread.

"You do if your crazy friend doesn't show up soon."

Sunny isn't known for punctuality. She's known for quite a lot of other things, but being on time has never been one of her biggest concerns.

I walk past the deep freeze, kick open the door, and step outside to the back parking lot. The ground under my canvas sneakers is cracked and red as dried blood as I walk over and heave the bag into the dumpster. I step back and stretch my arms out, still not fully awake. It'll be hot today. It was yesterday too. It's too hot for early June … usually I don't feel like I'm trapped in a locked oven until mid-July.

The screen door slams shut behind me and I turn to see Sunny tying up her apron. "Hey, girl," I say. "You're late again. Nick's pissed."

She shrugs and flashes her sly smile. "Are you kidding? Nick loves me. He tells me so every time he gets drunk." She digs a cigarette from her apron pocket. "Stay out here for a sec, Jess. It's real quiet in there. Just the boys so far." She offers me the pack of Export lights.

I shake my head. "Uh-uh. I quit again." I chew my nail. It's only been a few days. To tell the truth I'd rather go inside and scrub out the pots from yesterday than watch Sunny suck the smoke in and blow it out in to the morning air like a halo around her pretty, dark hair.

She turns her face up to soak in the sun. "Beautiful, huh? Sometimes I actually forget it's so horrible here."

"Come on, let's get in there before we both get fired."

"Jess. You okay?"

"Oh, you know. Yeah, I'm okay. Just tired." I could tell Sunny about last night, but when I play it over in my head and edit out the parts that would bore her, all that's left is a bad case of insomnia. I pull open the door and it screams on its hinges. "Door needs oil, Nick," I yell.

"I'll call the newspaper," he yells back, loud enough for the whole diner to hear, and possibly Annemarie's flower shop down the street. Nick is cracking eggs onto the grill with gusto as he rants at the guys at the counter, going on about the provincial smoking laws.

I pick up a spray bottle and sponge and start on the pie cooler.

"Your government treats you like children," he raves, waving his grease-splattered spatula in the general direction of Bobby and Mike. "Little children who can't control themselves."

I'm watching the guys openly stare at Sunny's rear end as she sways over to a table by the window. "Well, Nick," I say, "some of us can't."

He stops long enough to point a finger at me. "*You*," he says sternly. "You are the worst of all. You complain about smoking all the time and you still do it. No self-control. They have you right where they want you."

I pull the banana cream out of the case and inspect the wire rack it had been sitting on. "I quit three days ago."

Applause erupts from Mike and Jackson, and Bobby pounds the counter with his fist in mock frustration.

"Excellent, excellent," Mike crows. "Good job, Jess. Thank you once again for contributing to the beer fund."

I'm suspicious about the excitement. I've quit about five times in the last year, so it's not like a major newsflash or anything. Bobby takes a swig of coffee and winks at me. "Hey." I shake a finger at him. "You bet I couldn't quit? You're cursing me. It's your fault I can't quit for good." He makes a show of taking a five-dollar bill out of his wallet and handing it over to Jackson.

I can see a man signalling me from a window seat, so I grab a menu and the coffee pot. "Well, now I'll have to find something else to do with my hands. Maybe I'll take up martial arts and kick all your asses."

"I bet Daniel can think of something for you to do with your hands," Mike calls after me, and they all bust out laughing like it's the funniest thing they ever heard.

The guy by the window has papers spread across the table and he's bent over them making notes. I put the menu down in front of him.

"'Morning. Coffee?"

"Yeah, sure, that would be great." He doesn't look up. I hate that.

"Did you want to know the specials? Or should I just leave you alone?"

Now he looks up. "I'll just have some oatmeal, if you have it." He seems amused. Right away I can tell he's not from around here. One, there's only 2,426 people who live in our town and I don't recognize him. Two, he's wearing one of those necklaces made out of braided string with a coloured bead knotted into the middle. Men from here do not wear necklaces. Period. Guys from Nelson do, and Kaslo. Peachland,

Summerland, sure. I've even seen a guy wearing a sarong on the beach in Penticton, which had Daniel laughing so hard I thought he would choke on his Big Mac. But here in Grace River? No way.

"Sure. Hey, your eyes are the same colour as mine. Maybe you're my long-lost brother." They are too. Kind of a greeny-grey, like the river when the sun is shining on it..

He smiles. "Hmm. Well ... do Alice and Dean of Bellevue, Washington, sound familiar?"

"Nope. How about Gary and Sue of Grace River, BC?"

He pretends to think about it and I laugh and go to place his order.

Sunny follows me behind the counter and starts to pour orange juice for her new customers. I snap the oatmeal order onto Nick's spinner and glance over to the table. The out-of-towner is absorbed in whatever he's reading.

Sunny drums her painted nails on the counter. "Well. He looks like a very peaceful little hippie. He fits right in with the rest of you boys." She directs this at the guys, who are just starting to get their hard hats and gloves gathered up. "And he's cute, too," she adds. They toss change on the counter and glance over to check out my customer. His hair is long enough to get in his eyes and he pushes it back off his forehead as he reads.

"Ten bucks says he's here on his way to the Nelson Fairy Field Party or whatever the hell it's called," Mike says.

Jackson shakes his head. "No." He's watching thoughtfully as the guy studies his papers and ignores his coffee. Jackson notices things that other people don't bother to pay attention to. "Twenty bucks says he's an environmentalist type."

Bobby laughs. "Oh, Jesus, will those guys ever fucking quit?" He grabs his hat, and him and Mike start walking toward the door. Mike stops near my customer's table and holds up two fingers. "Peace, man," he says in a bad Cheech and Chong impression and heads out the door.

I shake my head. "Idiot."

I clear the plates and crumpled napkins and sticky syrup bottles off the counter and head into the back to dump the dishes. Nick is grumbling to himself as he doles out a gloppy mess into a white bowl. "Here you go. Two dollars' worth of oatmeal for half an hour of scrubbing the pot." He inspects the diner, which has practically cleared out now that most of the AXIS workers are gone. He grabs a folded newspaper from the counter and heads to the back. "I go outside. You call me if you need me to crack more eggs. I go read some more lies." He taps the paper meaningfully. "Lies, all of it. I might as well read *National Enquirer.*"

I pile the brown sugar and small pitcher of cream onto the plate. "I'll ask my mom for you, Nick. She's got a nice tall stack of them in the living room."

When I place the oatmeal in front of the customer he doesn't look up. I have to reach down and move some papers aside with my free hand, which startles him. "Oh. Thanks. Hey, could I get some more coffee?"

"Sure." I glance back at the counter where Sunny and Jackson are still chatting. "So. Are you just passing through?"

He tips some cream into the bowl and then spoons some brown sugar on his oatmeal. It doesn't escape me that he's taking his sweet time answering. I notice the light-brown freckles scattered over his arm as he stirs and consider counting them for something to do while I'm waiting when he finally says, "I'm just doing some work on the river."

"The Grace River?"

He stops stirring and looks up. "We're investigating some environmental concerns."

"Ahh. Environmental concerns." I check over my shoulder, wondering if I owe Jackson twenty bucks or if I managed to keep my mouth shut when he was making the bet.

"Are they serious concerns?" I tilt my head in that perky friendly waitress way that usually gets me good tips, but he just takes a sip of coffee and looks out at the parking lot.

"Sure," he says. "Yes. There are serious concerns."

I want to say "What else is new," but instead I say, "So ... are you going to shut us down?" I'm playing one of those inside jokes that you wouldn't understand unless you're from around here. Here's the joke: Environmentalists have been crawling all over this place since I was in diapers, since my parents were in diapers, for god's sake, and guess what? AXIS does prevail! Hooray for AXIS. The funny part is how seriously he seems to be taking it all.

He smiles, finally, and shakes his head. "Oh, I doubt that." I'm not sure what he's smiling at, but at least I know he's not delusional.

I lean in a bit. There are still some guys from the plant sitting at a table in the corner. "Most of the people I know work at AXIS," I say quietly. "Or else their husbands do."

He nods, his eyes flickering to my wedding band. "Sure," he says. He taps his fingers on his papers for a minute. "I'm just doing research on the river, salmon stocks, lead and arsenic content in the sediment. That's all."

"Hmm," I say, nodding my head in that sideways interested way as I check over and see that Jackson and Sunny are watching me now. "Well, according to the news we're all going to hell in a handbasket anyway, right? I mean, AXIS is just a little blip on the radar, isn't it?" Jackson rubs his fingers together like he's holding a wad of cash. Outside I can see Mike and Bobby pile into Bobby's truck. They wave as they pull away. I lift my hand in response.

"That's one way of looking at it," he says. He's watching the guys too. "That's not how I look at it. That attitude is the reason the world has ended up in this state."

I'm momentarily stunned, and in very un-Jessie-like fashion I can't think of anything to say.

"It's interesting, though," he says. "People are often terrified of change until they're shocked into seeing what's really going on around them. Sometimes they realize that the way things are right now is actually pretty bad. They just haven't noticed. Know what I mean?" He gives me a calm little smile.

I stare at him while I think about that for a bit. It's funny, but I'm not offended. I think he's got a pretty good point. But the fun has been deflated out of the conversation like it got pricked with a pin. "Well," I say. "I'll just go get that coffee."

After my shift I sit and melt in the front seat of the truck for a minute. My feet are swollen and throbbing so I reach down and peel my socks and sneakers off. God. I could go to sleep right now if I didn't have to pick Lily up from my mom's and get home to start dinner. The sun is so bright I have to squint even with my eyes closed.

I start up the truck and crank the window down as I pull away from Nick's, waving to Sunny and Glory, the girl who took over for me. Sunny is still counting out her tips at the counter inside. She can't see me, her dark head bent over, a beer cracked open and waiting near her elbow. If it were six years ago, before I had Lily, I would just wait for Sunny, we would grab a few beer from the cooler and pay for them with our tips, then head out to Jade Lake to float around and wash off all the work sweat and obnoxious comments and returned food and roving eyes.

So much changes when you have a kid. I wouldn't take it back, though, that's not what I'm saying. It's just sometimes my body still remembers what it was like before, it sends those little messages of longing like when you think of your first kiss or a fifth-grade talent show when you brought down the house with your dance routine to a Bee Gees song. It's hard to feel spectacular when you have to go home and take your kid out of her Kool-Aid-stained clothes and pull the hamburger out of the freezer.

At the end of Main Street I roll on to the AXIS Memorial Bridge, a small bridge that just crosses the width of the Grace River, which is only about sixty feet across. The bridge is named for five AXIS workers who were killed by a chemical explosion in 1962. The sunlight glints off the river, which looks cool and green and almost good enough to swim in, if you didn't mind the fact that the drainage pipes from AXIS pumped god knows what into it all day long for about a hundred years until pretty recently. I know, I know. But it's not like I never thought about these things before that environmentalist came along.

For instance, I can still remember the very last time I jumped off the bridge into that water. We used to do it all the time, all the kids did. It was the fastest way to cool off in the summer. This last time I was eleven, wearing my new yellow-striped bikini, and I was there with Sunny and Jackson. I jumped first, plugging my nose and point-ing my toes and slicing that water like a smooth knife. I remember the smack of cold, the moment when I couldn't breathe, when my heart pounded in my ears and my lungs felt full to bursting. I rose up to the surface, my long hair tangled with a floating river reed.

When I rubbed the water from my eyes I was still the only one in the river. I yelled up to Sunny to jump, but I could see her and Jackson standing on the bridge shaking their heads. There was someone else with them. I squinted, then shaded my eyes. It was my dad, glowing red, backlit by the noon sun. He was on his way home for lunch from the smelter. He hung over the rail, waving at me. "Get out of there, Jessie," he called. "Come on, now."

Sunny, her neon pink lightning bolt earrings swinging, gestured to me quickly, a finger sliding across her neck. *You're in trouble.*

But when I hauled myself up onto the rock wall and dripped my way over to Dad, he just shifted his newspaper to his other hand and scratched his head, looking like he wasn't so sure what he wanted to say. Jackson handed me my ragged old Holly Hobby towel, which I took and covered up with. Though I was only eleven, I was still pretty modest, especially since I had started the faintest hint of what my mother called "a chest."

I gave him a little wave for encouragement. "Hey, Dad." Water dripped from the end of my nose, and I wiped it away with a corner of towel.

He smacked the newspaper lightly in his hand. Smack, like a nervous tic or something. My dad wasn't the smoothest operator. My friends called him "Gilbert" behind his back, like the dorky guy from *Revenge of the Nerds.* He scratched his head again, then pointed out at the river. "You ... uh ... you shouldn't be swimming in there."

I nodded. I knew this already. I had been told I probably shouldn't swim in there, even our school had made a point of telling us. The thing was, we figured, what harm could it do? I mean, we weren't drinking it or anything. "Yeah, I know, Dad. But I was just really hot, so ... "

He looked expectant. I had this habit of ending sentences on "so" when I didn't have anything else to say. Behind him Sunny and Jackson were shifting their weight back and forth like they had to pee. I knew they still wanted to jump in too.

He just smacked the newspaper and frowned up at the sun. "You go on home now," he said. "You kids find something else to do."

Later that same day, when I was sitting in the living room with the fan pointed right at me while I played Chinese checkers by myself, arranging all those little marbles into patterns, my dad came home from work, his tie askew, his hair plastered to his face from sweat. He was carrying a plastic grocery bag, cradling it like a baby, and he called out to me. I turned, marble in hand.

He pointed to the door with his chin. "Come on out to the garage. I want to show you something." He seemed excited and nervous at the same time. It was enough to capture my interest, and I dropped the marble, untangled my long legs, and jumped up.

The hills in the distance shimmered with a haze of grey wisps. I hopped awkwardly out to the garage on bare feet, trying not to let them touch the searing-hot driveway for more than a second at a time.

The garage was cooler. It smelled like grease and gas, and the air tasted like copper pennies. I eyed the old fridge Mom kept in the corner for grocery overflow. There was a box of Popsicles in the freezer, but I had already had three that afternoon. I was pretty sure I wouldn't get away with a fourth. Dad dropped the plastic bag on a stained patch of cement and knelt down next to it.

He hadn't said a word, and now he just untied the knot carefully and peeled the plastic back. "Look at that." He was almost whispering, shaking his head like he could hardly believe what that wrinkled soggy plastic bag was holding.

I peered over his shoulder as he pulled the plastic back more. "So what?" I said. "It's a fish. So what?"

My father wiped his forehead with his sleeve. "Yes. It's a salmon, actually. Quite rare to see them up here. It's ... well, I don't know how it died, it could just be old age, but its heavy metal readings were through the roof. I ran a couple of tests on it yesterday." He looked at me now, his glasses slipping a little on his sweaty nose. "This fish is the reason I don't want you in that river."

I stared down at that fish, the sickly white clouds on its scales, the milky green of its head. The cold dead eyes looking like they had seen something they wished they could forget.

After the bridge you're on the other side of town, which is where most of the houses are. They all kind of look the same, little stucco and wood houses built in the 1950s, with their little square lawns and their little picket fences. Some of them are starting to fall apart now, the stucco coming off in chunks, the fences missing posts, but not my parents' place. There are sunset roses blooming in the front of the house, and a wishing well with a sign that says "Free Wishes" and a bunch of ugly garden gnomes, which my mother has made a habit of collecting from garage sales and repainting.

Lily is perched on the front porch watching Dad, who's hunched over the lawnmower, pulling it across parched grass that already looks about as short as you could expect grass to be unless you actually shaved it bald. He's wearing a button-up short-sleeved cotton shirt, and it's stuck to his back with sweat. You can see right through to his undershirt.

I push the truck door open and have to suck my breath in at the heat rising up from the pavement. I wave and call hello. Dad can't hear me over the drone of the mower, but Lily stands and waves back excitedly.

"Hey, Momma!" she shouts.

Dad turns off the mower when he sees her jumping around. He gives me a little salute. "How was work?"

I shrug. "The usual." I head across the lawn to Lily and settle on the porch beside her, hug her close. She smells like sunshine and cut grass.

"Grandpa let me mow," she announces solemnly, aware of the huge responsibility he had given her.

Dad inspects the patch he just mowed and then nods to himself, satisfied. He returns his attention to me. "Your mother is inside making your dinner. She figured you'd be tired."

"I'm okay. Just hot." I pat Lily. "Let's go in and see Grandma."

Inside the house it's dark and dank, the heat having worked its way in and found a place to die. The heavy orange drapes are pulled shut to keep out any trace of sunshine and the air smells of canned tuna and boiled peas.

"In here, honey," Mom calls from the kitchen. Lily and I look at each other and wrinkle our noses.

"Yuck," says Lily. "What stinks?"

"Grandma's cooking," I whisper.

The kitchen is even hotter, but at least there's a light on so you don't feel like you're in a cave. A small black and white TV is blaring from the counter, a gift my father gave to Mom about twenty years ago.

Mom is bent over the stove, just pulling her tuna concoction out of the oven. "How was work?" she asks.

I sit in a chair at the kitchen table, and Lily sits on my lap. "Fine. Good. You didn't have to cook, Mom, it's enough you had Lily."

She plunks the casserole onto the stove and pulls off the oven mitts. "Oh, please. You know it's no work at all to have Princess Lily-flower here."

Lily smiles, her body bobbing up and down on my lap.

"We had fun, didn't we, honey?"

"Yup. Grandpa let me mow."

My mother looks from me to Lily, then back again, as though this were the biggest news she'd heard all day. "Did he now? Well, you better go and get yourself a Pepsi from the fridge in the garage. You deserve it after all that hard work. And bring your grandpa one too."

Lily claps and wriggles off my lap.

"Mom ... " I want to tell her Lily can't have a pop right before dinner, but as usual she puts a hand up and silences me. I roll my eyes and wait for her to speak, but she's silent until Lily's out of earshot.

"What, Mom? What?" I whisper, irritated.

She points at me, looking at me long and hard over the rims of her giant reading glasses. "You look like shit, Jessie."

I look away, down at the table. There's a stain on the tablecloth that looks like dried tomato sauce. I start picking at it. The thing about my mother is, when she says something like that it comes out accusatory instead of concerned. Like I need to make more of an effort not to look like shit.

"Jess? Did you hear me?"

I pick another flake off, then dust my hands off and stand. "Thanks for making our dinner, Mom, but I don't think we can stick around. I've got to get home." I try to think of a good reason why. "Daniel will be home soon, so ... "

She shakes her head at me and gestures to the casserole. "It's already done. Just take it." More head shaking. I feel like I could just melt into a puddle around my bare feet, and part of me wishes I could, just to disappear out of this sweaty tuna-reeking kitchen. The TV is blaring about some movie star's Malibu mansion being up for grabs. Only 24 million! What a deal. "I can't believe you watch this crap, Mom," I say.

Mom leans back against the counter and folds her arms. She doesn't answer, still watching me like she's having some psychic all-knowing mother moment in which she can see right through me. If she could, all she would see is a tired waitress who wants to go home, sit on the porch, put her feet up, drink an iced tea, and just be left alone. I walk over and kiss her cheek. "Nothing's wrong. I'm just tired," I say in her ear. I wrap a dishtowel around the casserole. "Thanks for the food." I head for the screen door and kick it open.

"Anytime. That's what I'm here for, right?" The volume of the TV goes up a few more notches as the door slams behind me.

Lily has returned to the front porch, where she's sipping a Pepsi, some of which has spilled near her feet and is pooling in a small brown pond that she taps absently with her toe.

"Up, Lily." I nudge her with my foot. "Let's go." I'm halfway to the truck with the casserole dish burning through to my fingertips when my dad comes out of the garage and calls me.

He jogs over to catch up. "Let me get the door for you." He opens the truck door and I set the dish on the floor. Lily's legs aren't long enough to reach the dish so I don't have to worry about her burning herself.

I wipe my forehead. The sun is piercing, bouncing off the water shooting from a neighbour's sprinkler. "Thanks, Dad."

Lily hasn't moved. "Come on! Get a move on, little girl." My patience is wearing thin now.

Dad smiles at me. "You do look worn out."

"So I hear. Lily!" She rises reluctantly and meanders across the lawn, collecting cut grass on her Pepsi-covered feet.

"Why don't you go for a swim? Take Lily up to the lake. You used to go up there all the time, didn't you?" He picks Lily up and settles her on the seat of the truck. Dad is the polar opposite of my hidden-agenda-filled mother. He has no agenda. He really just wants to be pleasant, wants everything around him to be pleasant, doesn't like to talk about anything that isn't pleasant...

Lily glares at me. "Let's GO." She swings her pointed feet toward the casserole. They actually almost reach. She's growing fast.

"Fine. Okay." I close her door and my dad reaches his hand in the open window to give her face a squeeze.

"Until next time, Miss Lily."

I give him a quick hug. "Okay then. Thanks for everything."

"Sure. And say hello to Daniel. Oh ... by the way. It's not a big thing, Jessie, but he did say a while back that he would take a look at our carburetor. I can take it in to the shop if he's too busy, I just thought I would check in ... "

"I'll remind him." Daniel isn't the best when it comes to keeping promises.

We head back toward the bridge, then turn left and follow Route 36 along the river. Once you get out of town, which is about three blocks, there isn't much to see except the odd farmhouse with stacks of rusty metal and car parts on the front lawn, and then Tom Bailey's hobby farm with Black Rock stuck on one end of it. And then there's Drake's mechanic shop, which is part of Billy Drake's fifteen-acre property. But other than that it's just winding road, with the river on one side and those brown, waving hills on the other.

"I'm hot," Lily announces.

The breeze coming through the open windows feels like it went through a sauna before it got to us. "No kidding."

She looks at me. "You're grumpy. Where's Dad?"

I turn left onto our dusty dirt road. I think about the four loads of laundry sitting on my bed, the breakfast dishes piled in the sink. Daniel won't be home until nine. I lied to Mom to get out of the house. So it's just me to cook dinner—there's no way either of us will eat my mother's tuna surprise—and do all the housework and get Lily to bed. Lily looks miserable and she's absolutely filthy. Even her blonde curls are sweaty.

"Tell you what, kiddo. Let's run in and grab our bathing suits and head out to the lake. What do you think?"

"But it's a long drive. Super long. And I'm hungry! I only had a Twinkie for lunch."

"Your grandmother gave you a Twinkie for lunch?"

"Two."

"That's great. Super." I think fast. I don't want to cook, I don't want to serve, I just want to be in that lake. "We'll grab a burger from Dairy Queen. Okay?"

Her eyes widen and she nods, then claps her grimy hands together. "Yay!"

I let my breath out in relief. Okay. This will be way easier. As I turn down our driveway I consider calling Sunny but decide against it. Just Lily and me. It'll be good.

Later that night I'm sitting on the front porch when I see the headlights of Daniel's truck off in the distance like the shining eyes of a cat or a coyote or something even bigger and meaner. That truck is something else. We can't afford it, not even close, but that didn't stop Daniel from picking it out of a lot full of shiny brand-new vehicles in Kamloops and signing away on the dotted line. We barely make the payments every month, but god forbid I should mention the fact that if we took it back we might not have to buy the generic brand of coffee that comes in the huge yellow container and tastes like it's had rusty nails soaking it.

I'm drinking it now, which is why it's fresh in my mind. It's late, after eleven, and Lily is tucked away into bed, the smell of lake mud and fresh mountain water on her skin. I'm one of those people who can drink coffee anytime, and it doesn't seem to bug me. I can drink it right before bed, which is what I'm doing now, and then five minutes later my head hits the pillow and I start snoring away. Getting to sleep isn't the problem ... lately, *staying* asleep is another thing entirely.

I'm on the lounge-type lawn chair, the one that's long enough to stretch your legs out all the way, and I'm just enjoying the cool air, the way all the plants in the garden seem to release that earthy smell into the sky when there's nothing moving around anymore, when everything gets still and quiet. I can smell overripe strawberry from here, even though the little patch is over by the side of the house. And mint and lemon balm that Kali came over and personally planted after the last ones she gave me died a slow and painful wilting death in the pots.

I close my eyes as Daniel's truck gets closer. Take a few deep breaths. Not that he stresses me out or anything, I just know it's the end of the solitude. The silence. The lake wasn't as relaxing as you would think ... you can't exactly float on your back and forget all your worries when you have a six-year-old wrapped around your throat calling you a bad dolphin and ordering you to let her ride on your back. Luckily she wore herself out after a while of splashing and yelling, "Watch this!" every ten seconds and she went up and played on the shore, hacking at the sand like she was holding an axe instead of a shovel and singing the alphabet at top volume.

Then I swam out to the dock, just a floating raft about forty feet from shore, taking long strides, stretching every muscle I could as I swam, working out the tension. When I hauled myself up on the dock I just sat there awhile and watched Lily digging her trenches.

Now, as Daniel swerves his truck in beside mine, which is his old one that cost three hundred bucks and took him about forty-seven hours in labour to get up and running, I think how I could live out there at that lake. There are only a few cabins, maybe eight or nine. Jackson's family has one of them, and we used to go out there in the summer all the time and play on his rope swing, fish for rainbow trout from his dad's aluminum motorboat. But most of the year there isn't anyone out there at all, just the loons and the trees and the fish.

"Hey there, sexy." Daniel swings his gear over his shoulder and tramps up the stairs.

"Hey, yourself." I take a sip of coffee, then put it down beside me. It's cold now. I'm not a coffee snob, but I do have my limits. I can drink rusty nail water as long as it isn't cold.

"Long shift?" I say. He started at nine that morning, and ended at nine. Where he was for the last couple hours or so isn't much of a mystery.

He slings his bag down and sits on a lawn chair beside me. "Yeah." He yawns, but from where I'm sitting it looks a little fake. Daniel's dramatic. He might just feel a bit tired, but damn it, he wants me to know he worked long and hard because ... "I stopped in at Bud's for a beer. Man, that was a killer day." He yawns again.

And there it is. All that yawning served its purpose. "Yeah, I had a killer day too. I stopped in for a martini at the Steelworkers Inn. I just left Lily in the truck in the parking lot. She was fine. I tossed her some fries through the window."

He smiles sideways, that slow, devilish grin. "Know how I know you're lying?"

I rest my head back again. Close my eyes. Crickets are shrieking from the field, an excited screaming, the kind like when you're on a roller coaster and you're just cresting the top of that first hill, before you go down and let out a scream of full-blown terror. "Tell me, genius."

He reaches over and unzips his bag. Pulls something out. I open my eyes and he's holding out a can of Kokanee. "Steelworkers doesn't have martinis. Unless you call gin on the rocks in a greasy water glass a martini."

"Well sure," I say. "That's their specialty. Greasy Gin Martinis. All the girls are drinking them." I take the beer and crack it open. I'm not a fan of beer myself, but I can tolerate it, as it is the official beverage of Grace River. "Cheers," I say and look him in the eyes for the first time since he got home. He looks tired, and he hasn't washed off the smears of grease just above his jaw that he must have got from working the machines all day. There's a lot of things I could say right now. A lot of things that, five years ago, I would have been dying to talk to him about. Stupid stuff like my mom's disgusting casserole, or the tattoo Sunny wants to get of a drunk reindeer, or more serious stuff like me waking up and feeling like I can't breathe ... but I don't.

He tilts his beer at me. "Right back at ya, princess."

I lean back and close my eyes again, listen to those shrieking crickets. Feel the June air wrap itself around me like an old familiar blanket. It's not so bad, I tell myself.

I hear the flick of Daniel's lighter as he lights a cigarette, the strong smoke covering over the mint and the ripe strawberry with its big bully tobacco smell. I want one, bad, but I try to talk myself out of it. I think about driving along the river on the way home, the open road at dusk, the sweet smell of summer-blooming sage, the stars starting to prick the sky. The moon glowing over the river as we drove along beside it, lighting it up, transforming it into something enticing, something so old and magical and silvery cool that I could imagine for a while that there wasn't a thing wrong with it at all.

Jackson

"For Christ's sake, Jackson, keep your damn eyes on the road."

I turn in my seat so I'm facing properly. "Sorry. Brooks was choking." I only looked back for a sec at the kids. It's not like I endangered their lives. But she's right, I should be watching where I'm going.

We're in the truck, the old crew cab I picked up for cheap off a guy in Creston. It's a good truck, because I can haul work stuff in it, cords of split alder for the fireplace, the ATV when we go out to the lake, you name it. But the beauty is we can fit the kids in it too. We were driving a beat-up old station wagon before. The back end got accordioned while Caroline was driving home one night and that was that. I still got it in the yard out back on our property. I'll work on it when I get the time. I can't get it looking new, but I can replace the rear bumper and hammer out some of the dents. At least the engine still works good, so I might be able to sell it for five hundred bucks when I'm done.

Caroline leans back on her seat and shuts her eyes. "He wasn't choking, he was coughing."

She's still a little pissed because we left so early.

"Okay, well, we all survived." I pat her bare leg, the shorts riding up so high they look like bikini bottoms. "Right, Sparky?" Sparky's what I call her, since we first got together. You can guess why, but I'll tell you anyway. She's hell on wheels, that's why.

I guess she can hear the grin as I'm saying it, because she opens one eye and glares at me with it. "Don't call me that, Jackson." She shakes her head and then yawns. "Dammit. I need another coffee, babe."

Her first two were in styrofoam cups from 7-11, which are on the floor of the truck rattling along beside the sandals she kicked off when she got in.

"I'm firsty," Brooks calls out from the back. He was named after Garth Brooks, in case you're wondering. I put my foot down about naming him Garth. Anyway, he's eating goldfish crackers by the handful, straight out of the box, which is probably what made him choke.

"I didn't pack anything." Caroline jerks at me with her thumb. "Your dad was in too much of a hurry. So you kids will just have to suffer."

"Well, I'm thirsty too, Dad. Can we stop? Please?" Travis. The voice of reason.

We're about ten miles out of Merritt now, I can tell because the hills are changing colour, going from green to brown, from something living to dead old desert. "I got some bottles of water in the cooler, guys. Just a few minutes. Hang on." Caroline, she forgets stuff like that all the time. I was the one to pack all the crackers, and some of those fruit leather things, plus all the food we'll need for the next couple of days.

Caroline reaches over and turns on the radio. She plays with it until she finds a local country station. "Howdy, folks," some over-cheery DJ shouts. "Gearing up to be a hot one for us on this Nicola Valley Country Festival weekend. Grab your coolers and the portable barbie and head on down to the best show in BC ... "

She smiles now. "All right. We're almost there, boys. We're gonna have us some fun."

"Yay," calls Brooks, but Travis grumbles something about missing his soccer game.

She spins and swats him on the arm. "Soccer shmoccer. You can play soccer any old time. This is a real live cultural event, bud. And Momma's been coming here every year since she was fifteen. Except when I was pregnant with you two." She flips back to the front. "Since you both had to be damn summer babies."

"Damth a bad word."

"Well, thank you, baby. Momma didn't realize." She laughs, lowers her window, sticks her arms out. "Hello, Merritt," she yells. "Didya miss me?" A rig driver waiting to turn onto the highway honks at her and gives her a big grin.

Usually she goes with a group of girlfriends, but a couple of 'em are expecting babies now, so she talked me into it. "It'll be a nice family trip, Jackson." I don't know. I kinda remember there being kids and families and whatnot there when we last went together, before the boys were born, but I mostly remember pulling Caroline off the stage when she hopped up there to join in with Billy Ray Cyrus, and I remember it raining and I remember the mud. It was everywhere. All over us, all over our tent. It got so you didn't even try to wash it off. We just wore it like war paint and drank so much we didn't care how cold we were or the fact that the tent dripped. We came with Jessie and Daniel that year ... and I think Bobby too. That's right. I remember being in the beer tent with the guys and then trying to track the girls down. We found Jessie asleep in her tent, but we never did find Caroline until she crawled into my sleeping bag at first light.

I kinda wish they were all coming with us this weekend, but Danny and Mike are both working nights. Bobby woulda come, but he didn't want to be third wheel, since it's just Care and me and the kids.

To tell you the god honest truth I'm a little worried taking the boys. I mean, I guess people take their kids, sure, it's just ... they're probably the kind of people who bring their $100,000 RVs and cook steaks on their indoor grills and set the kids up with the DVD player in the bed in the back while they slip out to catch half an hour of music at a time. The kind who bring their own chardonnay in an econo box and drink it in those plastic wine glasses with an ice cube.

We're more the type who bring a cooler full of baloney and hot dogs and a case of Kokanee. But we got a good tent and everything, and all our gear is in pretty good shape. I checked it all before we left.

I look over at my wife, who's waving at people as we drive by. We're in the town now, driving slow down the main street. She seems happy. I check the kids in the rearview, and they're both staring out their windows, Brooks chewing another mouthful of crackers so big he looks like a chipmunk and Travis nodding quietly to himself. I wonder what he's agreeing to. What he's telling himself.

The street is alive with people, we can only crawl along as everybody heads up to the site just a mile or so out of town. Some of the girls are wearing bikinis and hats and not a whole lot else. A couple of them grin at us as we creep by, one of them holding up an open bottle of beer, her hat low on her head. "Howdy," she calls and her girlfriend grins at me. I lift a couple fingers out of politeness. She's close enough she could hand me the bottle for a sip if she wanted.

Caroline reaches across me. "Howdy there, girls. Have a great time!"

"Thanks," they giggle.

"Y'all be good." Caroline waggles her finger at them like a scolding mother, which is pretty funny. You'd know why if you knew Caroline. It's funny too how as soon as we get here she suddenly has this Alabama accent even though she was born and raised in BC. She gives me a soft kiss on the cheek before sitting back. "Thanks, baby," she says. "Thanks for coming." She smells good. Like cherry lip gloss or something, though she doesn't look like she's wearing any. I give her a grin. Naw, I think. This is going to be all right.

"Jesus Christ, let's GO already. How long does it take to eat a friggin' baloney sandwich?" Caroline is chomping at the bit to get down to the main stage. She's changed into her concert gear, which meant taking off clothes, not putting more on. She's wearing a bikini top like all the other girls, plus the cut-off jeans and no shoes. I figure she'll get sliced to shreds on broken beer bottles, but I don't say anything. Not much point.

I screw the cap back on the mayonnaise jar and give Brooks a nudge with my elbow. "C'mon, bud. Let's go hear some country music." Brooks shakes his head, his cheeks bulging with a pasty mess of white bread and mustard. He doesn't eat the meat.

I keep clearing off the picnic table while Caroline wipes crumbs off Travis's face and gives him a big, sloppy kiss. "You gonna dance with your momma?"

He looks horrified. "Uh-uh."

She just laughs, then strides over to a lawn chair and picks up her straw hat. She pulls it down low in front and pretends she's twirling a lasso. "Don't I look like a real cowgirl, boys?"

They laugh, Brooks spraying white chunks onto the table. I cram the leftover food into the cooler by the tent and grab my own hat. I'm trying to think what else we might need, since the tent is almost a half-mile from the stages, but I think I've got it covered. I got my wallet in my back pocket, a bottle of water and some snack stuff in the backpack, plus spare T-shirts for the kids. I wonder if I should bring sweaters for them, but one look up at that blue sky tells me not to bother.

We walk along the Concordia River. It runs straight through the whole festival, which is on thirty acres or so of flat farmland leased out by some country-music-loving business guy from the big city. The campsites are all along the river too, which is great. There's even a few trees for shade. We swiped a good spot right under a big fir.

The kids run ahead, sliding and squishing their feet in the sandy riverbed. There's people everywhere, girls shrieking, men laughing, high-fiving. Most of 'em are pretty young, they don't look much older than teenagers to me, but they might be close to our age. Not quite thirty-three but feeling forty-five. Caroline is reading the program, which she got in the local newspaper in Grace River and reads over every day like a bible, like there might be something important she missed the first time.

I poke her in the ribs, and her suntanned skin feels warm. She doesn't look up. I swing the backpack over to my other shoulder and poke her again. "Hey."

She swats at me like she would a pesky fly, but I just laugh. "I tell you what's happening at work?"

She looks up now, folding up the program. Man, she's a pretty lady. Those big blue-green eyes, the sun coming in through the woven straw in her hat and sending diamonds of light over her cheeks. Even with that little white jagged scar below her right eye from falling on a broken bottle she could be on a magazine cover. I'd buy it, that's for sure.

"What, that environmental guy?"

Brooks slips and lands up to his thighs in water, getting his shorts wet. "You okay?" I call, but he just shrugs and climbs back up the bank, clumps of sand sticking to his skin.

I look back at Caroline. "Yeah. I guess he had a meeting with management yesterday. He's just doing some testing. Don't know too much."

She smirks. "How many of these guys have you seen in the last fifteen years? It doesn't mean a thing. They come, then they go. C'est ça." Caroline took French in high school very seriously. I guess she was planning to go to Paris and be a model or something. I mean, that was the original idea. Probably around the same time I thought I was going to be the next Gretzky. Between my bad knees and her falling on that bottle at a lake party when she was sixteen, neither of us had much of a chance.

"Nah, I'm not worried." I watch Brooks slide down the bank, Travis holding his hand so he doesn't fall. Some big shirtless beefy guy is walking backward toward us while he talks to his buddies and he bangs into my shoulder before I can get out of the way.

"Watch it," Caroline says.

He stops and looks her up and down with a grin. "Whatever you say, honey."

I point at him. "She's not your honey. You got that? Is that clear, buddy?"

Don't get it wrong, I'm not one of those guys. I'm not looking for a fight or anything. There's just a line, is all. I mean, in some ways I shoulda been the guy that got picked on when we were kids, 'cause I was the tall one with the feet too big for his body, all gangly-armed and stooped over like an old man. But I didn't, probably because of Mike and Danny. Even when Mike was seven he had a reputation for being a scrapper. Once bit a kid's ear so hard the kid needed stitches. And Danny, well. The three of us got ourselves into some trouble, there's no two ways about it—stealing two-dollar bills from our parents' emergency money, throwing rocks at the neighbour's three-legged dog, riding our bikes off the hills and into the brush below like crazy people. People figured out pretty quick not to mess with us. No matter what happened we'd lie, cheat, and steal to cover each other's backs.

The beefy guy throws his hands up, gives us a smile. Friends. "No worries, man. No worries." He turns so he's walking forward and disappears into the crowd. Caroline watches him go, chewing her lip, then we keep going. I should say this is a pretty common thing that happens, on account of how Caroline looks. If I had my way she'd be covered up in a big raincoat all the time, but she's one of those girls who even looks good when she feels like shit, blowing her nose every three seconds, and hasn't washed her hair for a week.

Caroline was the kind with all the friends in high school, the girl all the other girls wanted to be, or at least that's what Jess and Sunny tell me. If Grace River High had cheerleaders, she would have been the captain. When I was a pimple-covered kid getting high under the AXIS Memorial Bridge and drag racing in my beat-up Z-28, I never thought in a million years that one day I'd be marrying Caroline Bennett, I can tell you that much for sure.

We're getting closer to the action now. I can smell the charbroiled burgers from the Lion's Club charity truck and the greasy fries and what I'm pretty damn sure might be corn dogs. Caroline fans herself with her precious program and calls the boys away from the river as we walk toward the network of stages. I wish we'd brought folding chairs. What the hell are we going to sit on? Jesus, I'd forget my head if it wasn't screwed on right.

"You got no reason to be worried, baby." It takes me a second to figure out Caroline's picking right up where she left off with the environmentalist.

"Yeah. It's not that. I'm not worried. It's just this lawsuit from down in Washington. Something about slag cleanup."

Caroline laughs. "Oh, good luck with that." She pulls Brooks in for a hug, then picks him up and he perches like a little prince on her hip. He's getting big. Another year and she won't be able to do that anymore. She weighs a hundred pounds soaking wet, if that, and she only comes up to my shoulder.

"Yeah. But it was weird, I met the guy ... " A mike check drowns me out, the feedback whining through the amp so loud a bunch of people instinctively cover their ears, still managing to keep their plastic cups of beer full.

I'm about to tell her more, about how I ran into that same guy who was at Nick's yesterday. I want to tell her how when I was walking out to my truck last night he was there, coming back from a meeting, I guess. He drives one of those fancy VW vans, not the old kind that break down full of hippies on their way to Kaslo, but the newer kind that's all white and has a double bike rack on the back and new hubcaps. He kind of looked me over as he walked up, but not in an aggressive way. Just sizing me up.

"You just get off shift?" he asked, and I nodded as I tossed my stuff in the back of the truck.

I was about to climb in, not to be rude or anything, but what do I have to say to this guy? But he stopped me, he actually put a hand on my arm for a split second before realizing what he was doing and pulling back. "Listen," he said, kind of quiet, like we were in a spy movie or something. "You get your lead levels checked here at AXIS, right? They have a doctor that does all the testing on the workers?"

I wasn't sure what to say. I wondered if he was recording the conversation or something. "You know, man, I don't really ... "

He shook his head. "It's okay. Just do me a favour? Next time you get your readings back, go and get your levels checked somewhere else. Like Nelson. Then compare them. Okay?" He held a hand up as though to say, *That's all. Totally reasonable request.*

I just stared at him as he walked away. It struck me as pretty damn odd, and that's why I want to tell Caroline. "So I met the guy ... " I say, trying again now that the mike check is over. "And he tells me ... "

"Holy shit!" she yells. She runs off toward a brunette with big hair, Shelly or Shelby or someone, an old friend of hers from grade twelve who moved to Vernon or Kelowna to work in a bank. She looks pretty wasted already, and her and Caroline jump up and down like girls do. There's a whole bunch of 'em and Shelby or whatever her name is introduces Caroline to them, giving me a little wave.

"Howdy," I say to the girls and they all laugh, Caroline punching me in the arm. "You remember Jackson, my darlin' husband."

They all say hello, and then I feel a tug on my shorts.

"I gotta pee." I look down. Brooks is looking up at me, lost and overwhelmed by all the people. Looking small.

Caroline is laughing at something, and she's already holding a beer someone must have offered her. She glances over. "You take him, okay, Jackson? I'll meet up with you in a bit. By the main stage there." She points to a crowd of about a thousand people milling near the main stage. "Travis probably has to go too, don't you, honey?"

Travis shrugs.

I pick up Brooks and smile at the ladies. "All right. I guess I'm on bathroom duty. See you in a bit."

Caroline gives me a wink, then tips her beer at me. "You're the best. Oh wait ... you wanted to tell me something ... what was it, babe?" But the ladies are starting to walk away, heading into the crowd of swarming bodies. Shelby grabs her arm and starts pulling.

I shake my head. "Nothing," I call. "I'll see you in a while." I watch Caroline saunter off with her arms around her girlfriends. I watch until I can't see her anymore, until she just becomes another body in the crowd. Then I take Travis's hand and we head off to find the bathroom.

"Dad?" Brooks says quietly, resting his head on my shoulder.

"What's up, bud?" Brooks feels small and light in my arms. Five is still pretty damn young, especially when I look down at Travis and see what two years can do.

"I don't like it here."

I sidestep a young woman who's yanking up her shirt and showing her boobs to some group of guys by the beer tent. I try to cover Travis's eyes with my free hand, but he twists away. "Yeah, me neither, bud. But we'll have fun. Do some dancing. Eat some corn dogs. It'll be all right." And it will. I'll make sure the kids have fun. Caroline'll have fun. It'll be all right.

Kali

*P*eople think I don't really belong here. To be honest, that was part of the appeal. When my girls and I first moved to Grace River last year I was used to all my friends back on Vancouver Island— vegans who only drank organic wine or smoked organic pot. They were all reading the latest spiritual how-to books and going to see the hottest Buddhist leaders at trendy retreat centres on the Gulf Islands. And even though I believed in and practised most of those things myself, when I left Kieran and Summer's dad, my partner of eight years, I was tired of being defined by anything and expected to act accordingly. Hippie, vegan, wife, mother. I wanted just to be whatever I was, not because it was expected of me, but because it was what I wanted.

I never thought we'd end up in Grace River. And it wasn't where I was heading anyway. We kind of happened into it, which is the way my life usually works. I can have all the best intentions and plans and goals and then something else entirely will fall in front of me.

I *was* heading for Nelson ... that's where Harry, my bio-dad, lives. I'll backtrack a bit. My mother was forty when she had me, courtesy of a turkey baster donation from her good friend Harry, a tie-dye-wearing, grey-haired bass player who toured with a Grateful Dead tribute band before settling down in the Kootenays to start an organic dairy farm. He still lives there, thirty years later, still has goats and sells the milk, still gardens and sells the vegetables, still has young dreadlocked people helping him for free food and crashing on his living room floor.

My mother was working on her master's in women and eastern religion when I was born, taking night classes and leaving me with various friends from her wide circle of transition house co-workers and political group co-protestors. I was raised by a network of women who lived in bright, messy homes with batik hangings on their walls and glass jars full of dried beans in their kitchens. They smelled like peppermint soap and didn't own TVs or go to doctors. They rubbed fresh calendula cream on my scratches, held garlic poultices to my neck when I had a sore throat, stirred brewer's yeast into orange juice and watched me while I drank it down. And all this time Harry was on tour or milking his goats, so I didn't see him much until I got to be five or six. Then my mother would drive me out to the farm and we would spend a few days hanging out with whoever happened to be hanging out there. As I got older, I would go there on my own, taking the bus or eventually driving a beat-up Nova full of friends to go and pick his apples for five dollars a basket in the summertime.

So anyway, I was heading for his place with the girls, craving that kind of distracted comfort he offered me whenever I was going through a transition and my mother wasn't around to help me through it. She's in India right now with some friends, working at an orphanage on the banks of the Ganges River. But it's funny—this time when I pulled up to Bio-dad's and saw all those old trucks and vans parked every which way and saw the cherry trees blooming and the goats wandering around the field I just felt overwhelmed by it all. I was healing from a painful separation, from someone I thought I might be with for the rest of my life. I had splintered my family, pulled my girls from their father, gotten custody, and destined them to a life of long weekend and summer visits. Not that I didn't have my reasons. But those aren't important. There was no great drama, no bizarre love triangle, no bruises.

We lasted two weeks at Bio-dad's. Until Sierra, a funky woman in her fifties who sold Harry's goats' milk and produce at her health food store in Grace River, came by to pick up an order and we got talking. It turned out she was looking for help at Earth's Bounty Health Foods. It was a small store, and she told me that in all honesty it didn't do too well considering where it was located—there wasn't much of a market for wheatgrass juice in Grace River—but she was committed to keeping it going for as long as she could and providing some healthy choices for the people who were interested. And something just struck me. I could stay at Bio-dad's and plant and harvest, sure, but this was his dream, this was what he had set up and worked at for years ... I wanted something that was my own. And although Harry offered sage advice when it came to the state of my soul and many times offered me a no-strings, easygoing, safe place to land when life knocked me around, the biggest gift he gave me was teaching me about herbs

As a small child he would take me out to his greenhouse or to his massive field of tangled greens and he would point them out, picking small leaves and crushing them between his fingers, making me smell them. *Rosemary for circulation. Clary sage for anxiety. Lavender for inflammation.* And of course, as a small child I was bored and wanted to go and run around with the gang of wild children shrieking and running through his forest. But it sank in and finally stayed with me, fitting into my life like a missing limb that had been found and suddenly made life so much easier.

What I wanted when we moved out to the Kootenays was to make my own soap, my own lotions and tinctures. It was something I had always wanted but found difficult to pull off when we lived in an apartment in Victoria and the girls' father was always at the university getting his philosophy degree and I was working at the deli down the street so we could pay the rent. I did make some soap and try to sell it at the local stores, but it was what you call a flooded market.

And although all the people who lived at Bio-dad's tried to convince me that Grace River was small-town, redneck, unhealthy, polluted, I still came and checked it out, went to look at the cottage Sierra just happened to know was for rent on the outskirts of town. It was on two acres of land with a stream, a meadow, and lots of room for a big garden. In the end it was that house that seduced me. Tiny gables, covered porch, an attic room to work with my herbs, endless fields for the girls to run in. A place of our own.

So now I'm walking to work from that sweet little cottage. It's hot, too hot, although the day has barely begun. The girls are safely off on the school bus to the Waldorf school halfway to Nelson ... it's a long ride for them, but it's better than being in the public school in Grace River. The sky is an uncluttered baby blue, and the hills are still green, although I remember from last summer that in another month they will start turning brown from the heat. Sage is blooming, foxglove is opening its magenta buds, wild daisies scatter themselves among the grass. I walk past fields that used to be farms, but they sit largely unused now, except for the odd horse or cow.

It usually takes me almost an hour to walk to work, but I don't mind. The store doesn't open until ten o'clock, so I have lots of time to get there after I get the girls off. This is what I wanted, anyway, a place where I could live in peace and be around nature, not some crowded apartment off a busy street in Victoria.

This is a different kind of beauty here. No majestic mountains, no shimmering inlets and rolling waves, no orcas or seals or bright purple starfish clinging to beach rock. Here it's quiet. Still. Not as dramatic and full of life and intensity. Simpler. Also, it hardly ever rains, which, while it is a challenge to grow what I need to grow in my garden, I can appreciate after so many years of dealing with black mould on my windowsills and endless days of being stuck inside with two small children who used the furniture as their playground. It's only once in a while that I'm sad to be so far away from the ocean, filled with some secret nostalgia as I lie there trying to recreate the soft crashing sound of waves breaking on the shore, pull it back to me. It isn't hard. The body clings to memories too.

I hear a truck coming around the bend behind me and it slows and pulls over, churning up the fine dust. I turn and shade my eyes.

"Hey, girl. You're gonna get burnt to a crisp out here. Come on." Jessie waves her long arm out her open window, smiling at me with that open way she has.

I shuffle dust out of my shoes and walk to the truck. "It's so *hot*," I agree. "And it's not even really summer yet."

She brushes her hair off her face and turns down the radio, which is blaring a Def Leppard song. "Sorry. Blast from the past. Daniel left it in here when he took my truck in for a new tire."

Def Leppard isn't really a blast from *my* past, as my teenage years were spent wearing black and going to intellectually stimulating alternative schools and listening to the Sex Pistols and Talking Heads.

Metal bands were frowned upon. Openly mocked, even. But I can still relate. "Sure. Brings back memories."

The sun is burning through the fabric of my white cotton shirt and I start wishing I had one of those Chinese paper parasols. I used to have one, when Summer was a baby. I would bring it to the park to protect her from the sun ... where did I leave it? I'll have to ask their dad if it's still in storage at the apartment.

"So do you want a ride? I was just picking up eggs at Jersey's." Jessie pats the seat beside her.

"Are they selling eggs again? I thought a fox got all their chickens or something." I love that, I love the small town-ness of it, all these people knowing what everyone else is doing.

Jessie shrugs. Her blue Harley-Davidson T-shirt looks damp with sweat. "Guess they got some new ones. C'mon. If we go fast enough we might get a cool breeze."

It feels better to be moving. I let my arm hang out the window like Jessie does, waving it through the air like a languid child on a summer road trip.

"I don't know how you can walk in this heat, Kali. Really. It's kinda crazy." Jessie turns up the music slightly and "Rocket" wails through the speakers.

I smile. I know "kinda crazy" is probably mild compared to what some people say about me. "I like walking. It's the only real exercise I get."

"Hmm." She doesn't sound convinced. She drums her fingers on the steering wheel thoughtfully. "So hey, do you make anything for people who are trying to quit smoking? Like some kinda herbal thing maybe?"

"I can make you up something to calm you down. Smoking is just a way of dealing with stress. You want a tea or a tincture?"

She shrugs. She's still drumming the steering wheel and I can sense her agitation.

"You know, you could try meditation."

"Oh, yeah, meditation. Sure." She smiles. "That's me. Heading off to the ashram any old day now." She changes the subject. "So has Mike said anything about the stuff at work?"

"What stuff at work?" Mike ... he's not a big talker. That's what drew me to him. When I met him last December he was wandering aimlessly around the store looking out of place in his work clothes, the heavy flannel and thick jeans. He was reading vitamin labels, peering at the bin of alfalfa overflowing in the cooler. When I asked him what he needed he looked sheepish and said he didn't need a thing, that he had just never been in the store before. He picked up a slim brown bottle from the flower remedies case. "What the heck is this?" he asked.

"It's called Rescue Tonic," I told him.

He raised his eyebrows at that. "Oh yeah?" He unscrewed the top with surprisingly gentle-looking hands. He sniffed and looked up. "Smells like booze," he said with a childlike smile.

I smiled back. "Yes," I said. "It's made from flower essence, but they preserve it in alcohol. You take a few drops whenever you feel stressed or anxious."

He looked at the bottle carefully. Screwed the cap back on. "Rescue Tonic," he echoed. "Sounds good to me." He grinned. "I'll take it."

And now sometimes we'll sit for a whole evening out on my back deck smelling the sweetness of my garden, listening to frogs croak from the riverbed, staring up at the stars. Sometimes we don't say anything, just sit, and it isn't at all like what it was before with the girls' dad, not a thing. That was too much talking, too much analyzing and discussing and criticizing. Searching for meaning, hidden layers ... And I'm not stupid, I know that the reason Mike's quiet is because there are a lot of things Mike doesn't want to think about, let alone say out loud, but I understand. It's not my place to push him. Besides, I want to be left alone too, so as long as he gives me my space, I'm happy. "What's going on at work?" I repeat.

Jessie's staring off at the horizon, her arm draped across the steering wheel as she leans forward. She has that kind of natural face that reminds you of the prairies, with her wheat-coloured hair and her big-blue-sky eyes. She shrugs her tanned shoulders.

"Some environmentalist from the States is up here. Something about the river being polluted down in Washington State." She shrugs again, but this time I see something forced in it, something unnatural. A show of nonchalance. And I notice now how tired she looks, that under the tan there is a lurking paleness ... I may drop off some nettle tincture later to strengthen her blood, and maybe some skullcap for her nervous system.

"Is it only polluted down there? How did they manage that?" I say lightly.

She laughs. "Nope, it's polluted all the way down. But the Canadian agencies have never really been able to do much about it. I mean, AXIS has cleaned up their act a lot, that's for sure. They aren't pumping slag in there anymore, for one thing." She indicates the river to the left of the road with a nod of her head.

"Okay." I'm still watching her, trying to figure out where this is going. "So are the guys worried about this environmentalist?"

Jessie shakes her head. Laughs. "No. No, they aren't worried. Just talking shit, I guess." She drums her fingers again. "I met him."

"The environmentalist?"

"Yeah. He's in town for a while, doing tests up and down the river. I guess he's gonna be travelling up north too. Kinda based here and there for a few weeks."

"Huh." I'm not sure where she's going with this. "So ... are *you* worried about something?"

She shakes her head slightly but doesn't look at me. "The boys are off to Ashville this weekend, hey?"

It takes me a minute to process the change in topic. "Right. The hockey tournament. It's so weird ... who plays hockey in this heat?"

She laughs. "Yeah. Only the die-hards. Anyway, this'll be the end of it until September. Then they let the ice melt and use the arena for agricultural fairs and stuff." She gives me one of those all-knowing wifely looks. "Don't expect Mikey to be in very good shape when he gets back Saturday night. It takes them a couple of days to be able to form a complete sentence."

"I told Mike not to come over Saturday night. It's better for the girls. And I don't really need to see him when he's hungover. He'll come over

Sunday after his shift." I dip my hand up and down on the warm current outside the truck window. I think about how much easier my life is now. Jessie has to deal with her husband the minute he gets home, whatever shape he might be in. But me, I have it easy. I still get the sweetness, the companionship of a man coming to my door a few nights a week without having to cope with all the day-to-day trials of a relationship.

"Well, I wish I could do that," Jessie says. "It would cut down on the warfare, that's for sure."

I don't like that word, *warfare*. "Why don't you try giving him some time to relax and come back to himself? It's a big transition to go from being with a bunch of men playing hockey and drinking beer ... all that testosterone ... to coming home to your wife and kids. If you give him a little space it might work a lot better for you."

Jessie stares at me for so long I'm afraid she might go off the road. And I know what she's thinking, I know what's going on in that head of hers. She thinks I'm nuts. I know women thrive on the conflict, they love to complain about their men in that tribal bonding way that women have probably done for centuries. It helps them feel connected, understood. It gives them a place to vent their frustration, their helplessness at the stubborn behaviours of their mates. But I don't do it anymore. I don't waste my time complaining. I just try to make things better now.

"Sure. I'll give that a shot. I'll let him go to his tournament even though Lily is in a play at school for the first time ever and he's going to miss it. And I have to work two shifts while he's gone. But then I'll give him some space when he gets back. Maybe make him a nice meal, get him his slippers. Let him sleep." She's joking, but she's also trying to make a point. I don't say anything. Point taken.

We are nearing town now, hugging the river as it winds beside the road. There are small groves of gnarled fir and pine trees dotting the bank, and I can hear the river singing over rock, rushing away from town on its journey south.

Jessie suddenly reaches over and turns the music off, which I am a little grateful for. "Hey, Kali ... did you hear what the environmentalist said to Jackson a few days ago?"

"No. What?

"He told Jackson that there was some big thing a couple years ago when some AXIS workers got tested through the smelter and then got tested in Vancouver and it turned out they weren't getting accurate readings. Like, the reading in Vancouver was way higher."

"That doesn't surprise me." The faith people put in that place, believing every public memo about cleaner water, cleaner air, down to the "scientific research" that proves it. They still don't seem to understand the power of money. Since I've been here I have been vigilant in giving immune-boosting vitamins and herbs to my kids, but overall I figure that living out in the country away from town is better than living downtown Victoria with all the car pollution.

"It doesn't?"

"No … what surprises me more is how much people want to believe AXIS. Remember that mommy group I took the girls to when I first moved here?"

Jessie nods and makes a left turn when we near the bridge on the outskirts of town. I have only four blocks to spit this out.

"Well, this one time the moms are all talking … "

"Who were they?"

"The moms?"

"Yeah, who were the moms?"

"I'm not sure. I don't remember their names. I've seen them around, though. Anyway, they were saying, 'Oh, Jimmy's a thirty-two, Sally's a thirty-seven,' and I thought to myself, What on earth are they talking about?"

"There is no child named Sally in Grace River," Jessie says, deadpan. She pulls into the gravel parking lot beside the travel agent's, which is right beside Nature's Bounty. She turns the ignition off and settles back for the rest of the story.

"So then I asked what they meant and they said that they were talking about the lead content in their kids' blood the year before. And this one woman, she was saying that her kid's was twice the normal amount, but that it was okay by her because it just made him sleepy so he was easier to take care of. She said that the 'lead task force' came from AXIS and ripped out all her carpets and stripped her paint and pulled out the soil from her garden. But they convinced her it would all be better then. She was totally secure with her new soil and paint and carpet. It's like she didn't even think about the fact that the lead particles were still drifting down from the smokestacks, seeping into her home and onto her yard." I haven't ever really talked to Jessie about the lead issue before. To be honest, I always thought of it as the elephant in the room.

"That must have been Eileen Caldwell. She is the laziest woman I have ever known," she says lightly. "Her kids watch about nine hours of TV a day, and they still go to school, so you do the math. Also, she lives downwind from AXIS. It's practically in her backyard, so she's probably sucked up her fair of share of lead particles too."

"Okay, but my point is that *that* is what really scares me. That blind faith. That unwillingness to see the truth. To accept it."

"So why didn't you take for the hills after the mommy group?"

"I felt like I could protect my girls by having them out of town. And I'm not judging anyone, Jessie, I'm just saying it's important to be aware ... "

But Jessie stops me when she leans toward me. "Kali," she says, "we are aware." She looks out the window of the truck at the main street of town, the hanging baskets spilling their indigo blossoms, the new awnings stretched proudly over doorways. People walk by in the sunshine with their coffee in paper cups, walking dogs, carrying shopping bags. "I guess we just all have our reasons for putting up with what we know we shouldn't." She pats my arm gently. "Even you."

Daniel

I'll tell you what I want to do. I want to go home, kiss my wife, her Royal Highness Miss Jessie Belle McAllister, park my ass on the couch with a beer, and watch some fucking hockey, that's what I want to do. But no, here I am, waiting for the goddamn meeting, standing out back of the lunch room catching a smoke while the sun sinks down over the hills, which means it's almost nine, which means the game is probably over anyway. Oh well. Last I heard Calgary was losing 6-2. They lose one more game and they won't make it to the last round of the Stanley Cup playoffs. That's something I don't really want to see.

It's bullshit, is what it is. Like I don't work hard enough, like all the guys don't work hard enough as it is without having to hang around and go to department meetings after their twelve-hour shifts. And at this meeting we have to listen to them talk crap about the environmentalists again, tell us to treat them with respect ... What the hell is everyone worrying about, that's what I want to know. We've been here for a hundred years, we just cut the cake at the Centennial last August, and we sure as hell are more environmentally friendly than we were in 1902. The changes they've made in the last five years have been pretty damn impressive.

Those people who come in from out of town and think they know something about our situation, the ones who sit in Nick's with their decaf green tea clicking their tongues at us when we walk in from a shift still wearing our gear, they haven't bothered doing the research. If they had, they would know that we've cleaned up our slag to the point that Forrester, our boss, lets his two-year-old twins paddle around in the water downstream from AXIS. Hell, they built a fucking water park there with money donated from AXIS and most kids I know go swimming in the river now. Except ours, of course. Jessie's still holding out that it'll turn Lily into some lagoon creature with mutant gills or something.

Anyway, it just pisses me off, the whole thing. And this time it isn't even the goddamn Canadian environmentalists. The fucking USA thinks they have a score to settle too. If they looked at the case histories of all the environmental claims made on us, they would see that we've won every time, except when AXIS screwed up here and there, which happens in the real world. And we always paid the fines. We cleaned up our soil, we reduced emissions. The lead content in the soil has gone down by, like, 50 per cent. What do they want? People have been living here right beside AXIS for a hundred years and we haven't been wiped out yet.

I guess I better get in there. I open the door and head inside, working my way through the maze of pipes and walkways to the staff room. Jackson's there already and so is Mike, hunched over the table, cups of coffee in front of them. Terry, John, and old Gus are all there too, and some other guys push past me to get in. It's just our department, the maintenance guys. When I say maintenance, please do not think I mean like janitors or something. No, I wouldn't work in a place for fourteen years to have the reward of some shit-cleaning job. We're the guys who have been here long enough that we know what the hell we're doing and how the hell the place works. We come in when there's a problem and clean it up—some of us, like me and Jackson, are mechanics, some are even engineers, although we don't hang with those guys much.

"That been on the burner all day or what?" I say to Mike, settling in beside him.

"Just about." He yawns and pushes his hat back on his head, rubs his eye with a filthy, calloused finger. "What the hell, man. If it can keep me awake, I'll fucking drink it. It tastes like the slag them Americans are bitching about, though."

Jackson rolls his head around on his shoulders. It's these twelve-hour shifts, that's what's wrong with him. I'm telling you. You'd think I was used to it, but I'm still worn out at the end of the day. The caged fluorescent light makes all the workers look green and unhealthy.

I shake my head. "Can't believe I'm missing the fucking game, man."

"We should demand they put up some flat screens during playoffs. We should strike until they do." Jackson smiles as he says it, but a couple of the guys stop talking and stare when they hear the word *strike*. Jackson holds up his hands. "Joke, man. I was kidding." Strike talk isn't usually something we joke about here, but Jackson has his own set of rules when it comes to this place. The silent code that most guys get, like not questioning too much, or not complaining about certain things, Jackson has never really stuck to. He's one of those guys who actually sees himself working somewhere else one day. He tried opening his own shop a few years back, fixing up people's trucks on his property, but the money was slow and he ended up back here, just like everyone knew he would.

Forrester comes in with one of his lackeys. The room is full now, about thirty or forty guys and Lou, the chick who looks more like a guy than I do. She's a welder too, and you don't want to piss her off or she'll weld your ass to a pipe. I'm not kidding. She once chased down a guy who called her a dyke. She had to drop her torch, but she tackled him and was trying to drag him back toward it when some guys intervened. Forrester won't can her because she fills his girl quota. I mean, she ticked off "female" on her application, but I think that's about the extent of her feminine qualifications.

Anyway, Forrester has some papers he's rustling around in his hands and he looks as tired as the rest of us. "Okay, guys," he calls out and the murmuring stops. "Gonna get right down to it here. We've got a few things on the agenda so let's get rolling. First, we want to keep you in the loop about some investigations going on in regards to that lawsuit down south." That's what they call it here, "in the loop." It's supposed to build a sense of camaraderie that they keep us in on all the behind-the-scenes crap we don't necessarily need to know about. Like this.

"We getting sued?" some guy—Paul, I think—asks.

"Not exactly. The EPA is having some formal negotiations with AXIS concerning the cleanup of the river around Native band land down there. We're just talking." He smiles, but only his mouth moves. His eyes don't crinkle up in the corners like a normal person's. He's the only man I know who can smile with half his face. "But there is a guy from another agency representing the band. He's up here doing a more in-depth study of the river, the sediment, what have you."

"So, what? We gotta worry about this?"

"Shouldn't be a problem," I say. "If the Canadians can't prove we're doing anything wrong, why should we be worried about the Americans?"

"This is a formality, guys," Forrester says. "Absolutely not something you should be worrying about. When you read over the sheets you'll see they're claiming much higher toxin levels than our studies did. It's basically a he said/she said situation. Also, they're complaining about something that we've stopped practising more than five years ago."

Everyone here remembers that. The slag is a by-product of the smelting process. It contains trace amounts of lead and arsenic and mercury, but in such small amounts it doesn't really do any actual damage. Even so, we started saving the slag, piling it up and then selling it by the truckload to the Ministry of Highways to blend into their asphalt for paving the roads. So if these guys had filed this six years ago, they might have a leg to stand on, but as it is I want to get the hell out of here, especially since I know it's a waste of time.

Mike raises his hand. He's bored out of his mind. "Teacher, can I be excused?"

The guys laugh, including Forrester. "Sure, sure. Like I said, just wanted to keep you in the loop. So listen, I do want to say one important thing." We all look up like good students. "I want you to treat this guy with respect. Show him that AXIS employees are civilized and that we care about the same things they do. We just have a difference of opinion in terms of who's responsible for what. Okay?"

Blah fucking blah. Like I said, I am getting pretty sick of this shit. We all nod and murmur our "Sure, yes suh, whatever you say, suhs."

"Okay. Next on the agenda, the maintenance shut-down ... "

There are cheers all around and Forrester holds up a hand in protest. "Gentlemen, I know you love a paid week's vacation in June, but I am the bearer of bad news. We aren't contracting out for the whole cleaning crew during the shutdown, so some of you will have to keep the beer chilling in the fridge for another time. I have a list here with the names of those of you who have been requested."

I groan. How much you wanna bet I'm on that list? That's one of the downsides to working here so long. They rely on the "expertise" during cleanup.

Forrester carries on, talking about the rotten-sandwiches-in-the-vending-machine issue, and I just tune him out.

After the meeting, as we work our way down a couple flights of steel stairs to the locker rooms, Mike catches up to me and Jackson, who, by the way, is reading his goddamn handouts as he walks. Part of me hopes he walks into a pipe. I tossed mine in the trash already. The only handout I was interested in was the one that told me that sure enough, I'm working during the shutdown and so is Mikey.

Mike slaps me on the back. "Hey, you guys want to go for a beer or what?"

"Absolutely," I tell him. There's never a question, especially on the day shifts. We get off at the perfect time of night to go grab a few and still get home before we get in serious shit. The night shifts are the worst because when you start at 9:00 PM you can't exactly go out for beer first. I've done it, don't get me wrong, but because you've been sleeping all day it's like drinking for breakfast, and by about 2:00 AM those chicken wings and beers are sloshing around in your guts like a lake in a storm.

"I'll meet you guys down there, okay? I gotta change." Mike jogs ahead of us, weaving through the guys and running down the last set of stairs to the locker room. There's a man who loves his beer.

"You coming, man?" I ask Jackson, who hasn't said a word.

He checks his watch, which he does a lot. I find it pretty irritating, especially when there's beer and the possibility of the last few minutes of a hockey game involved. "You late for a fucking manicure or what?" I ask him.

He smiles. "Nah. I better get home and check on the kids." He pulls open the locker room door and lets out the stink of work sweat and old socks. He settles on a bench and starts taking off his boots as I think about this.

I peel off my blue coveralls and dump it in the laundry bin. "Check on the kids? Isn't Caroline there? What are you, Superdaddy?" I keep it light, but I'm not an ignorant ass. I think I know why he's doing it. "Hey, man," I say, quietly this time, "you worry too much."

Jackson laughs it off. "I'm not worried. I just told them I'd read them a story when I got home. You know Brooks, he'll make my life hell if I don't keep my word. He'll fucking . . . I don't know, wait up for me on the front porch with my hunting rifle."

That crazy shit is just his nervous talking thing.

I change the subject. "What's the plan for Caroline's birthday?"

Jackson runs his hand through his thick hair, making it all stand up on end. He looks like a freakshow sometimes. Jessie told me once that all the girls think he's a real handsome guy, kind of James Dean or something, but I can't see it. "I don't know, man. I was gonna have that barbeque thing at the house with all the kids and everything, but Care wants a party." He rubs his face in his hands now, trying to wake himself up, probably. "I guess we'll do Laredo's. Thursday night. Can't do it on the weekend 'cause of the hockey tournament. I talked to Bud, and he's gonna sort out the food and stuff."

"Sounds good." I don't want to be an asshole, but if I had a choice between having a bunch of my friends' kids come over and get high on sugar and tear around my house while the adults all sat around the garden and tried to act civilized or going out to the bar with all my buddies, guess what I'd pick?

Mike has wrestled out of his coveralls and comes over. He jerks his thumb at Jackson, who is rooting around in his locker for his street shoes. I shake my head. Mike nods and points at me. "You and me. Let's do it. The night is young, I got no shift tomorrow. Let's get this shit started." Mike has it made with this Kali chick, I tell you. Every man needs a sweet little hippie girl like that. She feeds him homemade soup and gives him herb tea when he has a hangover and doesn't nag him about a goddamn thing. How is that even possible? It can't last, but he better enjoy it while he can.

As I change out of my boots I think about Jessie. The smart thing to do would be to give her a call and let her know I'm going out. But she's probably sitting on the front porch wearing some old sweatshirt from high school and thinking about the meaning of life. She seems to be doing that a lot lately. She sure as hell doesn't need me to help her out with that. I don't know what's going on in that pretty little head, but I can tell you I'm not so sure I want to.

Plus, she's no Kali. She's already seriously pissed at me because of the hockey tournament being on the same weekend that Lily is in that big end-of-the-year school play.

I already feel like shit about it, but what can I do? We've been planning this tournament for months. My mom will tape the play anyway, or someone will. Lily's playing a zucchini or something and she's only in it for about two minutes, so I can't give up the whole damn weekend. I'm the top scorer on the team. Anyway, after spending some time giving the situation some serious consideration, I say screw it all. A cold beer would taste damn good right about now.

Jessie

I decide this morning when I wake up. It's my day off. Daniel dropped Lily on his way to work, because he works the nine-to-nine today. So here I am, in my messy bedroom, still lying in bed staring out the window wondering what in the hell to do with myself. I know I should be doing all kind of things: laundry, dishes, vacuuming, watering my garden, *finding* my garden under all those weeds ... but I could care less about any of that and it's worrying me, like when you realize you just aren't fitting into your life the way you should, like you're just slightly off centre from the heart of things. So I think of jam.

Not jam for me, or us or whatever, I mean, I can buy a jar of Smuckers for $1.99 at the SuperValu. But there's this country fair every Sunday on the way out of town and people sell their stuff there. Why not me? Why not make up big batches of jam and sell them and make a little extra money?

I have never made jam before. That might surprise you, since I'm a country girl and all. But my mother, my tuna-surprise-casserole, white-bread-marshmallow-fluff-sandwiches, hot-dogs-are-good-for-you mother, didn't ever make her own jam. She bought it, just like most of the other wives of Grace River. It wasn't until we moved out to the farmhouse that it occurred to me to try to grow vegetables and bake bread.

When I first walked in the door and saw the big sunny kitchen with all the hand-made cupboards with little glass doors and the 1950s yellow Arborite table and the white lacey curtains I had a dangerous revelation. Married at twenty-one, any dreams I might have had about going to college in Nelson and becoming a social worker, or going to college in Kamloops and being a nurse, or even my grade-six dream of being an astronaut, just kinda dissolved into this misty-eyed vision from the movies about being a good wife and a good mother … and I wanted to make healthy meals that you roasted in the oven and use fresh milk from real glass bottles and hang my laundry on the line while the kids swung from an old tire swing under the trees.

But soon that dream dissolved along with my other ones. Because in my dream of the perfect family life, I forgot the fact that it wasn't the 1950s anymore, and that the 1970s happened for a reason, and that reason was so that women like my mother could go out and get a job, even if it was in the lingerie department of the local Zellers, and buy their damn jam and not have to worry about being judged for it.

The reality is, here I am, thirty-one next month, and I have a big beautiful farmhouse that it is such a bitch to keep clean, I barely try. The rooms develop dust out of nowhere, and there's so much dirt tracked in there in the summer and snow and slush in the winter, the carpets have turned from off-white to dark grey. And if anyone can tell me who has time to bake bread or roast a chicken when you get home from a nine-hour shift serving greasy food to truckers and smelter crews all day, please speak up now or forever hold your peace.

The point of all this rambling can be traced back to what I said about revelations. I've had a few over the years in my search for the perfect business. The stained-glass phase, the cookie-baking phase, hell, even the damn chair-making phase. All of these products were to be sold at markets and festivals around the Kootenays and beyond, but ultimately all I ended up with was a bunch of molten metal stuck to my clothes, a few unhappy cookie customers who didn't appreciate the fact that I accidentally left out the sugar in one batch, and of course the pile of useless scrap wood in the backyard from all the pieces I cut wrong. It's time for me to get off my butt and do something new. And I'm starting with jam.

So off I go. I don't even shower, just pull my hair off my face with one of Lily's pink elastics and throw on some cut-offs and one of Daniel's shirts and I am on my way to buy jars and whatever else a person needs to make jam. It feels good, driving along the road, the sun on my arm, the Tragically Hip singing out through the morning about wheat kings and pretty things.

I pull into the SuperValu and the lot is almost empty. It's still early so I guess most people are still getting kids off to school or having their coffee. Which reminds me ... Usually it's the first thing I do, but I was so excited about my plan I completely forgot. The store has a deli. I'll grab one there. I have to get going, because I figure making jam could take a while. Especially if you don't know how to do it.

I go into the store and wave at Tracy, my high school valedictorian, who works the lotto counter. I grab a cart and head ... where? The store is cool and eerily empty. A couple of the cashiers are chatting, but the rest of the checkouts are abandoned. There is one little old man tottering near the entrance to the cereal aisle, but I don't see any other signs of life.

Well, okay. I need jars, I know that for sure. And I saw some in the housewares aisle the other day when I was buying dish soap. I head over and there they are, all stacked in the middle of the aisle as though they were expecting a stampede of jam-makers. I inspect the boxes. It looks like three different sizes. I grab one of each and figure seventy-five jars will be enough to get me started. They also have a display of little boxes of pectin, so I grab one of those too. Then I head back to the checkout. I know I'll need sugar, but I have a five-pound bag at home. And the fruit I'll have to buy out at Jersey's. I don't know what they have now, but whatever it is will be fine.

"Hi there," I say, to get the ladies' attention. They're still chattering away and giggling like kids, even though they're both my mom's age. One of them is Sunny's Aunt Carol, and she comes over to the checkout where I'm unloading my boxes.

She runs the first one over the scanner. "You making jam, Jess?"

I figure that's pretty obvious, but I don't want to be rude. "Yup. I'm gonna sell it at the fair."

"Oh, good for you." She looks at me kinda strange. "So do you have more pectin at home?"

"Uh ... no. Why? How much do I need?" What the hell *is* pectin anyway?

She smiles in that knowing way those motherly types have. She's already figured out I don't know what I'm doing. "Well, it depends how many batches you're making, honey. You go grab a few more boxes. I'll wait." She pats my jars and I head back to the jam aisle. I pick up four more boxes, return to the checkout, and toss them down. "Okay. All set."

She's amused, I can tell. Maybe word has gotten out around town about my cooking ability. I wouldn't put it past Sunny to tell stories about me to her relatives, since they're the type who make fancy food out of homemade pastry and stick toothpicks in it.

Before she rings in my stuff she asks me, "Do you have a canner, honey?"

"A canner?" I imagine some strange-looking contraption with big steel arms sealing my jars shut.

"Uh huh. A canner. It's really just a big pot. So you can sterilize the jars."

Great. I nod. I have a big pot, so that's covered. And it's also good to know about the sterilizing thing. Aunt Carol smiles, glances over at her friend at the next checkout to see if she's getting all of this. She is. Her friend, "Alice" according to her nametag, chimes in, "You need a good recipe or you'll end up with runny jam. Nobody wants to buy runny jam. Sometimes those recipes in the pectin boxes don't turn out."

I would probably have thought of all this stuff if I had my coffee this morning, I swear. I mean, at least I would have thought of the fact that I don't know what I'm doing and might need some help. I just don't always think things through, and sometimes I end up missing things. I eye the deli and I can almost smell the coffee beckoning me over there. "Okay," I say. "I need you two ladies to help me out here. Tell me everything. What do I need to do?"

I leave the store with jars, although they made me take back the large ones because they said I wouldn't be able to make as much money from large jars as I would from the smaller ones. I also have six boxes of pectin, another ten-pound bag of sugar, and a recipe that Carol printed up on the SuperValu office computer. Tracy even got in on the action and told me to go for the berries because it was a pain in the ass to get the skins and pits off cherries. So now I'm headed for Jersey's to buy a flat of strawberries and maybe raspberries if they have them yet. I will say this ... jam isn't going to be the money-making prospect I thought it was. I've already spent about forty bucks and the ladies told me the berries will cost me about forty more. I'll have to sell the jam for, like, ten bucks a jar.

The road out to Jersey's is nice. You just take the road past town and turn left, except instead of turning on our road you turn a little farther down. So I pass Kali's cute little cottage and on I go to Jersey's, where I discover they have both the kinds of berries I want. I buy a flat of each and start heading for home. As I turn back on to Route 36, I can see a white van parked on a gravel turnoff near a grove of pines right by where the rocks of the river gather up into a wild whirlpool of water. As I get closer I recognize the van from Nick's parking lot and realize it belongs to the environmentalist. I wonder what he's doing there, and just as I'm wondering, the strangest thing happens. I put my foot on the brake, slow down, pull off, and park right beside his van.

I sit there for a minute questioning what the hell I'm doing and then I just chalk it up to the new me. The adventurous one. So I leave the fresh berry smell erupting in my truck and wander down to the river's edge. I can see him near the whirlpool up to his thighs in whitewater, scooping water into what looks like a plastic cup. I watch him for a minute, wondering if I'm being creepy, when he looks up.

I wave. "Hey," I shout, like I'm an old buddy who just stopped by to say hello. He looks confused, or at least I think he does. It's hard to tell from fifty feet away. But he puts a lid on his cup and wades back to shore, climbing up over the rock and then onto the grass by the trees. His sandals are under a tree and he slips them on, still looking over at me standing by my truck like an idiot.

"I was just ... " I say and try to think. I can't come up with anything clever. "What are you doing? Catching minnows?"

He walks over and sets the cup down on the hood of his van. "Oh, hey. The waitress. How's it going?" He wipes his hands on his cotton pants, which are rolled up to his knees and soaked to his upper thighs.

"The waitress. Yeah, that's me. I just saw your van and wondered what you were up to."

"I'm collecting water samples." He's smiling and I figure he's probably thinking, *What did it look like I was doing?*

I lean against my truck. I can smell the berries through the open window like the best perfume you could ever buy. "Why don't you monitor them up near where the slag used to come out under the bridge? That's where you guys usually take samples."

"I will. But we're more interested in the overall picture, especially since AXIS isn't dumping their slag into the river now. We're more concerned about the long-term effects, I guess. A Native band in Washington is claiming, among other things, that the salmon numbers are down and they're seeing changes in the ones they do have."

This is the stuff of McAllister family dinners, right from the age when I could finally understand what my dad was talking about. "They've been claiming that for a long time."

He shrugs, kind of a relaxed can-you-blame-them sort of thing.

"Not that I blame them," I say and instantly feel stupid, like one of those people who says *I'm not racist but* … I look around trying to will away the hot blush I can sense rising over my face. It's a nice spot here, almost big enough for a picnic if you felt like it. There are two or three trees, the river is singing along over the rocks. I don't know why I never really noticed it before.

While I'm looking around he takes the sample off his hood and walks toward his door.

"So do you live down there? In the States?" I say quickly, trying to keep him talking so he doesn't leave. I know he does, he already told me at the diner that his parents are from Washington. Plus, he has US plates.

He opens his door and puts the sample inside, takes out a bottle of water, then shuts the door again. He points over toward the river and says, "You want to sit for a minute?"

I shrug in what I hope is a nonchalant way and follow him over to a tree. We settle underneath it in the shade. I'm wishing I had water too and I'm suddenly conscious of my sweaty Vernon Ice T-shirt and Lily's pink fluffy elastic holding back my hair. I watch him drink from his blue bottle, the sunlight reflecting through the plastic.

When he stops drinking he says, "Yeah. I'm from Mount Vernon.

It's about an hour north of Seattle." He passes me the bottle. "Here. You look hot. I'm Liam, by the way."

"Jessie." I'm a little surprised by the offer, but I take the water. Consider. Do I drink out of a stranger's water bottle? He's watching the river, leaning back on his elbows, legs stretched out casually in front of him. He doesn't look like he'd be offended either way. And I'm thirsty. And he's becoming less of a stranger every minute I'm here. I unscrew the cap and take a long drink, then set the bottle down. "So ... Mount Vernon. I've never been there. I mean, I've been camping through Oregon once, but never to Seattle or anything. It's a pretty big city, hey?"

"It's cool. Yeah, Seattle's big. Lots going on. Lots of good restaurants, great shows, music. I've been living there for the last six months or so. I miss home though. I grew up on the mountain on a little farm. Lots of trees, creek, meadow. And it's a small town ... about the same size as this place."

"So why don't you go home then?"

He glances over, takes the bottle. Takes a drink, obviously not concerned about my germs. "My girlfriend works in the city. She's a documentary filmmaker. It's too much of a commute. And I travel a lot anyway for work. One day I'll go back home, buy some land, build a house, grow some food."

I chew on a ragged nail and wonder if it's too late to take the elastic out of my hair. It seems stupid, but I know I have bits of hair falling out of my ponytail and it probably looks greasy ... it's just that it's not often I get to talk to an environmentalist who lives in Seattle with his documentary filmmaker girlfriend and wants to buy some land and grow his own food.

He gives a little laugh and points out to the river. "See that?"

I shake my head, following his finger.

"Fish jumped. A big one."

"I should let my husband know. He'll be out here with his rod in two seconds. He has the worst luck ... " I trail off. "What was it, a salmon?"

He looks over. "No. Not a salmon. But if your husband is fishing for salmon in here it's no wonder he's not having much luck."

I nod. "Yeah. Right. There aren't too many of those in here anymore."

I knew this, I knew there are only about a hundred salmon every year that can make it up the fish ladders on those dams they built down in the States. A fact that makes that salmon my dad found all those years ago even more depressing. I guess there were only ninety-nine that made it that year.

"You ever seen salmon spawning?" His curly brown hair is shot through with these gold streaks, probably from the sun, and it's rumpled, almost tangled but not quite. I figure this guy is outside a lot. His skin is tanned and smooth; his bare calves are corded with muscle.

I shake my head. "The only salmon I ever saw was a dead one my dad scooped out of the river and did metal tests on." I say this to get some sort of environmental conversation going so he knows I'm not as much of an idiot as I suspect he might think I am. But he doesn't respond to this.

"You should see it sometime," he says. "It's an amazing thing. You see those hundreds, even thousands of fish, all battered and bruised, fighting their way over rocks and through shallow water just so they can get back home before they die."

"It's so weird," I say. "Why do they bother? Why not just have your babies any old place? Why not just give up and live out your last few days in peace? It doesn't make sense to fight so hard just to get back to the place you started from."

He smiles. "Yeah, it's a bit of a mystery. I guess it depends on whether you *liked* the place you started from."

"How do they even know where to go? All those hundreds of miles and out to sea and they somehow find their way back."

"Also a bit of a mystery, but they figure that the salmon use some sort of internal magnetic compass that gets them close to their stream, and then they can smell the soil and the plants from the place they were born and they start heading toward it. As for why they bother ... I don't know. I guess familiarity is a powerful thing."

"Do any of them ever just say 'screw this' and go somewhere else?"

He laughs. "It's coded into their genes, so not very often. But it does happen."

"There's always a rebel."

"Yes, there is."

"Don't you ever get depressed?" I say suddenly.

He looks over. Waits for me to go on.

"I mean, don't you ever just think it's not worth it? Hasn't this river already put up with canneries, dams, the smelter … it's been polluted for hundreds of years. Isn't it just too late?"

He doesn't answer for a minute and then he says, "There's a Chinese philosopher who said, 'The mark of a successful man is one that has spent an entire day on the bank of the river without feeling guilty about it.' There's a couple of ways of looking at that, but to me it means living your life in a good way. Not just sleepwalking through it, causing damage, and living with that low-grade guilt from the aftermath."

He checks his watch, which is on one of those fabric bands that can probably support your weight when you're rock climbing or something, and then starts to rise. I guess our time is up. I stand too. He reaches out his hand and I stare at it for a moment before realizing that he wants me to shake it. "It was nice to meet you again, Jessie. Sorry I have to run."

I give him my hand and he just holds it in his firmly, more of a squeeze than a shake.

"You too." When he lets go of my hand I fold my arms in front of the biggest stain on my shirt, which is right over my belly button. A raspberry squished into it while I was carrying them to the truck. "I'm sure I'll see you around."

We walk back toward our vehicles and when he passes my truck he stops and says, "Wow. That's a lot of berries."

I look in the window at the crates. "Yeah. I'm making jam."

"That's going to be a lot of jam."

I wave my hand as if to say "no big deal," which it doesn't seem to be after all this life-and-death salmon stuff and finding home and documentary-filmmaking girlfriends. "Yeah, well. I'm planning on selling it at the fair in Ashville. It's my latest thing. I tried stained glass, but it took me ages to make and people didn't seem to want to pay two hundred dollars for a little piece of glass to make it worthwhile." I point to my rear-view mirror. "I made a few. One of the little ones is hanging there."

He looks in politely, brushing my arm as he bends to see into my truck. "Hey, the river. Very nice. I like the colours."

Although it's sweet of him, I know it isn't my best work, which is why it's hanging in the truck instead of a window back home. It's just a little circle about the size of my palm, and it has a blue ribbon of river at the bottom and a few green hills and then blue sky at the top. I fit a little piece of amber-coloured glass in the corner for the sun, but it was too big and ended up looking like the sky had caught on fire. "Yeah. I don't know. It kind of looks like something my little girl would make. That's why I moved on to other things. I also tried making those wooden chairs people have on their decks. I got the plans and everything, but on my first one I ended up with three arms and a missing slat for the back. I guess I haven't found my groove yet."

He moves away from the truck and looks at me. "Well, you'll never find it if you don't keep looking." He seems like he's about to say something else, but he chews his lip for a second and then says, "Hey, jam is cool. Jam could end up being your groove." He looks out over the river. "Man, it is beautiful here. Have you lived here a long time?"

I lean against my truck, the sun glaring down on me. "My whole life." I shade my eyes. The sun doesn't seem to bother Liam. He's not even squinting.

"Do you like it?"

I can tell he wants the honest answer, not just the *Yes, the weather is lovely and there are some nice hiking trails* answer. I can tell he's the kind of guy who always wants the honest answer. "Yeah, I like it, I guess. It's nice to live in a place where everyone knows you and there's all that history and stuff … " As I say it I'm not convinced I mean it. Parts of it, sure, but it's hard to sum up in one sentence and have it be real and completely true. It's hard to sum up anything in one sentence and have it be completely true.

He points a finger at me. "See? There it is. The familiarity. You have that coded in there too."

And before I can tell him that it was only a half-truth and that sometimes the other part of me wants to bolt from my home stream like a rebel salmon and find somewhere new and fresh and easy, Mike drives by in his Camaro. And there I am leaning against my truck like I've been hanging out all day and there Liam is standing two feet away from me pushing his gold-shot surfer hair off his eyes in what I now know is an unconscious habit and doesn't really have anything to do with whether he can see or not. I think, *Oh, great. Here we go.* But I wave. Mike must have been at Kali's. He looks at me strange but waves back. My heart trips a little, but I just ignore it. I get myself together. Stop lounging. Stand up straight. I wish I could shake Liam's hand again without seeming like a dork, but I know that's not possible so I just say, "Well. I guess I'll see you around. How long are you here for?"

His eyes are following Mike's car. "Not long. I'll be here for a couple more days, then I drive up north to the source for a few days. I come back though town for a day or so at some point again before I head home." He seems distracted now. Something's brewing behind his green eyes that I can't figure out, some private worries. I wonder what his life is like at home with his moviemaking girlfriend. I wonder if she has dyed-black hair and wears red lipstick and drinks espresso straight up with no milk or sugar. I wonder what his house looks like.

"You take care, Jessie," he says and heads toward his van.

At his door he looks back and gives me the half-smile again, turning those eyes on me full force for the first time. There's a moment, one of those moments where for some reason you keep looking at someone and you can't look away, like your eyes are just the right ends of two magnets. I let it go longer than I should, past when the little alarm bells start going off, when I have to remind myself I'm a married woman and all that crap.

I tell myself that it's just curiosity about someone from out of town and it has nothing to do with how he looks or his soft mellow voice or how he's so different with his lounging and his hand squeezing and his slow smile that spreads out over you like a warm blanket. Even so. He's the one that looks away first, hopping in his van and peeling out onto the road, leaving me standing there with my stained T-shirt and dirty hair and a truck full of berries.

Jackson

*C*aroline's in the shower singing to herself while I make the boys some dinner. Nothing fancy, just canned ravioli, but I grate on the extra cheese like my mom used to and it tastes pretty damn good, if I do say so myself.

It's Caroline's birthday. I was planning that little barbeque at the house, have everybody bring their kids kind of thing, but she nixed that real quick and we're off to Laredo's for a big party instead, after we drop off the boys at my mom's.

I pull the pot off the stove and pour the ravioli into two plastic bowls. Then I sprinkle on the cheese and set it in front of the boys.

"Yuck," says Travis right away and as usual.

Brooks gives his a little stir, thinking about it while he lets the cheese melt into the noodles. "Yeah, yuck. This is gwoss, Dad."

I start to rinse out the pot. "Too bad. Eat up, guys." I check the clock and see it's almost six, which means we only have about half an hour before we have to leave to drop off the boys. I dry the pot and set it on the counter.

"Travis, you keep an eye on Brooks, okay? I gotta get ready." I give him a pat on the head as I walk toward the door.

"So you can go partying with Mom?" He's got that tone now, you know, like a teenager. The thing is, he's only eight, so I wasn't expecting it so soon. It wasn't so long ago he was still asking to be carried to bed and wearing pyjamas with feet in them.

"That's right, bud. Partying with Mom," I holler back over my shoulder.

I can hear her in the shower, singing away like she's on a stage in Vegas or something, loud and happy and brave as hell.

"Jesus, Jackson, just park anywhere. Stop circling around like a buzzard." Caroline is checking her hair in the rear-view mirror, which she twisted away from me while we were on the highway. I had to shoulder check before I changed lanes to get on to the exit. I finally pick a spot not too far from the doors to Laredo's. The parking lot is almost full, which means we're in for quite a night, because it's only 7:30 and most of the real partiers haven't even left home yet, so everyone here is here for Caroline.

That's what happens when you go to school in a town and then never leave when you're done. You get 197 people at your birthday party, and most of them know too much about you. Just for an example—there's people in there who know who she kissed in Billy Perkin's wood shed when she was fifteen and who she showed her right boob to in the boy's washroom at a school dance when she was sixteen (it wasn't me ... I didn't see it until a couple years later. It was worth waiting for, believe me). Some of them know her mother left her father for another woman and now lives on some hippie island on the West Coast making sculptures out of garbage, and most of them know that her dad is a drunk and has been ever since her mom turned gay.

I look over at her now, scrunching her blonde hair to make it curlier, checking her makeup. She's checking for lines too, I can tell. Wrinkles. A sure sign that it will be over some day, all that clear smooth pink skin. "You look fine," I tell her.

"Fine?" She narrows her eyes like I just told her she was a fat pig.

I shake my head. "Sorry. Gorgeous. Red hot. How's that?"

She gives me a little smile, showing those small white teeth. She has a pink rose in her hair, tucked behind her ear. "You look like a Spanish dancer or something," I say, just to keep things moving in the right direction.

She turns back to the mirror and runs her fingertip under her eyelid. "Spanish dancers wear red roses, Jackson. Not pink."

I pull the keys out of the ignition and open my door. "Well, you would know, Sparky."

She presses her lips together, smacks them open, looks at herself one more time, and then opens her own door. "Yeah. I cut the stem too short on this one and I couldn't fit it in the arrangement. Annemarie doesn't mind, as long as it was an honest mistake and you don't 'accidentally' cut a whole dozen wrong."

I meet her at the front of the truck and we walk toward the entrance together. "You get tomorrow off?"

She nods. "No problem. We only have the Wakefield funeral anyway. I did most of the arrangements today and left them in the cooler. Yellow carnations." She says this like yellow carnations are only fit for people with names like Lester or Leroy on their way to the prom with their second cousin.

"I know you're ... " I start to say, but I'm drowned out when she shouts over to a group of people near the door.

"Birthday girl's here!" she yells, waving her hand in the air in case for some crazy reason they didn't hear her. "Let the games begin."

What I was going to say was that she's more the type of girl who's into exotic flowers, like ... I don't know ... orchids, maybe. Something beautiful and tough to keep alive.

"Here's the thing right here, okay? If you're gonna fucking work your ass off to make it to the Cup, then why the hell would you sit back and let yourself get fucking slaughtered in the last game?"

"Oh come on, Danny, they lost by one goal. They played strong. Their defence was awesome." Mike is chugging a Bud, slumped back in his chair, Kali sitting beside him with her hand on his leg. She looks kinda out of place here with that crazy orange-and-purple-striped dress and her black hair and those dark gypsy eyes. I wonder what she thinks about the dart boards and the peanuts and all the drinking and carrying on in there. She doesn't say much, hasn't all night, unless something political comes up. She had a few things to say about AXIS, let me tell you. But hockey, not so much.

"Nah ... they're pussies," Daniel says. "Sitting there on their big fat contracts. They don't give a shit anymore. Why should they even give a shit about the Cup when they get paid so much?"

Jessie takes a haul off her wine cooler and swats Danny with her free hand. He's pretty drunk by now and it's not even worth trying to argue with him because he just cuts you off. I crack a peanut shell with my fingers and pop the nut into my mouth. The table is covered in shells, and there's a big pile of them by my feet. The weird thing is, I'm the only one eating them. For some reason I just can't stop. It's like some nervous tic or something.

Daniel swats her back, just playing, but he catches her arm as she's lowering her drink and it sloshes over the rim of the bottle onto her white T-shirt, spreading across her chest. She sets her bottle down. "Jesus! How many times do I have to tell you I'm not entering a wet T-shirt contest?" She pulls the shirt away from her body to check out the damage. Daniel is laughing. Good thing Jess could care less about clothes. It's not like she was dressed up like Caroline, who would have had a fit and demanded to be taken home to change.

I crack another nut and look around. The place is hopping. It's almost eleven now, so the banquet table with all the potluck salads and cold chicken wings and Jell-O moulds has been cleared away and people are pretty much concentrating on getting wasted. Bud is looking happy there behind the bar, pouring out shots and pulling pints like he's in the bartender Olympics or something.

"Hey, guys. This place is jumping! That Caroline can draw a crowd." Sunny pulls up a chair between me and Danny and grabs a handful of peanuts from my bowl.

Jessie points to her shirt, which is sort of stuck on her chest. "Check it out. If I dance on the bar, maybe I'll make enough tips to buy the next round."

Daniel signals for the waitress. "If you're lucky."

"You're drunk, Danny," Sunny says, chewing on a mouthful of nuts. "The night is young. Save some obnoxious comments for later."

He grins at her. "Oh, I got some saved up for you, honey, don't you worry."

I look away, back out at the crowd. I don't know where Caroline's got to, I haven't seen her for almost an hour. I'm not worried, though. This is the way it goes when you've been married for ten years. Why the hell would you want to sit and talk to the person you wake up next to every morning when you get a chance to see other people, right?

"Okay, so, Sunny, what do you think about this environmentalist asshole? Do you think it's cool or what?" Danny's shifting gears again.

She looks confused. "Why would I think it's cool?"

He shrugs, takes another swig. "I dunno ... seems like Jess here thought it was cool from what she said. Something about striving to save the rivers even if there's no point to it or some such crap." He sounds like an ass, but you can't tell if he's really serious or not. That and he's petting Jessie's hair like she was a cat or something, which she doesn't look too happy about.

Kali reaches for her red wine. "He's just doing his job, Danny. Just like you." She smiles and tilts her drink at him like a private toast.

I have to agree with that one. "Yeah. It's not his fault he got sent out here," I say, crunching on peanuts. We're getting down to the last few now that Sunny's helping herself. "He'll just do his thing and bugger off again. It won't make a bit of difference."

"You never know ... " Kali says, but Mike cuts her off with a sloppy kiss.

"That's my girl, eh?" he says. "Gonna save the world."

"One plant at a time," Daniel says. "Hey, Kali, you ever think of growing something more profitable in that garden of yours? I got a few ideas ... "

"Hey!" Sunny calls out. "Can I speak here? I believe a question was addressed to *me*." She taps herself in the chest. "Okay. I say the hippie is kinda hot, so let him be." She grins at us.

Daniel raises his eyebrow. "Is that so? Hmm. Jess here forgot to mention that."

"Whatever," Jessie says, looking away. "I don't think he's hot. Too scraggly for me. I like my men clean-cut and obnoxious, don't I, honey?" She's joking, but it comes off a bit more serious than she means it to be. For some reason she looks over at Mike, and he looks back at her, a little smile on his face.

Daniel puts his beer down. "Yeah? You gonna save the world too, Jess? What's it gonna be? Pottery for world peace? Deck chairs for orphans?"

There's silence as everyone stares into their drinks like they just lost something in there and then Jessie shakes her head and stands, wet T-shirt and all. "I'm gonna go dance. I love this song. Come on, Sunny." It's the Eagles singing "Desperado," and I have to say I'm curious to see the two of them swaying together in a slow dance. Sunny scrapes her chair back, grabs the last two peanuts, and salutes me, following Jessie off through the crowd.

Just then I spot Caroline. Her halter top is pulled down low on one side, almost exposing that famous chest I was talking about. I know it's not possible, but her skirt seems shorter somehow too and she's listing heavily to one side.

"Shit," I say and rise up from my seat. Daniel turns around and laughs.

"Don't sweat it, man. It's her birthday. She's having a blast."

I work through the crowd just as she's climbing up onto a barstool with her bare feet. She stands on the stool and people start cheering. I grab on to her leg. "Hey there, Sparky. Come on down now."

She lifts one foot and twirls it around, skimming the top of the bar with it as I hold her other leg steady. Some of the people cheer, and Bud just grins from behind the bar. "We in for a repeat of last year, sweetheart?" he calls.

Jesus. Last year. I'd rather forget all about that. "Caroline." I'm trying to sound firm, and I grip her leg more tightly.

"Fuck off, Jackson," she slurs, placing her foot on the bar and trying to pull her other leg away.

Daniel appears at my side, a fresh beer in his hand. "Let her go, man. She wants to dance. Right, Care? Go on, girl. Show us what you got."

She shakes her leg away and I let go. She leans down toward me, points in my face. "It's my fucking birthday. So let me do what I want. Right?" She yells out to the crowd for encouragement. They yell back, cheering. "That's right. I'm gonna do my birthday BAR DANCE!" She hops up and holds her arms in the air as the crowd cheers her on.

She smirks at me, but I can see something sad behind those blue eyes too, before she turns them away from me and starts moving her hips. She's disappointed in me for trying to stop her. And she's right. Who do

I think I am? It's her birthday. Everyone gets wasted on their birthday, it's like a town rule here. I look around and it seems like everyone's staring, wondering what the hell's the matter with me. Jess and Sunny are at the other end of the bar. Sunny's got a smile on her face, but Jess is watching as Daniel starts climbing up on the bar beside Caroline. I just shake my head and back away.

Somebody punches in Shania Twain's "I Feel Like a Woman" on the jukebox and Caroline starts bumping and grinding. Daniel can't keep up, and he won't put down his beer, so I'm worried he's gonna get a good bump from those tiny hips and go sailing into the wall of liquor bottles behind the bar.

Jess walks up. "Sorry, Jackson." She sounds tired. Fed up. I know that feeling.

I shrug. "Hell, they're having fun. And I wasn't about to get up on that bar with her."

"Thank god for that," she says. She pats my shoulder as she walks away, heading for the front door.

I watch them up there, my wife and my best friend, and it's hard to put my finger on what's wrong. I'm not jealous, it isn't that. It's just some part of me thinks I should be the one up there with her. That there's something wrong with me for not being able to just let loose and relax and have a good time with my wife on her birthday. I watch Daniel catch her elbow as she gets too close the side of the bar. I watch how she's starting to lose the beat, how her movements are changing from a sexy dance to a drunken stumble as she laughs and claps along, off beat, to the music. I watch how the crowd around her claps too, smiling and thinking what a fun gal that Caroline is. Then I have to look away.

Daniel

I'm dreaming I'm climbing Black Rock when Lily wakes me up, landing on my back like a sack of potatoes. She's lucky I don't swat her off me. I don't always wake up too good. But this time I figure out it's her pretty quick and just let her curl up next to me.

It's weird. The sweat on my face and my arms is making the sheets stick to me. In the dream I was sweaty and hot while I tried to climb. And I was freaking out, heart pumping, breathing hard as my feet were slipping and sliding on the rocky face of the cliff before I finally made it to the top. From up there I could see all of Grace River, the brown hills, the grey highway, the houses and the stores on Main Street, AXIS sending out white smoke into the blue sky, and the Grace River looking like a big black snake someone had run over flat.

I open up my eyes and give Lily a little pat on her back. She's pretending to be asleep, making loud snoring sounds. I look over at the bedside table for the alarm clock ... 8:15? Shit! I sit up quickly, knocking Lily on her side.

"Hey!" she yells, her blonde hair all knotted around her freckled face. She puts her hands on her hips. I can't get over how much she looks like Jessie. Well, except for the knotted hair, I guess. Lily hates it when Jess tries to brush her hair, so mostly she just doesn't bother.

She gives up on being pissed off and starts bouncing on the bed. "Hey, Dad. You're going to a hockey termament, right? Today you're going to it?"

I check the clock again. Shit. "Yeah, bug, I gotta get a move on too."

She pouts. "But WHY can't I come too, and Mom?"

I head to the closet. Bobby and Jackson will be here in twenty minutes. I gotta hustle or we'll miss our first game at 10:45. Ashville is over an hour away, and I definitely need a coffee before we play. I didn't get home from Care's party until almost five. I guess I stayed a little longer than I planned to. "Your mom has to work. And you have school today. And your big play, right?"

"Right," she agrees, nodding like crazy. "Don't you wanna see my play? I'm gonna be broccoli. I practised and everything."

"Geez, Lily, I know, kiddo. I just . . . " This is a tricky one. I come back to the bed and hold her little face in my hands. "I gotta be there for the team. You know? I made a promise, right, and you gotta keep promises. I made it before I knew you were gonna be the broccoli." She narrows her eyes at me but finally kind of nods her head and I let her go, give her a big kiss on the cheek, and head back to the closet.

I look around for some clean jeans and stuff them in my travel bag. I already got the hockey gear packed up and waiting in the garage.

"It was fun last time when we went with you. I watched your games and Mom was there and we ate at ABC and I got to have butterscotch pudding, remember? It *sucks* when I can't go. I wish I wasn't even the broccoli. I wish Kevin Albert could be it instead. The broccoli sucks. I only get to sing one song."

I have to smile at that one while I'm hunting through the overflowing laundry basket for underwear. "Well, why don't you sing it to me? For practice?" So she starts belting out this song about the greener the better and the king of the veggies while I look for my underwear with no luck. Laundry just does not seem to get done around here. Fine. No underwear. I'll go commando. I toss the bag onto the bed, just missing Lily, who's got her mouth open wide like an opera singer or something while she yells out, "Four delicious servings a daaaay . . . " which seems to be the grand finale.

I give her another kiss on my way out the door. "Sounds like you're gonna rock the house down. I don't think Kevin Albert could pull that off. And good thing you're not coming with me, anyway. You'd have to share a room with Daddy and Big Bobby and Jackson. You don't want to sleep in the same room as three stinky old men, do you?" She wrinkles her nose and I pat her cheek and head to the shower.

After my shower I head down to the kitchen, where Jess is making coffee. I wonder how she even found the coffeemaker, the place is such a fucking mess. Dishes are piled in the sink, all over the counters. She's been distracted with this whole jam business, I guess.

"Hey, babe. How long do you figure that coffee's gonna be? I gotta get moving." I drop my overnight bag on the floor. Jess doesn't answer. I grab two six-packs of beer from the fridge and stuff them on top of my socks and deep cold muscle rub. I look over at her. Is she sleepwalking or what? "Hello?"

She shrugs "I don't know, Danny, I guess it'll take as long as it always does. Just stop at the 7-11 or something." There's this icy edge to her voice that she can't really hide. I'm used to that, trust me. But, man. Her blonde hair is shining in the sun coming through the kitchen window, and my faded blue Harley-Davidson T-shirt is hugging her in all the right places. I can see a peek of striped panties and consider missing my first game for a sec, but I know it's not even worth trying.

I take a wild guess. "So, what, are you pissed about last night?" She left way before me, around midnight, and I got a ride with Mikey later. I can hear Bobby's Ford pickup churning up gravel in the driveway as I zip up my bag.

"Who, me? Come on. I'm never pissed off." She shoots me a smile. There are dark circles under her eyes. She looks tired. I think about asking her if she's okay, but I don't want to open up that can of worms right before I take off. What if she says no?

I laugh instead. "Sure, you're the calmest woman I know. Absolutely. That's why I married you." Bobby honks from the driveway. "So I'll see you tomorrow night. It'll be late, though. If we make the finals, our last game is at 9:15, then we gotta shower and drive home. I guess it'll be around two or three in the morning."

Jessie pops some bread in the toaster. "Yeah, well don't wake me up. I work the early shift Sunday morning."

I come over and wrap my arms around her waist, turning her around to face me. "That might be tough. You are one hot chick, you know that?"

She rolls her eyes. "Go on. They'll start panicking if you don't get out there soon with that beer. And don't wake me up, Danny, I mean it.

I'm working late tomorrow night and then first thing Sunday." She stops nagging a minute and lets me hold her close, breathe in her soft, flowery smell. Then I head out the door, a free man.

I toss my gear in the back of Bobby's black pickup and climb in beside Jackson, who hands me a styrofoam cup of 7-11 coffee.

Bobby nods from the driver's seat. "Hey, Danny. You made it out, did you? How'd it go last night?" His eyes are puffy. He was working night shift, so he hasn't slept at all.

"Awesome party, man." I look at Jackson. "How about you? What time you make it home?"

Jackson's staring through the windshield at the road. "Oh, like five-thirty. I think Bud was ready to pull his rifle on us by the time I finally got Caroline to leave."

We drive along the main street of town, past the row of shops and restaurant, then crest a small hill and pass Nick's and head out of town.

We roll into Ashville just in time for our first game. It's an easy win for us, embarrassing for the Fernie Fireballs ... we cream them 10-2, despite the fact that most of us haven't had more than a few hours' sleep. Then we spend the rest of the day hanging out in the motel room watching football and eating Chinese takeout. We win our second game that night, thanks to an overtime goal by yours truly, have a few drinks at the Ashville Ice Sports Pub, and then bring some beer back to our room and hang out until we all pass out. Saturday we play our morning game and then just chill all afternoon watching the other teams play until our last game.

After that awesome start we kinda lose it in the fourth game later that night ... guys are hungover and tired, and we get too many penalties for roughing and fighting. We lose the game by a goal, cheating ourselves out of a place in the finals. We decide to have a few beers before we head home and announce our defeat, so we go back up to the pub. It's packed, almost all the guys from the tournament are there, plus some wives and girlfriends. We're sitting around the table rehashing the game when Mike, already right pissed from drinking beer at the arena all day, comes over with a bleached blonde, her unbelievably long legs stretching out from a skintight pink dress. I figure she must be all of twenty-one. Here we go.

"Boys, this is Kansas. My new friend." Mike hangs his arm like dead meat around her shoulder, whispering something in her ear. She giggles like a little girl and swats him away. He pulls out a chair for her and sits down next to her.

There's a weird silence for a minute and then Bobby gives Kansas a smile. "So, Kansas. That's a different name, eh? Is there some, uh ... meaning to it or something?" He looks intimidating, because of his size and his black T-shirts and biker jacket, but he's just a soft-spoken teddy bear when it comes to women, which works out pretty good for him. He's also the polite one of the group; I couldn't give a shit where she got her name. I check out the big picture window in front of us. It looks out over the ice below, where the Haley Hurricanes and the Johnson River Rockets are battling it out in a three-all game for the final. I put my money on the Hurricanes. They're a faster, younger team, and Johnson River doesn't look like they want it bad enough.

"Oh, yeah, like, my parents? They like, conceived me in Kansas on this road trip? So they figured, Hey, nobody's named Kansas, right?" She winks at us. Well, mostly at Mikey. Jackson is eating pretzels and watching the game too. I look back down and the Hurricanes have the puck; their beefy centre is weaving through a useless line of Rockets and coming up on the left side of the net. I rise up halfway to my feet, but the puck is knocked away by a speedy Rockets defenceman who comes out of nowhere. I sit back down.

"Jesus." I nudge Jackson and it makes him drop a pretzel. "Did you see that? That guy is fucking fast."

He scans the game. "Yeah? What number?"

"Thirty-seven." We watch as number thirty-seven grabs the puck again and sails across the ice toward the Hurricanes' net.

He whistles though his teeth. "We don't have speed like that. Not even close."

I find that a bit fucking offensive, since I'm the only one on the team who ever played on Grace River's junior team, and if I hadn't busted my knee I would have had a chance in the draft for the NHL. But I know that was a lifetime ago. I know I'm getting slower: I haven't told anyone, but I think I can feel the signs of arthritis in my knee, and I can't dig in like I used to when I'm on a breakaway. I take a long swig of beer and keep my mouth shut.

"Hey, guys." Mike snaps his fingers in our faces. "Guys. Kansas here says there's this great club over town. They got $2.50 tequila shooters. What do you think?" He's slurring. I know I should be looking out for him. Mikey, he's like the retarded kid brother when he drinks. He can't control himself. He's always doing stupid shit. I know he loves Kali and all that, but I don't have it in me to raise hell over him wanting to hang out with this chick. She's just a plastic blonde, man. It's not like he's gonna leave Kali and shack up with her or anything. He just wants a few laughs.

I look around the room. Most of the guys are starting to leave to find the real parties, except for the ones who brought their wives and kids. They'll be going back to their rooms to watch pay-per-view movies and order pizza. For a second I almost miss Jess, but then I remember the last trip we took out here. I mean, yeah, it was fun for Lily, but me and Jessie fought the whole time over stupid things like where to eat or when to stop for gas. She got pissed at me for going out with the guys after one of the games too because she said she didn't come to sit on her ass in a motel room while I partied it up. She'd been asleep when I came back to the room anyway, I don't get what the big fucking deal was. Fuck it. I stand up. "Party's dying down here. Let's go." I grab my jacket.

Jackson and Bobby do the same, but Jackson's looking at me like he wants to talk to me privately. I'm not in the mood. Kansas is all excited, and she pulls a tiny cell phone out of her tiny purse. "Oh, you guys are gonna totally love it. I'm just calling a couple of friends, okay?" She starts punching numbers. I can see that Jackson looks terrified as he watches Kansas tell her friends to meet them at the bar. Mike is playing with Kansas's hair as she talks. I make a mental note not to let him drive.

We all pile into Mike's Camaro, with Jackson driving. Mike sits in the back with Kansas on his knee. I'm in the passenger seat, a beer between my legs. Not a bad place to be. Aerosmith blasts from Mike's new speakers.

"Turn it up! Crank that baby!" Mike yells from the backseat. I can feel the buzz start taking over as I watch the town's lights whiz by the window. I settle back in the leather seat, sinking into it.

"Hey, you guys?" Kansas is leaning between the front seats, her head inches from mine. I can smell her cheap perfume, like baby powder and dying roses.

"What's up, Kansas?" I like saying her name, I like how it rolls off my tongue. I check out her perfect Barbie profile as she leans forward. Her boobs are falling out of her pink dress and I don't think she's got a bra on to help the situation out. "Kansas. So are your friends named Montana and Texas, or what?"

She laughs this short little shriek. "Omigod, that's so funny! No! But, you know, I do know a girl named Montana, I met her in Cancun? She was, like, a model?"

Mike growls from the backseat. "Get back here, Kentucky."

She swats him away, still talking. "Okay, anyway, I was going to say we should ... oh, hold on, look at that, look at that ... " Me and Jackson peer through the windshield into the dark. We're driving through the rural part of town now, past farms, flat fields, and small hills. She points at a rocky hill with a smattering of coarse trees circling the perimeter. "We should totally go there later. It's like a big rock, but there's this path on the other side, and trees and stuff? And you can hike up to the top." I stare at that rock.

"We've got a rock like that in Grace River," Jackson says.

Kansas sits back. "Cool," she says, her voice muffled. "Can you climb it?"

Jackson looks over at me, I can feel it, but I just ignore him. I won't look back. I hit the button for the window and toss my beer can onto the road. The air is cold on my face. It feels good.

Jackson looks back at the road. "Yeah, you can climb it."

The club is called The Jungle, and it's a warehouse-type building with green vines painted on the walls. There are some stuffed parrots hanging from the ceiling and a large mangy-looking stuffed gorilla by the front entrance. I'm definitely feeling the beer now, my whole body vibrating with the thumping of the club music. There's a bunch of writhing bodies on the dance floor and the huge bar lit up with Christmas lights. Kansas pushes us through the club, waving at people as she goes, pulling Mike by the hand. We get to a table at the back and settle into the cheap red velvet chairs as Kansas runs off to the bar. She comes back with three blonde girls wearing tight jeans and high heels.

Kansas shows us her friends like one of those girls on *The Price is Right*, with a big sweep of her arm. I hear their names and forget them pretty much as soon as they leave her mouth. One of them sits beside me, gives me a bright smile. Her hair reminds me of Jessie's, it's long and smooth and more natural than her crispy-looking hairsprayed friends'. I smile back. Just to be polite.

Kansas and her friends are so bubbly and excited it's hard not to have a good time. They order a couple rounds of tequila shooters and soon it's like we've been hanging out together for years. Even Jackson has warmed up a bit. He finally takes off that goddamn plaid work jacket and he's listening to one of the girls babble on about her job at an insurance place like it was the most interesting thing he ever heard. I know better than she does if she thinks it's going anywhere, though.

Even drunk Jackson would never flirt with girls. Not even as a teenager. It's a fucking miracle he ever worked up the nerve to ask Caroline out and an even bigger miracle that she said yes. It's only because of that goon Ricky she was with before. He played D on our high school team, but he was a real asshole. Sucker-punching, running the goalie … anyway, he slapped Caroline around a bit and one night they got in a fight at a party out at the lake and he pushed her and she fell on a piece of broken glass. She still has the scar on her cheek, but at least she got something good out of the deal, 'cause guess who was there to drive her home and wipe her tears?

"Wanna dance?" The girl next to me—Mel?—is holding out her hand. I stare at those cheap rings and silver bracelets. Think for a second. Dance. Yeah, what the hell. I stand up, and that's when I can really feel the beer and the shooters. I almost trip over the leg of my chair, but I recover pretty quick. "Absolutely. But take it easy on me, I'm an old man." She's nice enough to laugh.

She's wearing one of those tops that ties up around the neck, and when she starts to dance her shirt rides up over her hips. I'm wondering how old she is ... twenty? Twenty-two? And then I make myself look away and just focus on the dancing. My fucking head is throbbing, pounding along to the beat. Then I get shoved by Bobby—him and the others have all made it out to the dance floor too. It's a funny scene, actually. All these young girls with their cheap shoes and their cheap jewellery and their tight shirts and then Bobby and his black leather biker vest and his big belly and skinny Jackson with his plain white T-shirt glowing in the lights and his hair sticking up. Kansas raises her arms and lets out a rock concert scream. "YEAH!" The other girls scream too. I laugh my ass off. Everything seems so hilarious all of a sudden. I watch Jackson try to keep a safe distance from his girl, dancing without moving most of his body. He just swings his arms from side to side and smiles like he's at a Sunday school picnic or something.

Mel slides up and starts moving her body against me and I can smell that sweet, soapy smell of her hair. I think of Jessie, which is probably a good idea, and I can't remember the last time we danced together. Mikey's birthday last year? No, she didn't come.

And then Jackson looks over, sees Mel dancing with me, swinging her hips with her eyes closed, and he kind of gives me this warning look and points his head toward the door. He wants to go, which is fucking funny. I just laugh.

The song changes to some slow, annoying Shania Twain song that Caroline always plays on the jukebox at Laredo's. Mel says, "Do you want to sit this one out?" She lets her lips brush against my ear and I can kind of feel the pit of my stomach give out. *Shit.* I tell her yeah, and then I kind of stumble over to the table, waving at the waitress as I go by. I need a couple more drinks.

A few hours later we're all piled into the Camaro. Jackson is driving again, but this time there are girls on all the laps except his. He's been flat-out ignoring his girl, Alex, since she tried to kiss him on the dance floor. He would have gone back to the motel, trust me, he really wanted to, but I pointed out that everyone else was too drunk to drive. Which is true. Definitely true. Right now I gotta mouthful of Mel's hair, and I reach around her to get it out. She's leaning heavily on me, and I wonder fuzzily if she's passed out. She was going at the tequila pretty hard.

I squeeze her thigh, just because it's right there. It's so toned and thin, I wonder what she does for exercise. She's probably told me, she kept talking for most of the night, but I can't say as I wasn't really paying much attention, the music and the words blending together into the background. Tennis? I squeeze again and she sighs softly. I pull my hand off her leg and rest it on the armrest. *Shit.*

"OOOOH!" There's a shriek from the back. I try to crane my neck to see who it was. Kansas is bouncing on Mike's lap, pointing out the window. "Let's climb up the rock!"

"Holy, are you crazy, Kansas? We'll get killed. Everybody's wasted." It's the other girl, Tammy, perched on Bobby's big knee.

I see the rock as we get closer. The moonlight is lighting up the drooping shapes of the trees. It's a rock hill, maybe five storeys high. About the same size as Black Rock, but wider. Not as treacherous. What the hell. You only live once, right? "Let's do it!" I shout, and Mel laughs and covers her ears.

Jackson slows down. "No. Really? Guys, it's getting late." He points at the clock on the dash, which tells us it's already 2:00 AM. "We need to get back home. I said we'd be back by now."

"Why?" Mike hollers. "They're all sleeping anyway. What the hell difference does it make if we get back at two or fucking seven?"

"Yeah. Come on! Don't be lame," Kansas pleads.

Jackson just shakes his head and I can see that muscle twitching in his jaw, but he turns off onto a dirt road, heading toward the rock.

We park and stumble out of the truck. Mike grabs a couple of old blankets from the trunk and I start toward the hill. The girls hang back giggling and trying to light smokes. Jackson catches up with me. He doesn't look at me as we walk along the narrow dirt path, and I know exactly what he's going to say, but he says it anyway. "Danny. Think about what you're doing, man. You been down this road before. Think about it."

Behind us, the girls have started singing an old Bon Jovi song, and Mike joins in, wailing along to "Wanted Dead or Alive." I know what he's talking about. But hey, I'm just having a few laughs. I'm not planning on doing anything I'm not supposed to. "What are you talking about, brother?" I pat Jackson's shoulder, but I kind of miss in the dark and end up patting his chest instead. "Come on. Lighten up. We need to chill out. Just chill out." I pat Jackson again.

Jackson shakes my hand off and looks behind us to where Mel is wandering up the path. "I've known you since kindergarten, man. You *do* this, you do stupid things, then you regret them later." He's hissing at me like an angry cat, which surprises me a bit, but to tell you the truth I'm not feeling much pain, so it doesn't bother me.

Mel comes along and winds her arm around my waist. "I need help walking, 'kay?" She smiles sweetly up at me, her perfect little teeth glowing in the moonlight. I ruffle her hair and Jackson shakes his head and walks away.

Cute kid, I think. She's just a cute kid. I used to date a girl who looked like her in high school, before Jessie came along in grade twelve. What the hell was her name ... Amy? Amanda? She was a cute kid too. All blonde and sweet-looking.

It's not much of a climb, because this hill is a lot wider than Black Rock and it has a gradual trail running around the outside. Soon we get to this plateau that looks over town. The lights in the distance are blinking as I settle myself down on the rock. Mel lays down with her head on my thigh. I ruffle her hair again. I'm not thinking too much at this point, see, I'm just kinda going with the flow. The rest of the group flops down too. I look around and see some dark shapes around the edge of the plateau. Some of them stand about six feet high.

"Those are kinda like caves," Kansas tells us, and then she picks herself up and pulls Mike to his feet. The poor boy hardly knows who he is anymore. He's grinning like a fool, his eyes hardly more than slits. "Come on, you." Kansas pulls Mike toward the shadows. "I want to show you something." Jesus. That was fast. No small talk for this chick. I think for just a second about Kali and how much she'd like him looking at caves with Kansas, but then I let it go. That's his business, not mine.

There's this big silence now while the rest of us figure out what we're doing. Bobby's propped against a large rock with that Tammy chick curled up next to him sipping on a cooler. Jackson plays with some sticks while Alex fiddles with her purse strap. I reach down and touch Mel's hair, running it through my fingers. Not as soft as Jess's but still pretty nice.

"It is kind of like Black Rock, eh?"

I look up. I was thinking that too, but I don't like what I see in Jackson's eyes. He's staring right at me when he says it. For Christ's sake. Here we go.

Now the girls have perked up, interested. Mel looks up at me. "What's Black Rock?"

I shake my head. "Nothing. Just this rocky ridge in Grace River. Kind of like this one, that's all." I'm watching Jackson, who's back to playing with the sticks.

Jackson nods but doesn't look up. "Kind of. Except more dangerous. A guy was killed falling off there once."

"Jackson." It's Bobby, his deep voice sounding like a warning. "Let it go."

Tammy stands. "This sounds too heavy." She offers Bobby her hand. "Let's go for a walk."

He hesitates for a second, looking from me to Jackson, then back at her. She smiles at him, her lips glossy in the moonlight, and he takes her hand. "All right." Good choice, man, I think, and he stands and brushes off the seat of his pants and they head off into the darkness.

Mel is watching Jackson now too. "What happened?"

"Oh, you know." Jackson shrugs, kind of an exaggerated *Oh, I don't know*, and says, "A bunch of guys were drunk, and this one kid climbed up and fell and broke his neck."

"That's so sad," Mel says, watching my face. But I just stare off into the darkness, focusing on the lights of the town twinkling in the skyline. "Did you know him?"

I don't answer. Jackson stands up suddenly. "I'm going to go crash out in the car." He looks at Alex. "You can have the backseat if you want." She shrugs and follows him toward the trail. Not what she was hoping for, but what did I tell you about Jackson?

"For fuck's sake," I say and stand up, knocking Mel on her side. I didn't mean to, but I'm a little unsteady. My buzz is almost gone, and now I just feel depressed and sober. What the hell is the matter with Jackson?

Mel brushes herself off and stands too. "What is it? Some deep, dark secret?" The way she says it makes it sound delicious or something. "You can tell me. You'll probably never even see me again." Her skin is glowing; she's still just wearing her halter top and cut-offs even though the temperature has dropped.

I shake my head. "Nah. It's just ... something we don't really talk about much, is all. Kind of an unwritten rule. Jackson was just trying to give me shit, in his own special way." I can see a purple blanket lying on the dust a few feet away and I walk toward it. She can wrap it around herself. She's probably freezing. Suddenly I can feel the breeze and I wish I'd brought my jean jacket from the car.

Mel follows me. "Shit about what?" I pick up the blanket, shake the dust off. She steps in front of me. "Shit about what?" she whispers.

I wrap the blanket around her shoulders. "About me being married and out here with you, that's what."

"Hmm." She moves closer, opens the blanket to wrap me in it too. "So he was kind of telling you he would throw you off the rock if you cheated on your wife or something?" She wraps her arms around my shoulders, pulling me closer.

I just stand there for a second, feel the warmth of her next to me. Feeling that gnawing sensation in my guts like an animal is in there trying to get out. I can still taste the tequila, and the night sky seems to spin around me. And then I circle that smooth little waist with my hands. Lower my mouth to hers. "Something like that."

The house is dead silent when I get home Sunday morning around nine. I am so fucking thankful Jess is working the day shift because man, do I need a shower. I dump my gear in the kitchen and sit at the table. I am bone-tired from getting three hours' sleep on that freezing cold rock.

Lily's stuffed unicorn is on the table, its horn lying on the butter. I move it over, and a pang of guilt stabs me right down to the toes. Jesus Christ. I run my hands through my hair. I need a shower. Wash it all away.

I think about waking up in that small dark cave, wrapped in the purple blanket. Mel was snoring, her breath reeking like stale cigarettes and booze. I untangled myself from her and dressed in the cold morning air, my head hollow and aching. I thought I might throw up, but I managed to make it down the hill to the car. I didn't even want to look at Mel anymore with her makeup all smudged across her face and her hair tangled and covering her eyes. How could I have thought she looked like Jess? No fucking contest, man. Jess has her beat by a mile.

So I banged on the car door, waking Jackson and Alex, who were asleep in separate seats with all the jackets piled across them. Jackson let me in and then went up the hill to get the rest of the group. He didn't say a word to me, didn't even look me in the eye, and I didn't blame him. I just sat in the front seat, watching the sun spread over the fields.

I climb the stairs now, already pulling my gross, sweaty shirt off. I bunch it up and toss it on the bedroom floor as I go by. I can't wait to get clean, change my clothes. I haven't slept outside like that since I was a teenager, and now I know why. I'm just turning to go into the bathroom when I hear Jessie call, "Danny?"

I freeze, my hand on the bathroom doorknob. Part of me wants to go in and lock the door, start the shower, pretend I never heard her. But I know I can't. She's heard me stop now. Damn hardwood floors ... "Yeah, it's me, babe. Just heading into the shower. I'll see you in a minute."

And I'm thinking that should work but then there she is, standing in the doorway of the bedroom, all sleepy and beautiful. "You can't say hi first?" she says, brushing hair from her forehead and yawning. That's when I notice she's holding my shirt. She holds it up. "What am I, your maid?" She smiles, which is a sight I haven't seen for a while. "You just throw your laundry at me and I go do it or what?"

"What are you doing home?" My voice cracks a little. Probably dehydrated. "Thought you were working the day shift." I keep my eye on the shirt, willing her just to put it down.

She shakes her head. "Sunny took my morning shift for me 'cause

I worked the late shift. I'll take her shift tonight. Come in here for a sec. Tell me how it went." She nods her head toward the bedroom and I wonder for a minute what she means by it ... but it doesn't matter because I can't get within ten feet of her right now with the smell of Mel's cheap perfume in my hair.

I shake my head, my hand still on the damn doorknob, and say, "No, I better jump in the shower first. Hockey smell. It's pretty gross. But I'll be there in a sec. Just ... just toss that shirt in the laundry for me, will you?"

She stares at me for a minute. "You missed a hell of a show. Lily took the house down dancing a tango with the bermuda onion at the end." There's that cool edge in her voice again.

"Sorry I missed it."

In the bathroom I peel out of my clothes. Jessie's lotions and hairbrushes are scattered across the counter as usual. I pick up this bottle of crazy organic lavender bath stuff I bought her at the health food store for her last birthday, remembering how stupid I felt going in there and asking Kali what she thought Jess would like. Well, Jesus, how bad a guy can I be, doing something like that? I could have just gotten her a box of chocolates from the Pharmasave.

I scald myself in the shower, trying to get rid of any trace of last night. Then I turn on the cold water, full blast, let it burn my skin with those icy needles.

I walk back into the bedroom with a towel wrapped around my waist. Jessie is curled up under the covers in a sunbeam, her eyes closed. I take a breath. I gotta keep going. Pretend nothing happened. I sit on the edge of the bed and pat her through the blanket. "So why are you sleeping? Late night? Out partying again?"

She doesn't answer.

"Hello?"

She opens her eyes, staring at the ceiling. "No, Daniel. I wasn't out partying. I worked late. Then I ... I woke up in the night again. Had a hard time getting back to sleep."

"Right. Sucks when that happens. You should take it easy, Jess. Maybe you're working too hard." I'm just talking shit. She's working as much as she ever has, which is as much as most people. I don't know what that weird sleep thing is. Nightmares she won't tell me about, maybe.

"So did you lose? Were you drowning your sorrows last night or what?" She sounds like she couldn't care less about my games.

"Yeah. We came close, but not quite." I feel this weird panic rise up, and I'm afraid I'll blurt the whole mess out to her, like someone with Tourette's, just start yelling how I got wasted on tequila and screwed some girl on a rock.

She doesn't say anything. I stand and walk to the window. Black Rock rises up off Bailey's field, shimmering in the morning sun. I grip the windowsill. I can't take my eyes off that mountain of rock. And suddenly I'm thinking about something else, not Mel and the club and the dancing and halter tops and the shrieking Kansas. I'm remembering Jackson, how he brought up the Rock, the way he'd looked at me. I can feel it all bubbling up inside. I turn from the window. "Remember Greg Smart?"

Jessie keeps her eyes closed, her face turned toward the sunbeam. "Yeah, of course. The guy who fell off the Rock. What about him?"

"You don't know the whole story."

"The whole ... what are you talking about?" She opens her eyes and sits up.

I keep going. It's the strangest thing, but I have to. I just have to tell her. "You haven't heard the real story, Jess."

She looks confused. "Yeah, I have. A million times. You and Jackson and Bobby and some other guys from your team were at the Rock and the new guy tried to climb it to show off and he fell. It was an accident. It sucked. But why are you talking about that now? What does that have to do with anything?"

I shake my head. "No, no, you don't get it. I'm trying to tell you what really happened. He wasn't trying to show off." I laugh, and I sound crazy, even to myself. "He wasn't. You didn't know him ... well, none of us did really. Didn't get the chance. But he wasn't the type to show off. He was one of those quiet boys. You know. Like Jackson. Thinks too much. He would have made a great team captain someday, if he lived. Strong, but smart, you know? No. We dared him. I ... I dared him."

"Daniel … " She's looking at me like she doesn't want to believe it.

"More than that. I more than dared him, Jessie, I called him a pussy, I told him if he didn't get his skinny white ass up that Rock I would kick the holy shit out of him." I laugh that crazy laugh again.

And even though I can't stand that sad look she's giving me, I have to keep going. I have to tell her the truth. I want her to forgive me. I want that so bad. "I said we'd tell the whole town what a pussy he was. The other guys, Jackson especially, they tried to stop him, they told me to lay off, told me he was just a new kid, not to take it too far. But I just kept going. I wouldn't let it go until that kid did what I told him. I wanted to make him do it. And he looked so scared, Jess. We didn't even have a flashlight or ropes, nothing. And it's so steep, nothing to grab on to with your feet. I told him lots of guys had done it, that we all had."

A lump swells up in my throat, and I have to fight to keep my voice steady. "And he did it. He started climbing. At first I felt bad, watching his shoes slip on the rock, watching him scrape his knees. But then I thought it was okay, I thought maybe he would make it. He started getting the hang of it, climbing like they do on those rock walls, slow, finding just the right place for his next move. But then he just … fell. And that was it." The lump in my throat bursts and I feel sick to my stomach.

Jessie watches me for a minute, and I can't tell at all what she might be thinking. She just says, "That's terrible, Daniel. That's just fucking awful." And she gets up and I think she's going to leave the room, which was not what I had in mind after telling her all that, but she stops by the window and she gives me a pat on the arm. It isn't a real warm, loving pat. But I take it. And then she says, "You were just a kid."

As she walks away I stare out that window and think about Greg, think hard. It's my own quiet punishment for what I've done, for all the things I've done. I try to imagine how scared he must have been. How the sweat must have dripped off his nose, how his eyes must have squinted in the darkness, looking for a safe place for his feet to land. How he almost made it to the top before he fell, spilling like a dark comet to the ground below.

part two

Kali

I'm washing the dishes late Sunday night when I remember that there's a herbal tea for heartbreak. I don't know what made me think of it, but while I'm stacking plates on the bamboo drainboard it just pops to the surface. The recipe was in one of my old Wise Crone's Magical Herbs books from when I was a teenager and I first started to get into herbs and aromatherapy. I was the one at parties wearing a Clash T-shirt with black fishnet stockings, rubbing ylang ylang oil into the temples of some half-drunk guy who was sure it would lead to something more. I was the one forcing my girlfriends to drink raspberry leaf tea when they had their periods, leading my boyfriends into the forest on rainy Sundays looking for nettles that I could dry and pulverize into an iron-boosting brew.

But I haven't used those books for years now, having moved on to the more advanced, more respected, more mainstream books. But I remember the recipe perfectly, the names of the herbs rolling through my mind like a familiar river ... *Vervain, peppermint, calendula, chamomile, lavender. Crush together with the dried petals of a red rose, steep in boiling water for ten minutes.*

I made that tea a lot, of course. Who couldn't, with a name like "Heartbreak Tea," plus the fact that I was seventeen and that I wanted so desperately to fix, help, make better all the people I loved so much. And of course it was much in demand in those days. What is teenagehood but a series of heartbreaks, dramatic love affairs that, alas, are not to be? I made it for girlfriends, for their boyfriends after they had separated, I even made it for one of my ex-boyfriends. Sage. I dated him for two months, then told him it was time for me to move on. Actually I had a dream about him, that he had sprouted eagle wings and lifted off, soaring high above me and away. In the dream I was devastated as I watched him go, heartbroken, desperate for him to stay. I broke up with him the next day, sure he would hurt me if I didn't.

Instead he was the devastated one, red-eyed, bewildered. We had such a *connection*, he said. I comforted him, made him lie on my mother's couch, holding a rose quartz in his left hand to heal his heart while I anointed his forehead with lavender oil and steeped a batch of heartbreak tea. I remember the feeling of power I had, being the healer and not the victim. I remember thinking I had definitely made the right choice. But now I think what a silly girl I was. I shake my head at my childishness, my illusion of power that I held to be so true. What did I know about love, about heartbreak? I hadn't had a child yet, I hadn't had a husband. I hadn't had to stretch my heart to the point that it sat strained and bulging in my chest, threatening to burst with every feverish wail in the night, with every kiss on the cheek from pursed sticky lips. The terrible wash of loneliness when the man you love doesn't love you back anymore, the man you had two children with and set up a home with, shared everything you had with for almost ten years. What I had with Sage, that wasn't love. That was practice.

I put the last dish in the drainboard right when Mike knocks on the door. There's that divine intervention and synchronicity thing again. Well, to be honest, it isn't really. I was expecting him. It's late. Almost midnight. I was actually expecting him around ten, but it doesn't matter. After I put the girls down and watered my garden I went into the spare room where I keep my soap supplies and started a new batch. If you weren't used to it, the smell of that room would knock you over, but I am used to it and it's like inhaling a sweet medicine. I'm making a batch of tea tree oil hand soap, so it's especially intense, that harsh tang you get in the back of your throat like childhood nights spent lathered with Vicks VapoRub. The tea tree is for the guys who work at AXIS. It has antibacterial properties, which I only hope can somehow wash away some of the toxic chemicals they come into contact with. I sell it at the store, but so far only Mike and a couple of his buddies have caught on.

I don't walk toward the door, because Mike just comes in on his own. I wait by the sink, a slight merciful breeze moving my curtains and carrying in the scent of the night-blooming jasmine that curls around the drainpipe outside my kitchen window. He comes in hunched over, carrying a six-pack like it's a stray dog he picked up on the way and is afraid of showing me. I just smile. His hair is messed, tousled like a child's, his T-shirt clean but his jeans filthy.

Mike has become a part of us, woven himself into the fabric of our lives in the last six or seven months. That quilted work jacket, those big clunky boots, they have a place by my kitchen door. The work sweat and beer and the oil from cleaning gears, that smell of a hard day's work I had never experienced before with my bohemian parents, my cultured husband.

"Hey," he says softly, finally looking up at me.

"Hey, yourself." Normally he would have already swept across the kitchen and pulled me to him, carried me off to the bedroom. A hard day? "How was work?"

He shrugs, sets the beer on the counter. "Brought some beer."

"Thanks." He looks like he showered, which he doesn't always do after work. It depends what they had him doing. If he was cleaning out a boiler, he showers. If he was operating a forklift, he doesn't. When he hasn't I usually entice him into a bath, which I will draw for him myself, pouring in a few drops of oil of oregano when he isn't looking. Once he asked me why my baths smelled like spaghetti. Usually I get in with him, since it's one of those huge clawfoot tubs.

"Sorry I'm late. I, uh … got a little delayed there." He looks sheepish but not particularly sorry. I'm used to this.

"I was making soap," I tell him.

He nods. "Good." He reaches over and pulls a beer from its plastic net, tilts it toward me. "You want one?" His arm is strong and muscled as he flexes it toward me.

I take the beer. Then I put it down on the counter and take the few steps toward him. I wrap my arms around him, hugging his shoulders to me. He pulls me in without a word, digging his hands into my hair, inhaling. He smells like stale beer and cigarettes, but he has the soul of a beloved child. I kiss him softly, then lead him into the living room. He grabs the beer off the counter on his way.

We settle onto my old red sofa, the one I got from the thrift store in Grace River. It's made of some sort of fancy brocade from the 1970s and there are patches that are shiny and almost worn through, but I love it. It's a fainting couch if I ever saw one.

He sits with me beside him with my legs swung over his. I take a sip of the beer, then set it down on the coffee table, which is actually an empty grape carton.

"So, how was it?" I ask.

"What?"

"The tournament."

He fiddles with the top of his beer can, flicking the tab back and forth so it makes a faint metallic springing sound. "Yeah, it was good. We didn't play so great, but what the hell. We had a good time, I guess." He looks off in the corner of the room, vaguely in the direction of my bookshelf. He's not himself. Not present, loud, joking, teasing me about my messy house, the clumps of earth and leaves that get tracked in by the girls.

I get a strange feeling. An unpleasant tingling where my legs are touching his, where any part of my body is in contact with his. It's like he's suddenly toxic, covered in something I don't want to get on me.

I have good instincts. And all the times I've trusted them, all the times I've really listened to them, they've turned out to be right. When I was with my ex-husband, I think they shorted out. When your instincts keep telling you something and your conscious mind doesn't want to hear it, something in the wiring just gives out and you start getting scrambled messages. He used to tell me I was crazy when I would say I didn't believe he had spent half the night at a professor's house discussing his PHD, or that I didn't believe it had really taken five hours for the mechanic down the street to change the oil in the car.

So here I am again, struck with a strong feeling that something is wrong. I swing my legs slowly off Mike's lap, sit up straight. I take another sip of the warm beer. I look over at my bookshelf now too. Mike stands awkwardly and walks toward it, feigning interest in a book, his head tilted to the side. He takes a swig of beer with one hand while he pulls a book on Italian architecture off the shelf, turning it in his hand.

"What happened?"

He looks over. "What do you mean, what happened. Where?"

"At the tournament." My voice is calm, level, because that's how I feel. There's no judgment here. I just need to know.

He looks irritated now, the book held in his hand like a useless prop in a bad play. "With what?"

I study his face. "Something happened."

To be honest, it sucks that I know. It would be easier not to. But as soon as I moved away from my husband, I got my instincts back. Right away. It's uncanny ... One night about two weeks after I moved into the little blue house, I had been planting madly all day, and I had herbs spilling out of planters, mounded into fresh earth in the beds I had dug up, flowers and seeds scattered everywhere. I was sitting down with tea waiting until it was time to walk the girls to the bus when I had a sudden feeling that I had forgotten to water one of the transplants. I went over the checklist in my mind and was fairly sure that I had watered all of them, which is completely necessary when transplanting, otherwise the plants go into shock. But just the same, I wandered out and sure enough, I had neglected a basil plant by the back door. It would have survived, I'm sure, but still. It was the start of the new phase. And the problem with listening to your instincts is that you have to be prepared to deal with what they might tell you.

"Kali, what the fuck are you talking about?" Mike says this with that slightly crooked, slow sleepy smile that he uses when he wakes up with me in my bed on a sunny weekend morning, when we don't have to get up because the girls are at their father's or Bio-dad's and we can just lie there for hours and forget about divorces and hard jobs and clothes that need to be washed, soap that needs to be cut and packaged.

I play with the folds of my skirt. What am I doing? Am I his mother? Did he ever promise me anything, ever? No. I just need to somehow make him realize I'm not going to give him shit, I just need to know that something has changed, for my own sanity.

"You're not in trouble here."

"Good to know." He takes another swig of beer, comes back over to the couch. I hold my hand out to him and he takes it and sits beside me.

I can feel it again, that creepy, prickly feeling travelling up my arm from his hand, crawling like black baby spiders. I let go of his hand.

He shakes his head. "What is with you tonight?" He runs his fingers through his hair. He has an edge to him, a sharpness that I'm not familiar with. I've seen glimpse of it here and there, especially when we're out with his guy friends. The swearing, the lewd jokes. But with me, he's always had a softness. The flipside. What attracted me to him in the first place. Protector/lover. The alpha male with the good heart. At least that's what I've imagined him to be.

The faintest sliver of irritation wedges its way into my self-imposed calm. "Mike, I just know things sometimes. And I know something happened. Something you don't want to tell me. What are you afraid of?"

He sets his beer on the table. "Jesus." He has a wrinkle between his eyes, an angry indentation. "Nice to see you too. I just got off a twelve-hour shift, there's shit going down at work, and I haven't seen you for days. What the hell, Kali. What the hell is wrong with you? It was a tournament. We played hockey, we goofed around. What do you want me to tell you?" His indignation is overblown, bad acting in the increasingly bad play.

"I don't want you to tell me anything. You don't have to tell me. I just can't be around you until you do. I can feel it all over you." I move away to illustrate, hugging myself.

"Well, this is fucking great." He stands to go.

"This is not what I had planned for tonight either."

He holds a hand out. "Do me a favour. Don't bother telling me about it. I can guess. Some hippie bath with fucking dead flowers floating in it, right?"

I'm stung and I don't respond. He looks sorry for a fleeting moment. For that moment I can also see the broken man that I know lives under his skin. The one I'm always trying to soothe, make better.

He sighs. "You know, Kali, you're a great girl." He sounds reasonable, like I'm being the hysterical one, the one who's crazy. I've been in this position before. "But you think you know everything. You think you're a friggin' psychic or something. And now you think I fooled around on you? Is that it?"

I take a sip of beer, meeting his eyes. "I don't think it. I know it."

He doesn't answer for a moment, his mouth slack. Then he closes it with a snap. "You're crazy."

I get up and walk past him toward the kitchen. I stop at the doorway and turn. "The joke of it is that if you would just admit it, I could work with it. I'm a very forgiving person, I understand that things happen sometimes. But I can't be lied to. Not anymore."

He just stares, not sure what to make of me. Of what I said. Then he brushes past me and grabs his boots, pulling them on and not bothering to tie them. I follow him into the kitchen and am just sitting down at the table when a sleepy figure appears in the hallway.

"Mike?" It's Kieran, rubbing her eyes, disoriented.

He stands up. "Hey," he says. "Hey there, Kieran."

"I heard yelling. Were you guys fighting?" Yelling? I guess we were a little loud, but it didn't seem like we were yelling.

Mike looks at the door, then back to Kiernan. Trapped. "Oh. No, we were just ... we were just talking."

Kieran comes over and sits on my lap, her warm eight-year-old body heavy and comforting. "Oh. So everything's okay, then?"

Mike looks at me. I meet his gaze. I don't look down. He scratches his head, stares at the ceiling. Then he looks back at us, Kieran curled in my lap like an oversized cat, the glow of a candle burning on the table casting shadows across her round face.

"I guess your mom thinks I did something she didn't like too much, is all." I feel like I'm sinking, the relief lifting the terrible heaviness away from me.

"Like what?" Kieran doesn't move, she isn't perturbed by this. She probably things he stepped on a pansy on his way up the front walk.

He drops his hands back down by his sides. "Something ... I don't know, something that maybe woulda ... hurt her feelings, I guess."

"Oh." Kieran yawns and uncurls herself. "Well, you should say sorry then."

She gets up and wanders back toward her room, stopping to give a slight wave to Mike. "See ya."

He waves back. "Okay. See ya."

I don't move, not a muscle, wondering what he's going to do now. He already almost admitted it. Come on, Mike, I think. Just one more step.

But he grabs what's left of his beer, slinging it on his finger as he digs in his jeans for his keys. "Guess I'll see you around then." His chin juts out like a child's, like Kieran's when she's been wronged.

"Guess so." I smile a little sadly as he turns to go, pulling the door shut behind him. I sit there awhile. I know it isn't over, not even close. This will resolve. I know how much he needs me to stay on track. I know what he's capable of falling into if he doesn't. When I started seeing him I knew it would get hard someday. I could feel it. But I also knew I was meant to be with him, that it was happening for a reason.

Still. I can't lie and say it doesn't hurt. I wonder who she was, what she looked like, although I know it doesn't matter. I just envy her somehow. That for one night she got the uncomplicated Mike, the one with the slow, sleepy smile and the muscled arms. Not the one who needs coaxing to eat healthy food, who drinks too much, who is still trying to live down a childhood that could have destroyed a weaker man.

I brush dried candle wax from the table, the names of the herbs for heartbreak tea coming back to me like an old poem memorized in grade school. *Vervain, peppermint, calendula, chamomile, lavender.* Old friends. I wonder if I should brew up a batch to drink in my bath but decide against it. Not tonight. Not yet.

Daniel

I'm just slinging my bag over my shoulder and headed for home when I see Mike walking toward the locker room all hunched over like he's carrying something heavy even though I can see he isn't. He gives me a nod and yanks the locker room door open. I want to spend another minute in this place like I want to jab myself in the eye with a broken bottle, but I still grab that door before it swings shut and go in after him. "Hey." I drop my bag with a thud on the concrete floor.

Mike stands at a row of lockers peeling out of his coveralls. He doesn't look over, just keeps on peeling. Must be having girl trouble. That's about the only thing can get Mikey down.

"So you wanna go grab breakfast or what?" I ask him, even though it's pretty obvious he's not feeling too sociable.

He shrugs, doesn't say anything, working out a knot in his boots. Then he looks up. He's pale and the circles around his eyes are so dark it looks like he took a couple of punches. "What the hell," he says. "Sure."

I got a bad feeling about why Mike's looking the way he is. "Meet you at Nick's in twenty minutes."

"Yeah. See you there."

I head out of the locker room, yawning all the way. It's the end of the night shift, a seven-to-seven, my worst nightmare. You have to sleep until about five, then you grab dinner and go to work and you don't see the light of day until it's time to go home in the morning and go back to bed. Usually I hang out with Jess and Lily before Lily goes to school, but I'm not too much in the mood for that today. Breakfast with Mike sounds like a better plan to me.

Nick's is packed, on account of most of the guys had the same idea. The place is hopping and all I can smell is grubby work socks and machine grease. We find a place at the counter and settle in. Sunny's on shift, making her way around the tables with the coffee pot. I wave her over.

She gives us that shit-eating Sunny grin. "Hey, boys. What trouble are you two stirring up this fine morning?" She flips our white cups over and fills them up, then reaches into her apron and tosses a few creams at us.

"Oh, it's too early for trouble, darling." I look over at Mike, but he's just stirring his coffee, watching the spoon as he moves it around. Yup. He's in one of those moods. Here we go. Babysitting time.

Sunny scans the room like waitresses do, but she stays put for now. "Yeah? I heard you guys sucked bad at the tournament. Were you hungover or what?"

I catch her eye, but it seems like a pretty innocent comment. And pretty accurate too. "You guessed it. We're getting too old for the all-nighters now. We shoulda eaten some porridge and got tucked in to bed in the morning, not gone and played a bunch of twenty-year-old NHL prospects."

"Right, yeah, you guys are getting a bit old for that crap. Right, Mikey?" She gives him a nudge with her elbow, somehow keeping from sloshing coffee all over him.

He doesn't look up. "Yeah. It ain't worth it anymore," he mumbles.

She raises her eyebrows at me and I just give a *Your guess is good as mine* kind of shrug. Somebody shouts out her name from across the room and she's off.

"The hell's the matter with you?" I say it quiet, so the other guys around us can't hear. I think I know what the problem is and I don't exactly want to broadcast it.

"Nothing, man, everything is perfect. Fucking perfect." He slams back his coffee and wipes his mouth.

"Dude," I whisper. "You been doing coke again? You look like shit."

He just shakes his head and holds his empty cup up in the air for Sunny to somehow notice from the grill where she's standing talking to Nick about an order.

"Hey."

"What? Jesus, Danny, I thought we were coming for breakfast, not a fucking interrogation."

"You look like shit, is all."

"Yeah, well I feel like shit. Happy? I'm sleeping in my old room at my mom's and she gives me the goddamn third degree every time I walk in the door. I don't need it from you too."

"Why the hell are you at May's?"

"Lost my room at the fucking house a few days ago. Had a little ... altercation with my landlord there. He was pissed about me being late on rent again."

"Rent?"

"Yeah."

"Why? You short?"

"Obviously I'm fucking short, Danny. Jesus."

There's no reason he should be short on cash, not one goddamn reason I can think of other than drugs. The guy's been working full-time at AXIS since he was nineteen. He makes close to sixty thousand dollars a year. Far as I know, the rent for the room in the crappy house he rents is about six hundred dollars a month. But he's always been good at blowing it on benders, which I'm guessing is what he's coming down from right now. I've been keeping my head down the last few days and it never even clued in that he wasn't around. But I play the fool anyway. "Why didn't you ask me for help? I woulda helped you out. Or you coulda stayed with me and Jess."

Now he just looks at me and I know what he's thinking about me and my lovely wife and our perfect marriage out there on Grandma's farm. I'm no idiot. But I don't deserve to be judged. I mean, it was Mike who got us in trouble in the first place. "Give me a fucking break, man," I whisper, keeping my eye on Sunny as she swishes around the diner, making sure she's far enough away she can't hear. "You picked up that Kansas chick. You're the one who said we should go for the shooters and ride around the fucking countryside with the drunk blondes. So don't give me that righteous shi—"

"Kali and me are done."

I can see it now, the whole ... what do you call it ... heart of the matter or whatever.

"She find out?" I can feel this thin kind of fear creeping though me. I mean, if Kali knows, then why wouldn't Jess? She's no idiot. Anyway, I got a pretty good arsenal of reasons, if she felt like asking. How about a wife who can hardly look me in the eye, who goes to bed early every night and turns off the light as soon as I start walking down the hall toward the room? Still. I don't want her to know.

Mike shrugs. "Says she just knows. I told her she was crazy."

"How'd that go?"

"Guess."

"Well. Maybe she'll come around."

Mike shakes his head. "I don't want her to come around, man. I don't want it to be like it was before. I don't want to fucking admit anything and then have her 'forgive me'"—he makes those quote things in the air with his fingers—"and have this big fucking thing with us. All the bad shit Mike did, just this big pile of shit that she has to ignore or try to fix or hug or pray about or light incense on or whatever. I'm fucking done with it." His eyes are red-rimmed and he looks like the walking dead. He needs to go back to his mom's and sleep it off.

"She was good for you," I say because it's true. You don't know much about Mike before, but he wasn't doing too hot. Not in the last couple of years. He always had a temper, even as a kid, and if you knew his dad you would have understood why. Guy disappeared off the face of the earth when Mike was twelve without a note or anything. And it was a good thing, trust me, but some people around town still think that if you dug up old May's prize peonies you'd find a little more than dirt and fertilizer.

So Mike got into a lot of bar fights and stupid shit like that, and he was always into drugs, but it was getting out of hand, even by my standards, before he met Kali.

Sunny walks back over with the coffee and Mike says, "It's done, Danny. I'm not pretending for some chick anymore. I'm through with that shit."

Sunny frowns. "What shit? You and Kali break up?"

"Yup." Mike dumps cream into his coffee and gives her a big grin. "Best thing that ever happened to me. Don't have no woman telling me what to do. You are bossy goddamn things, you know that?"

I wait for Sunny to say something smartass back to him, but she doesn't. She doesn't say a word. Mike holds up his coffee. "Cheers," he says. "Now can we order some goddamn breakfast, or what?"

Jessie

*T*he kitchen is already thick with heat as I stand at the sink to rinse out the camping cooler. Last night Daniel and I slept with just a thin sheet covering us, while I tried not to let any part of myself touch his sweaty body. He's like a furnace when he sleeps, burning up with some invisible fire that lives under his skin.

I'm not fully awake, and I can see the sun just peeking over Black Rock through my window so it's no wonder. I pry the lid off the cooler and start pulling out the empty beer bottles. Daniel took it to Ashville for his hockey tournament last weekend and obviously he didn't bother to clean it out. As usual. I swear, I try not to let these things bother me, but when you add them all up it's hard not to feel like a maid or his mother. I clank them on to the counter, maybe just a bit louder than I have to. Daniel is hunting through the fridge for the food we'll be bringing up to the lake. We're off to Jackson's cabin for the night, Lily settled in with my parents. She loves it out there at the lake, but it wouldn't have been any fun for her without Jackson's boys anyway. They're spending the night with his mom. Any chance Caroline can get for a babysitter ...

"Hey, babe?" His voice is muffled by the fact that he has his head stuck in the back of the fridge.

"What?"

"Did you grab the pillows?"

I keep clanking. God, I need a coffee. "Yes, they're already in the truck. Did you ... " I get to the last bottle, which is a different brand than the others. It must have been from one of the other guys. Something is wrapped around the glass neck, and I pull it off and examine it. What the hell? I try to think, the morning cobwebs trapping all my rational thoughts and tangling them in a soft grey heap. Ah. A hidden suspicion bubbles up and a question surfaces, but I stuff the thing in my pocket and turn toward Daniel.

He thumps a packet of hot dogs on the table and looks at me, waiting for me to finish my sentence. His hair is sticking up in dark tufts on his head like a baby chick's, his brown eyes still puffy from sleep. Lily's eyes. The one thing she got from him. Those deep pools that seem almost black until you get close enough and see how complicated they are, with their little flecks of green, their swirls of amber.

"I need coffee on the way," I say.

"So do you think that hippie guy is single?" Sunny's voice travels through my sun-soaked half-sleep and I open my eyes to the piercing glare of bright sky. I'm floating on Jade Lake on my cheap air mattress, the lapping water licking the sides of my legs like a persistent kitten, while Sunny floats on one side of me and Caroline on the other. We've been bobbing on the waves unevenly, sometimes bumping each other softly, sometimes floating so far we have to yell to hear each other.

"Hippie guy?" I drip lake water onto my chest lazily. Sunny had interrupted my dreamy mixed-up thoughts, and I have to say I'm almost grateful. I've been thinking things over since this morning, turning them over, chewing them up in bits and pieces. Now all I'm left with is the bitter core.

Caroline pipes up, "That environmentalist from Seattle, right?" Caroline has a throaty Kim Carnes voice that belies her baby-doll appearance. She's so small she could shop in the kids' department for her tiny bikinis, her eensy little T-shirts that stretch across her tiny breasts. I could never believe that body was ever home to those two scrappy, yelling boys. "He was in the diner a couple weeks ago, wasn't he, Jess? He's not still in town, is he?"

Sunlight bounces off the water and white spots dance in front of me, blurring the tree line at the edge of the lake and the endless span of blue-green water. I close my eyes again to escape the brightness. "Yeah. I mean ... I don't know. He said he was coming and going. He might be here again." Then I think about what Sunny just asked and I turn my head to look at her. "Wait. Sunny, you seriously have a crush on that guy?" She's rolled onto her front and I can't see her face to determine if she's just kidding around.

"How many hot guys do you know who roll into town on a mission to save the freaking world, Jess?" Sunny seems unperturbed, or at least the tanned back of her legs do.

"Well," I say. "He doesn't seem like your type."

Caroline laughs. "Too smart for you, honey. What you need is a nice lumberjack or maybe a trucker with some naked women tattooed on his arms. Right, Jess?"

I shake my head. "That's not what I meant."

"What *did* you mean?" Sunny is offended now, thanks to Caroline.

A wave from a passing motor boat laps over me, taking my breath away with the shock of cool water. "Nothing," I say. "Just forget it. I don't know if he's single. You'll have to ask him yourself." It's a lie, I know, but for some reason I want to keep my conversation with him to myself. It's mine. A small, sweet secret.

Later that day us girls are trying to scrape up some dinner from the slim pickings we brought with us when the men roll in from fishing, sunburned and drunk. They are quickly forgiven when they show us their bucket full of steelhead.

We eat the blackened fish fried in Labatt Blue on Jackson's family's cranky old gas stove in his cabin, along with some seriously overcooked corn on the cob courtesy of Caroline, who was on the porch painting her toenails and forgot to turn off the burner.

It's weird not having Kali here. Not that she always came—she wasn't exactly a party girl, but she did come to the lake with us sometimes. And she was damn good with herbs and spices too. Our burnt fish and overcooked corn would have had some minted baby potatoes and a big, leafy salad to go with it.

Caroline is right wasted on vodka coolers by about eight and persuades Jackson to dance with her by the beach fire while the rest of us clean up. She's singing "I'm Still Standing" by Elton John. She dressed up like him last Halloween, in a shiny white suit and a feather boa and those huge heart-shaped glasses. She had a great old time dancing on the tables at the AXIS costume party.

There are two tiny bedrooms in the cabin, and as I pass by the one me and Daniel are supposed to stay in on my way to the garbage can I feel a stab of dread. I don't want to sleep in there with him. Not one bit. In fact, even before today, for the last week or so I haven't wanted to sleep beside him. Not that I was feeling particularly warm and fuzzy about him before that. Not for a long time. But especially now.

I stuff the handful of corn husks into the garbage and go join the others around the fire. Jackson has collapsed into a lawn chair, and Caroline is settled onto a stump chattering to Sunny, her cooler bottle perched between her knees. I sit on a log beside Sunny, across the fire from Daniel.

"I don't know," he's saying. "It's just getting so fucking irritating, you know? Like give me a fucking break. You use a battery for your fancy hippie van, don't you? Where do you think the goddamn lead came from?"

Mike laughs. "For sure, man. And hey, you got a stomach ache and you take Pepto-Bismol? Guess where the fucking main ingredient came from?"

Daniel nods, takes a swig, points out at the black surface of the water. "Fish are jumping." We are all mercifully quiet for a second and I can hear a splash off shore. Then he continues. "Fucking hippie doesn't know what the hell he's talking about. We test that river ourselves all the time, and it's fine. Seriously, I'd like to wipe that fucking smug look off his face. Saw him at the SuperValu when I was getting milk last night. Has he moved here or what? Setting up a protest camp or something?"

I take a breath. He *is* back. I like that. I like knowing he's here for some reason.

Mike laughs. "Yeah, maybe Kali'll join his camp. She can supply the soap," he says. "Asshole."

Jesus Christ, I've had about enough of this crap right now. "Mike, shut up. What's wrong with you? You dump Kali and now it's all 'fucking hippie' this and 'fucking hippie' that. Give me a break." It slips out before I can stop myself and it isn't fair. Mike isn't really the one I have an issue with, although I am pissed at him for being such an immature moron and ditching a woman he clearly cares about, a woman who could have finally helped him get his shit together. "He's just doing his job. He's not a bad guy. Why does it even matter?"

Mike stares at me for a moment and I feel a small chill down my spine. "Well, hey, if anyone would know, Jess, I guess that would be you."

All eyes turn to me. "Hey, guys, let's bring it down a notch," Jackson says quickly. "This was supposed to be fun, okay. Let's go up and play poker or something."

"What's this?" Daniel says and I hate it, I *hate* that belligerent tone he gets when he's drinking. "Why would Jess know?" He looks at me, bewildered.

"Uh-oh," Caroline singsongs.

I shake my head. "I met him at the diner. So did Sunny. So did all you guys except Danny."

"Yeah. Jesus, Danny, relax," Sunny pipes in, but she's looking at me strangely too and I suddenly feel like one of those pinned butterflies under glass.

Daniel looks at Mike. "What are you on about then?"

Mike nods like an all-knowing sage. "Yeah? So that's the only time you ever met him? You weren't hanging out with him by the river?"

"What the fuck?" Daniel grinds his bottle into the sand.

To be honest, I'm surprised it hasn't come up yet. I mean, it's been more than a week. I would have figured Mike would have been all over that and I had a great excuse planned out. Not that I need an excuse for talking to another human being ... it's just that I knew I would need one in this particular instance. And yes, I probably should have come out and said, *Hey, so I was talking to the environmentalist today by the river* ... but the time just didn't present itself. So now I get to give it a shot in front of everybody, and believe me, they're all riveted.

"Yeah, so what? I ran into him by the river when I was out at Jersey's getting berries."

"He was at Jersey's?" Daniel sounds like he wants to understand, he wants to think it's nothing, but he can't convince himself. Which is a joke. Which makes my blood start to boil under my sunburned skin.

Mike scoffs. "No, they were fucking leaning on the truck standing two feet apart like they were best friends. Or something like that." He looks over meaningfully.

I'm stung by this seemingly senseless betrayal, but I roll my eyes. "So not. That's ridiculous. No, he wasn't at Jersey's. He was on the side of the road by this van and he looked ... lost. So I stopped and asked him if he needed help. Or directions or whatever."

"That was nice of you." Daniel is calm, which is always scary when he's drunk and in a mood. Calm means it's about to get real bad. Calm means he's gathering up his strength, composing himself for battle. Soon there will be no reasoning with him at all.

But I've had enough now. And I have good reason for having had enough. I stand, brush my jeans off. "You know what? I'm not on fucking trial here. If I want to stop by the side of the road and have a fucking conversation with somebody, that's my fucking business, Daniel. Got it?" I point my finger, jab it toward him, although he's a good ten feet from where I'm standing.

Sunny clears her throat in the thick silence that follows. "So do you guys want to go play cards or what ... " But she trails off when Daniel stands too and starts toward me, some determined look I can't quite recognize in his eyes. He has a point to make. Jackson gets to his feet and moves between us, his shoe hitting some coals and sending sparks drifting like red stars into the sky.

But Daniel stops a few feet away and holds his hands up to Jackson. "Hey, there's no problem here. I just had an idea. Forget cards. You want a game? Let's play 'Find the fucking hippie and beat the crap out of him.'"

"YEAH!" Mike raises his fist in the air and smiles this crazy, lop-sided smile.

I'm composing myself behind Jackson, heart racing, shocked that I'm in a situation like this. Is Jackson actually having to protect me from my own husband? Is this my life? And of course I think of Liam, of course I do, and yes, I've thought about him too much for the last week, but I haven't done anything wrong and neither has he and I will be mortified, devastated if my husband . . .

Daniel nods his head. Calm again, his hands still up in the surrender position. "Anyway, Jess won't mind, right, because it's not like she's friends with the guy or anything. It's not like she was hanging out with him. So where's he staying? That motel on Church Street?"

"Daniel." Jackson's voice is a calm warning.

"Come on, Jackson," Caroline pipes in. "Maybe he's right. Maybe this guy just needs a little scare." She's excited, a sheen of perspiration on her smooth face, her eyes shining with vodka. Jackson ignores her.

"I'm serious, bro, let's do it." Mike is almost vibrating now.

"You guys . . . " Sunny sounds scared now, she knows, like I do, that they will do it. They've beaten guys up for far lesser reasons before.

Daniel and I are locked in a staring contest. I break it. Look away. "I don't know where he's staying, Daniel. How would I know that?"

He shrugs. Turns to Mike. "I don't know. Mikey, how would she know that?"

Mike walks over and joins him. Puts his finger to his chin in mock thought. "Hmm. Well, maybe he told her when they were having their picnic."

That's it. I push Jackson's shoulder aside and walk past him, right up to Daniel. "This is insane. You know what you're doing? What *both* of you are doing? You're so full of shit." I'm close to tears, which I hate when I'm trying to make a point, I hate sounding like a weak little female. "Mikey. You know this is bullshit. You're just upset about Kali, this has nothing to do with Liam."

He just laughs like this is the funniest thing he's heard in ages. "Yeah . . . ooohh, I'm so sad. I better go kick someone's ass."

"Liam?" Daniel says quietly.

"Yeah, Daniel, that's his fucking name. LIAM!" I shout it and Jackson pulls me back, whispering for me to shut up, and I know he's right. I know he's right. I'm making it worse.

Daniel eyes Jackson. "What the fuck are you doing, Jackson? You think you gotta protect my wife from me? You think I'm gonna hurt her or something?"

Jackson shakes his head. "No, I don't think you're gonna hurt her. But you're not right in the head, Danny. You're acting crazy. You know that. We been here before. Come on. Just chill out, let's go play cards. Come on."

Daniel waves Mike over. "Let's go." He points at me, ignoring Jackson. "You can defend that little hippie piece of shit all you want, Jess, but I know what's right."

I can hardly speak for a moment, the irony of this slaps like a wet towel across the face. "What's *right*? Are you kidding me?" All the things, all the things come bubbling up to the surface, I can see them as clearly as my own reflection in a mirror. "Goddamn it, Daniel, you do so many things wrong, I can't even remember the last time you did something right." I'm so enraged, I swear if he were two steps closer I would take a swing at him right now, but I'm afraid if I move, my shaking legs will give out.

Daniel stares at me, stunned, and then I see it all registering behind the alcoholic shine. I can tell he's wondering if I know. He looks away and digs in his pocket for keys. "We'll take the truck." He stoops to pick up another beer out of the case and Mike starts to pull his sweater over his head.

"Daniel!" I yell. "Don't you go down there."

And he looks back at me with this look of quiet betrayal that makes my heart break into even smaller fragments and then he keeps walking. I'm panicked now.

"Danny. Sit down. Have a beer. Cool down." Jackson is using his big brother voice, but Daniel and Mike are already halfway to the truck.

"Yeah, guys, come on, come back, *sit down*." Sunny calls after them, but they keep walking.

"Jesus Christ," Jackson says and starts after the men. I have an idea now. It wasn't how I'd planned it, but then again, I didn't really have much of a plan anyway. I run up to the cabin, race into the room and root in my shorts' pocket. I can hear the guys fighting with Jackson, yelling and swearing at him. Jackson is holding his own, but I know even with Sunny yelling right there beside him that it won't work. I run out and over to the truck, just in time to see Daniel shove

Jackson back in the dirt, sending him sprawling in a heap of long arms and legs.

Sunny helps Jackson to his feet while Caroline shouts, "Asshole" from the fire, but she sounds more amused than horrified. I stop Daniel as he opens the truck door. His shoulder is tense, every muscle tightly coiled.

He looks at me fuzzily. "What's up?" He gives me a grim smile, his eyes hard. "I got some work to do." I pull his beer bottle out of his hand, which surprises him so much he doesn't have time to hang on to it.

"Here," I say, and I wrap a woman's hair elastic around the neck of his bottle. It's the kind that's wrapped in cotton, and this one is shot through with silvery threads. He looks confused.

"What the hell is that?"

Jackson comes back toward us, pissed now, but I wave him off frantically, I'm so sure this will do it. It's our last chance, me and Daniel. I know it is.

"Let's GO!" shouts Mike from the passenger seat. Daniel is still staring at the elastic.

"I found it wrapped around a peach cider bottle in your beer cooler this morning," I say. I poke him in the chest now, stab my finger into the muscle. "I'm guessing it belongs to that slut you were with in Ashville."

He doesn't look up, still looking down at his bottle, but I can see a flush come over his face as he realizes I know. "I could smell her on you, Danny, I could smell her cheap perfume on your fucking shirt. You listen to me," I whisper, inches from his face. "I want you to forget about this hippie guy and just go back to the cabin and go to bed. Nothing happened between me and him. Don't make a fool out of yourself."

He looks up and his shock and embarrassment has turned to defiance. I know I've blown it. Daniel hates to be cornered; it doesn't matter what he's done wrong, he'll claw and fight his way out every time. Instead of heading back to the cabin and calling it a night he grabs the beer and takes a long swig of beer, watching me over the lip of the bottle, that stupid elastic blooming like some strange flower around the bottle's neck.

"Thanks," he says. He pulls it off and wraps it around his wrist.

"I'll use this for good luck." He hops in the truck and slams the door. I watch him peel out up the dirt road, big clouds of dust billowing out around the truck until it disappears, only the red glow of his tail lights showing through the dark night. I can already hear the sound of Jackson's truck starting up behind me. I just hope that we get there before any more damage is done.

Jackson

These dusty roads are burned into my mind like the old maps me and Danny and Mike made on paper grocery bags when we were kids and they used to visit me out at the cabin in the summer. We plotted out the property in steps. Forty-seven steps from the cabin to the old pine where the frayed rope swing still hangs with its thick knots, twenty-two steps from the swing to the water. Close enough that if we timed it just right we could hurl ourselves from the swing into the lake, where the shock of cool water hit us like an electrical current. Time it wrong and you went sprawling into the shallows, inhaling a mouthful of rotten lake mud and tiny pebbles.

Me and Jess don't say much, but we're both thinking the same thing. Gotta get there before it's too late. I can go pretty fast, even though I'm driving the truck through that pure blackness of the country sky ... no streetlights, and no stars either. They've disappeared behind cloud for now.

They've got about a three-minute lead on us, since I wasted a good two minutes trying to convince Jess to stay behind. Also, Danny's driving like a bat out of hell, which I'm prepared to do once we get to the highway but not on this winding, potholed road. The last thing we need is to go through the trees and end up in the ravine. So maybe we'll be five minutes behind. Enough time to do some damage, that's for sure. Hopefully he'll still be banging on the door when we get there.

A few more minutes and we'll come out onto the highway. Funny—me and the guys never paced the two-mile distance from the cabin to the highway. We meant to. We even made bets ... 2,000,468 ... 12,000,642 ... but we never got around to it. I guess nobody will ever bother now. There wouldn't be much point. Still. Some old part of me kind of wants to know.

Jess is leaning forward to look onto the dark road that twists like a nest of snakes through groves of pine trees and fields of dry grass.

We get to the end of the turnoff, and the grey four-lane highway stretches out in both directions in front of us. I swing the truck right and we start picking up speed. Jessie looks so tense and worried. "Don't worry. We'll get there," I tell her.

She twists her hands in her lap and I notice she forgot to put any shoes on. Her feet are black from the soot of the campfire. "Yeah yeah, I know, I know. God. What is he thinking? What is he thinking, Jackson?" She slams the back of her hand against her door for emphasis. "Ow." She holds her injured hand against her chest and sits back in her seat.

"You okay?"

She nods. "What was *I* thinking?" She rests her head against the door.

I shrug. "Guess you gotta stand up for yourself sometimes. It's not your fault." We're humming along now, way too fast, but this is a straight stretch with no side roads for several miles. It's also pretty late, after midnight, so there shouldn't be too many cars on the highway.

I figure it might be a delicate question, but I ask it anyway. "Hey, Jess … you know this guy, right? You've talked to him a couple times. What do you figure? You think he's gonna fight back or is he just gonna let them beat the crap out of him?"

She looks over at me first, to see if I'm riding her about knowing this guy, but she can see that I'm not. "Let him? No. He won't let Daniel kick the shit out of him. He'll probably try to talk some sense into him. But if that doesn't work, I don't know what will happen. He doesn't strike me as a fighter."

"Well, people surprise you sometimes."

She starts hunting around on the floor of the truck, then hits the button on the glove compartment.

"What are you looking for?"

"A smoke … what are my chances?"

I laugh. "Not too good. Caroline brings hers with her everywhere."

"God, I would settle for one of Caroline's old butts right now." She smiles when she hears what she just said, then starts chewing her nails. "Yeah. I guess people do surprise you sometimes. Like you."

"Nah. I don't get in fights anymore. Not since high school."

"Are you kidding me? Don't you remember you guys all going nuts on that guy a few summers ago? The one who kept trying to put his hand up Sunny's skirt when we went dancing in Ashville? Remember? He followed her outside and you guys ... "

"Well, that guy. Sure." I smile. "But he deserved it. That was different."

Jess shakes her head. "This guy doesn't deserve it. Danny knows it too, that's what's so sick. He's just looking for someone to pound because he's pissed at me. Me! What a fucking joke. He's the one who ... "

She doesn't finish her sentence, but I know what she was going to say. And she knows that I know. Which makes me feel like shit. I kick a guy's ass for putting his hand up Sunny's skirt, but I don't do a damn thing when Daniel screws Jessie over time after time.

The lights of Grace River are on the horizon now, just below the crest of the hill. Almost there. I have to think now. Daniel is drunk, which I know from experience means he can't be reasoned with. So the only hope is to get there before any damage is done to Liam and then somehow physically restrain Daniel. And Mike. Mike's so drunk he can't see straight, which works good for me. He's not much use in a fight when he's wasted. His equilibrium goes off and you can pretty much breathe on him hard to make him go down. Maybe I can throw him over my shoulder and toss him in the truck. Put the child safety locks on. Danny, on the other hand ...

We pull up to the Big Sky Motel, which is just off the highway, hidden by an ugly row of big brown hedges. The tiny blue cabins are scattered around the dry grassy field like kids' playhouses. In the dim glow from the neon sign I can see the paint is peeling off the cabins in strips. Daniel's truck is parked at a weird angle in front of one of the units, right beside that white Volkswagen van with the Washington plates. I pull in beside the van and open my door, steeling myself for the shitstorm I'm about to enter.

"Hey!" somebody yells. "I'm calling the cops if there's any trouble." I turn and see it's a guy wearing boxers with a grubby T-shirt stretched over his belly. He's standing at the entrance to the office, which is across the parking lot at the edge of a dark grove of trees. He sounds scared, but he doesn't look like he's about to leave his porch.

I raise my hand. "Just seeing if my friend's here, buddy. It's okay. We'll be leaving in a sec." I hear the metallic slam of Jessie's door as she hops out of the truck.

The manager points his remote control at us. "No trouble. I'll call the cops this time, just try me. Get your drunk friends out of here." Out of the corner of my eye, I can see a man and a woman huddled nervously in the doorway of the unit beside Liam's. Danny must have made quite the grand entrance. I nod at the manager just as Liam's door opens, and Danny and Mike kind of tumble out and weave over to Danny's truck. Shit. We got here too late. They don't look roughed up at all, so maybe they weren't fighting. Or maybe Liam just didn't fight back.

They see us and stop dead. "Well hellooo, Princess Jessie," Danny slurs.

"What did you do, Daniel?" She starts toward them, but I grab the back of her shirt and pull her behind me. He's too far gone. I can't trust him not to hurt her. Far as I know, Danny's never laid a hand on Jess, but things have heated up so much they're boiling over. Exactly why I didn't want her coming here. She's too mad, she won't be able to stay calm.

She's trying to look around my shoulder at Danny and Mike, who are lighting smokes and lounging against the truck. "Go in," I tell her. "See how he's doing." Sparks are flying out of her eyes, but she goes, marching past the guys and into the cabin. I do some calculations in my head as I walk toward them.

"Danny," I say calmly. "What the fuck happened?"

Daniel breaks into this slow smile as he tries to focus on me. "Hey, buddy." The smile isn't friendly. I know it, and I know I don't have a lot of power over him now. In his head it's him and Mike against the world. Everyone else is the enemy.

"Jack-*son*," Mike says. "Buddy. You missed the fun." He takes a swig of beer.

Daniel starts to open his door. "Yeah, too bad. I know how much you wanted to help out. Don't worry, we did the job for you. As usual."

And that's it. I walk over to him, pull him back from the door, and shove him hard against the hood of his truck. I hold him there by his collar. "You listen to me, you son of a bitch. You think you're a tough guy? You think you're the man, Danny? You're nothing but a fucking coward."

I'm right in his face and I'm so mad I'm almost spitting, but instead of fighting back he just kind of goes limp a little, lets me hold him up, staring at me with those tired, watery eyes. This close up I can see the black circles and how pale his skin is. He doesn't say a word and I know he agrees with me. Just for that split second. I let go of him just as Mike is grabbing me and pulling me off and Daniel gets that meanness back in his eyes. I think for a second he might take a swing at me, and I almost want him to, I almost want this to just break out into a full-on fight. But he doesn't make a move and Mikey releases him and they both hop in the truck. Mike throws his beer bottle out the window. It hits the v w van and smashes onto the ground.

I head into the cabin and notice that the door is hanging funny on the hinges, which means it was probably kicked in. I'm not too excited about what I'll find in here. I can hear Daniel's truck screech out onto the road, the guys shouting something, probably at the manager, and then roaring away.

"Hello?" I call through the empty front room. It doesn't look like anything has been disturbed out here. I can hear voices from the bedroom and I head back there.

Liam is sitting on the bed holding a towel to his face. Jessie is beside him with her head in her hands. This is the room where it all went down; I can tell that right away. The sheets have been pulled off the bed, the dresser is pushed over on its side, there are water glasses and books scattered all over the carpet.

"Everything okay?" I ask quietly.

She looks up at me. "Bloody nose. He's okay." She sounds cold and far away.

I nod. Liam lifts his head and gives me a little wave with the bloody towel. I guess Jessie has filled him in on what we're doing there. "Hey." He looks at me for a minute. "Oh ... the guy from the AXIS parking lot."

"Yeah." I look around. "So ... you okay?"

He doesn't answer for a minute, looking from me over to Jessie, who stands and starts trying to straighten the room, picking up some clothes that have fallen out of the dresser drawers. "Don't," he says firmly. "I can do that." She drops some socks and then picks up a water glass, carrying it into the bathroom without a word.

His nose is bleeding again, so he holds the towel back to his face. "I was sleeping," he says, muffled through his towel. "They just came in here and pulled me off the bed." His eye is cut, a small river of blood runs down across his forehead and over the bridge of his nose. His cheek is red and already looks bruised. He points at the overturned dresser. "They threw me into the dresser." He sounds like he's in some sort of strange dream or something. Like he can't believe it happened.

I nod. "Sorry, man. I tried to get here in time. He was driving like a fucking maniac." I'm still standing awkwardly in the doorway. If he doesn't want help cleaning up, I don't really know what else to do.

Jessie returns from the bathroom with a glass of water. She hands it to Liam and he takes a sip. Hands it back to her. "Thanks." He doesn't look at her, and I know that even for those sensitive hippie guys it still sucks to be hurt and bleeding in front of a woman. Especially when her husband did the damage. I want to tell her to get the hell out and give the guy some space, but I don't.

"Look, man ... if it's any help, I don't think he'll come back. He was just proving a point. You know. Just had too much to drink." Liam is shirtless, wearing only a pair of cotton boxer shorts, which are now covered with a pattern of blood drops. He reaches up to touch his eye. He probably caught it on the edge of the dresser when he went down. He might need stitches. Shit.

"Don't," I say. "Don't touch it. You should get it looked at. It's deep."

"I'll get another towel." Jessie disappears into the bathroom, probably happy to have something to do. She comes back with a wet towel, which she places on his forehead. "You should go to the hospital. Do you want us to drive you? And you know what else? Call the cops if you want to. Go ahead. I don't mind. It serves him right. You *should* call the cops."

He takes the towel from her.

"I want you to call the cops." She's fighting tears, I can tell, because she gets this high, squeaky sound in her throat when she's trying not to cry. "And I don't agree with Jackson. They might come back. You never know."

Liam stands and holds his hands out, bloody towels in each one. "I'm okay. See. I'm fine. I just need a shower and some Band-Aids. I have a first aid kit in the van. If it's still bad in the morning I'll go in for some stitches."

I pick the rumpled brown bedspread off the floor and toss it on the bed behind Liam. "Do you need a ride somewhere?"

"No, man, I'm okay." He sounds like he means it. "I'm leaving tomorrow anyway. Thank you for coming out here. I'm serious. You didn't have to do that." Then he looks at Jessie, who is picking up a book off the floor and inspecting the cover. "And I'm not calling the cops. It's not a good idea for anyone concerned."

She starts to say something, but I stop her. "Jess. Just let him be. He can make his own decisions."

Personally I don't give a shit if Danny and Mike spend the night in jail. The only thing is, it could be a serious problem at work. If they get busted for assaulting the environmentalist, they could lose their jobs.

"You know what? If you're okay, we should get going. I'm sorry we didn't get here in time, man. Really. Come on, Jess."

But Jessie doesn't move. She's still staring at that book. "You go ahead." She glances up at me and clears her throat. "I'll stay awhile. In case he needs me to drive him to the hospital."

"No," Liam says quietly. "I appreciate that, but you go. I'll be okay."

"Jessie. Let's go."

She puts the book on the night stand. "Just give me a sec, okay?"

I walk out and leave her alone with Liam for about two minutes.

I can hear them talking, their voices raised at one point, heated, but I don't know what they're saying. Finally they come out and she walks over to me. I nod at Liam and turn to go. "All right, man. Take care of that gash, okay?"

"Hey," Liam calls. "Thanks."

But when I'm just about to open the door Jessie pulls me back gently and says, "I'm staying here, Jackson. I know you think I'm stupid, but I'm not leaving. I don't even know where the hell to go." She's whispering, but I'm sure Liam can hear her. He's standing at the door to the bedroom.

"No. No, that's crazy, Jess. You can't stay here." I can tell she's not hearing me. She looks shell-shocked, her eyes sunken, her hair tangled. Her filthy bare feet. "Come on. I'll buy you a pack of smokes, for god's sake. You can come back to the cabin and smoke the whole goddamn pack out on the porch all night. Don't be nuts, Jess."

But she just shakes her head and pats my arm and I know I lose. She's staying. I look over at Liam to see if it's even a choice and he nods slowly. "Okay," I say. "Okay." And I open the door and walk out.

I realize as I pull away that the damage was already done before Jessie decided to stay. Whatever salvageable scraps were left of that marriage had already been tossed out like the trash. I think about Caroline, probably passed out, still dressed in her shorts and halter top, her sandals leaving piles of Jade Lake's bone-white sand on the sheets. Breathing vodka into the stale air of the room.

I crest that small hill at the edge of town and the moon pops up over the hills, glowing red like a blood orange. I feel tired, like an old man who's already lived his life once and has to start again. I don't even want to think about what will happen next. I don't even want to know.

Jessie

*Y*ou know how when you're just going along in your life, keeping
everything together, holding it all tightly knit like a scarf or
something and then one day you catch the scarf on something sharp
like a barbed-wire fence and it snags and then it rips and then slowly,
no matter how you try to stop it by tying little knots or using clear nail
polish, it just starts to unravel? It might take a while, but after a bit
all you'll be left with is a big old pile of used-up wool. That's my life
right now. That's how I feel when I pull up to that motel and see what
Danny and Mike have done, what my husband, the man I married, has
done. And I add that to the long fucking list, excuse my French, and I
just know. You know what I mean. Maybe everyone knew before I did.
Maybe everyone thought I was a fool all this time.

Anyway, as soon as Jackson leaves after giving me that look that I
would have given anything not to be on the receiving end of, that look
that seemed to just be saying, *Come on, Jess, you're not really this stupid, are
you?* it gets real, real quiet. Just me and Liam, him still holding a bloody
towel to his nose and staring at me, trying to figure out what the hell I'm
still doing there. Like I know myself.

So I make myself useful, picking up the books that fell or were
thrown off the dresser, tossing a torn sheet from the bed into the corner
of the room, picking up some pieces of a smashed dresser drawer. I
don't say a word while I do this, because what can I say? How do you
apologize for the disgusting, unforgivable actions of someone you
actually vowed to spend the rest of your life with? After a while Liam
gets up and pulls some jeans over his boxers and zips up a red sweatshirt
over his bare chest. When he walks into the front room I follow him
like a puppy.

He opens the fridge and takes out a bottle of that organic honey ale micro-brewery stuff, holding it up without looking at me. "Want a beer?"

I clear my throat. "Sure. Okay."

I sit. I sit and stare at him for a minute as he pulls another bottle out of the fridge, flips the tops with the wall-mounted motel opener, and walks over to the table. I stare at those cuts and scrapes that my husband inflicted on him and I think about how much it must have hurt and I wonder strange things like what he said when they burst in his door, what he did. Did he protect himself, did he try to reason with them?

And then I just look down at the table, at the melted cigarette burns, the spiraling galaxy pattern on the aqua Formica. Suddenly I can feel it again, that feeling I get that wakes me up at night, that clutching in my chest. My breath catches and the room starts to spin. I'm afraid I might lurch forward onto the table ... what the hell is wrong with me?

"What?" Liam is alarmed. He grabs my arm. "Jessie ... what's wrong? Are you okay?"

I gasp for breath, press my palm against my hammering heart. The room is still spinning, Liam a bobbing red figure in front of me. *This is what it feels like when you're dying,* I think. I am overwhelmed with the sense of falling, disappearing. I close my eyes, terrified that when I open them the room will be gone.

But the hand on my arm shakes me back. "Jessie. Tell me what's going on."

I blink, try to stay focused. "I ... can't breathe ... " I choke out, but as I say it I know it isn't exactly true. I can breathe, I just feel like something is pressing all its weight against me. "The room is spinning ... feel like I'm gonna pass out ... "

"Okay. I think you're having a panic attack. Have you ever had this happen before?" He holds my arm tightly, anchoring me to my chair. It feels good to be anchored.

I nod. "Only at night." I take a breath and the weight has lightened a little. The room doesn't stop spinning, but it slows down. My heart continues its mad panic to bust out of my chest. "Something is wrong with me ... something must be wrong with me ... "

Liam shakes his head firmly. "Nothing is wrong with you. You're having a panic attack. It's probably already starting to go away, isn't it?"

I shrug, the fear not allowing me an out.

"Jessie, repeat after me. Okay? Say, 'I'm just having a panic attack.'"

I shake my head, still holding my heart inside my ribcage with my palm.

"Say it ... just try. 'I'm just having a panic attack.'"

I shake my head again, annoyed. Shouldn't he be calling an ambulance instead of playing repeat after me? But I can see the look of determination on his face. Fine. "I'm ... just having a panic attack."

"Good." He smiles. Smiles! While I'm dying ...

I think about what I just said and try to believe it. My heart slows a little. I notice that the room and Liam have stopped spinning. I can see the table, our arms intertwined, the bottles of beer. I can breathe. The pressure is lifting. I try taking my hand from my chest and my heart stays where it is.

Just like that I cover my face in my hands and start crying. Not those delicate quiet tears you see in the movies that don't make the girl's mascara smudge or make her nose run or her eyes get all puffy and red. No, just flat-out sobbing, shoulders shaking, the whole thing.

Liam lets me cry. He doesn't say a word. He gets up and goes to the bathroom and returns with some Kleenex, which he sets by my beer. I can see all this through my fingers, because by this point I've stopped sobbing and I'm just kind of hiccupping. Finally I take my hands away and wipe my face. Then I pick up the beer, watching my host over the bottle as I take a big gulp.

He puts the bloody towel down on the table. He seems to have stopped bleeding for now. He kind of looks like a boxer with the cut over his eye and that bruise forming on his cheek, but I would imagine that's something he's against on principle. He gives me a tired smile. "Better?" he asks. I nod. He touches his cheek where the dark purple is starting to spread.

"You need ice," I say.

I stand to go get some, but he grabs my hand and pulls me back down. "Listen," he says, quiet, way more in control than I am even though he's the one who just got beat up. "You don't need to take care of me. You don't need to fix this. You should go be with your friends and family. I'll be okay. There's no way that manager is going to sleep tonight. He'll probably be sitting on his front porch with the phone all night waiting for them to come back." He lets go of my hand and takes a sip of beer. "I don't hold this against you, Jessie. It's not your fault. You can go home. I'm leaving in the morning anyway. I'll be fine."

"Home? Go home? Are you serious?"

He kind of bites his lip and then seems to taste blood because he touches his lip with his finger and winces. "I can drive you anywhere you want to go."

I wonder if Daniel will drive back out to the lake looking for me. I hope he's long gone, that he's off on a bender for a couple of days, maybe as far as Nelson until he cools off. But he could be sitting on our front porch with Mike right now, well into his nineteenth beer of the evening, waiting for his loving wife to come home so he can have a talk with her. I stare off toward the cheap gold-coloured drapes that are half open, out into the dim-lit motel parking lot where I can see the reflection of the neon sign blinking on the pavement. *Vacancy vacancy vacancy.* I keep looking at that blinking pink, that hot bubblegum colour melting into black pavement. I'm suddenly exhausted.

"Do you ever feel like your girlfriend, what she does and who she is, that it sort of reflects on you as a person?" I ask. "Like when she does something stupid when you're out in public, says something or maybe doesn't get a joke or uses the wrong word in a sentence or something ... do you ever feel like everybody's looking at you and thinking what an idiot you are for being with someone like that?"

"Nobody thinks you're an idiot," he says. "We're all attracted to people for different reasons. There's a good point to that. Otherwise we'd all fall in love with the same people. And to answer your question, no, not really. I don't get embarrassed by Taylor. I mean, I'm with her because I love her, I love who she is. You know?"

I nod, but I don't know. Not really. "I am. I'm embarrassed. I mean, take all that other stuff I said about saying stupid things in public and times it by ten, that's how embarrassed I am. " The tears start rolling again. "All this time, I just thought it couldn't get any better. I thought I was being selfish for being so unhappy. I thought he was all I deserved."

Liam is watching me. I feel bad for him that he has to listen to all this, I do, but I can't seem to help it.

"Jessie."

I don't answer, blowing my nose on the wad of Kleenex.

"Jessie."

"What?"

"He wasn't what you deserved. It doesn't work that way. It's not like you did something terrible and that's why you ended up with a husband who didn't treat you well."

I snort, which is very unladylike, and which, combined with the puffy eyes and the nose blowing pretty much supports my argument. "Okay," I say, "so how does it work? I mean, do you think I didn't notice things early on, that I didn't know he was sleeping with that slutty waitress from Laredo's for a year and a half, or that he went through a phase where he spent half his paycheque at the casino in Penticton every second weekend? I knew and I let it go. I thought I just had to put up with it, that there wasn't any other option."

"Why do you think there is now?"

I shrug. That's a good question. "I guess I just see it too clearly now," I say. "I guess when something moves out of the shadows and right up in your face you can't exactly ignore it anymore."

A car pulls into the parking lot and Liam leans over and checks out the window. The car parks in front of another unit and a woman gets out carrying a 7-11 bag. "Listen. I really think you should go. Just in case he comes back. It's one thing if he comes back and it's just me and the manager here, it's another if you're sitting at my kitchen table. I don't want you to get hurt."

I consider this. I find it strangely touching that he doesn't want me to get hurt, even though I know that he wouldn't want anyone to get hurt, that he doesn't want the salmon in the river to get hurt. But I'm more important than a salmon, right? At least, I want to believe I am. The truth is that lately I've been feeling about as significant as a fish. Not even a live one, more like one that's been hooked and tossed into the bottom of the boat to gasp and choke and fight its last little hopeless fight.

I know he wants me to go for my own safety and probably his, but I don't want to go anywhere. Where the hell am I'm supposed to go? My mother's? Crawl under the knobby pink comforter with Lily and stare at the gold-framed puppy paintings and the rosebud-covered wallpaper all night? And then have to listen to her the next morning while she cooks piles of pancakes and sprinkles them with icing sugar and puts gummy bears on them for Lily while she tells me quietly that all men stray and that now is the time I should be standing by my troubled husband? I don't think so.

Back home? So I can confront my drunken, enraged husband who could be waiting for me like a grizzly in a leg trap, cornered and tired and confused and furious, ready to eat his own leg off to get out? No. Not tonight, thanks.

And my friends ... let's see, there's the drunk and newly separated Mike, who's probably still crashing on his mother's sofa bed, there's poor Jackson and his less than comforting and supportive wife, and then there's Sunny, who will have her own long and very opinionated take on the events of the evening. Can't do it.

So. I look over at Liam and then something rises up in me, some sort of rebellious desire. I take a breath, watching his thoughtful green eyes, which as far as I can tell have already figured out what's coming and are starting to cloud over with some sort of apprehensive sadness. I ignore it, ignore the alarm bells screaming in my head, and I say, "Can I stay here with you?"

He shakes his head slowly and I feel the disappointment and shame like a wet blanket. He smiles. "No. The couch is hard as a rock. I can't even sit on it to watch the news. I have to sit on the floor with a pillow ... "

"That's not what I meant. About the couch. I didn't mean that." He doesn't say anything, just looks out the window. "Never mind." I pull my hand away, cover my eyes. "Oh god, this is just a nightmare. I mean, it just doesn't end, does it?"

"What doesn't end?"

"Look at you. Look at your face. And I feel so bad and so guilty and I also just feel, I don't know, like I just want to stay here with you. And you don't want me to." I sniffle, and yes, it does sound pathetic, but hey, that's pretty much what I am. "And Daniel obviously never really wanted me. I don't know, Liam, I just don't remember a time ever in my life where I felt so unwanted. I just can't."

"Oh god, Jessie. Come on." He's angry, which surprises me what with all the soul baring I just did.

"What?"

"You think that's it? You think no one wants you? You think Daniel cheated on you because he didn't want you?"

I don't say anything. Liam leans forward. "Wrong. The reason he cheated on you was because he wanted more of you."

I blink. A few times. "That would be convenient way for a guy to look at it. It doesn't mean it's true, though. I mean, look at me. I just threw myself at you. Does that mean I want more from my husband, or does it just mean my husband is an asshole?"

"Same thing. Don't you get that? That's what I'm saying."

"You're saying Daniel cheated on me because *I'm* an asshole?"

"No." He's all hunched over and looking me straight in the eyes. "No, Jessie. It's not that black and white. I'm saying we can never give another person everything they need to feel wanted and loved and secure and in Daniel's case maybe like a man, strong, sexy, whatever it is. It's just some people are needier than others. More insecure. Have a bigger void to be filled up. I don't know."

"Have you ever cheated on Taylor?"

"Yes." His honestly shocks me and it takes a second to recover.

"But I thought you 'loved her.'" I make the quotes with my fingers and don't bother disguising the snotty tone in my voice. "So you're saying it wasn't anything against her, that actually you wanted more from her?"

"Yes. That's what I'm saying. I'm not saying that the 'more' is even attainable. I'm just saying that's why people cheat. I'm saying it isn't because you aren't desirable. It was something Daniel was missing, not you. Something he saw in someone else that could fill up some empty place he had."

"So you're not missing that thing you were missing before when you cheated on your girlfriend? You don't have an empty place anymore?"

He looks at me for a minute and I feel ashamed of myself, I feel small and spiteful.

"Do you really want me to answer that question?"

I shrug, embarrassed now.

"The truth? If I could stay with you tonight and not suffer any of the consequences there wouldn't even be a moment's hesitation, Jessie. Okay? Not a split second of indecision. And it isn't because I don't love Taylor. It has nothing to do with her and everything to do with me. And you. And what's happening right now."

"And the empty space between us?" I'm being sarcastic, but I don't get the delivery quite right and it kind of comes out quieter and more thoughtful than I meant it to.

He doesn't answer. I can still feel the sparks coming off him, it warms me, overheats me. I want to press up against him, disappear into him, just for a while. To disappear. And I know all the other stuff, about how it's wrong, and how people would get hurt. It's just that it doesn't matter, because my wanting him is bigger than all of that, bigger that Daniel, than Taylor, bigger than this whole town and how people would judge me. I wonder if this is how Daniel felt. I figure it must have been. It funny how we end up doing the same things that enrage us, how capable we all are of inflicting damage.

He runs his fingers through his hair "You should go," he says and then starts to stand. I grab his arm and stop him, pull him toward me. I wish I could be sophisticated like the beautiful French women in those foreign films Nick loves, I wish I was wearing dark sunglasses and a tailored suit and that I could just lower my glasses and peer at him without any shame and say, *Darling, make love to me. And then when we must separate, think of me when the autumn leaves turn to gold, like all beautiful things that must fade and die . . .*

But I'm wearing jeans and a an old T-shirt and the best I can come up with is "Please." Like a child, just like a sad child, clinging to his arm, desperate not to have to go, desperate just to be wanted by him.

And then he's reaching for me, pulling me up, holding me tight to him, his heart thudding through the bright red sweatshirt. And then he pulls away. Walks me to the door. Opens it for me. And I can tell he wants me to stay even as he takes me to his van. I hold on to that feeling. Maybe it's all I needed.

part three

Kali

I haven't heard from Mike in days. Jessie has filled me in and it doesn't sound like he's doing well. I've used the time to focus on the girls, help them with end-of-the-year school projects. Trying not to let my suspicion that our relationship is actually finished overwhelm me. What if it is? It wasn't meant to be, that's all. Still ... I can't help but worry about Mike. Jessie says they think he's using drugs again, that he might have been for a while. How could I not have known? Perhaps the freedom I had, our many days apart every week, had offered him his own, less healthy brand of freedom all this time.

And my dreams the last few nights ... so terrifying, so detailed, so precise. Not nightmares exactly, but ... well, here's an example. Last night I dreamed of falling. Jumping actually. A purposeful fall, not an accidental one. A leap, even, from the top of what looked like Black Rock, or at least some mammoth, imposing rock like it. I should mention that Black Rock is not part of my own history, not enmeshed in my childhood memory like it is for everyone around here as a monument to youth, to overcoming challenges, to the thrill of conquering your own fears.

I know, I've heard the stories from Mike. The triumph of making it to the top, young, drunk on cheap beer, tired, blinded by the glare of headlights illuminating the sheer sleek rock face at 3:00 AM. The temporary hero status given to those who succeeded, like Mike, Daniel, and the legendary Bill Scott who climbed it seven times, once with no shoes. The tragic story of the one who didn't.

So though it isn't part of my past, or even my present, in the dream it seemed to be, it seemed like it was a place I had always known but never bothered to explore. A dark, terrifying place that I had somehow never noticed.

In the dream it was a blazing, molten summer day and I was climbing to the top, up the smoothest, most impossible side of the rock. I could feel the heat of it burning through my fingers, the heat of a thing that has been sitting for centuries, storing up the elements into its pores.

It was surprisingly easy. My hands found small outcroppings wherever I reached, my feet somehow managed to step onto imperceptible ledges and push off. I remember concentrating but not being tired. Just focused. Almost pleasantly so. And when I finally hauled myself up and over the last perfectly sheer piece of rock, I stood, opened my arms wide, and jumped.

I've often had dreams about flying, soaring above treetops, catching an ocean breeze … but this was different. I didn't consider what I was doing. I didn't know I could fly. I just jumped. And then fell. Fast. It wasn't delicate or slow, not like those movies where people jump from planes and slowly drift to the ground. I rushed, all limbs, hurtled to the ground below, the low hills around me dead brown instead of the lush green they should have been. I didn't see myself hit the ground. At least I was spared that.

Before I jumped I remember looking at the town below. Seeing it. Seeing it very clearly, the long rows of square Monopoly houses, the twisting blue river, the steel arc of the bridge, and the smoking columns of AXIS spreading like a metallic cancer over the hill. There was a moment, a tiny, imperceptible nod. A fleeting sense of painful discovery, an acknowledgment of something I would really rather not know. And then I stepped off the edge.

Daniel

The weirdest fucking thing happened at work today. It's the week of the shutdown and me and Mikey and Lou the welder and a couple other contract guys were working our third day of cleaning out this boiler on the lower level, and out of the blue, Lou just passes out. They had to call an ambulance and everything. The weirdest thing. Just like that, one minute she's loosening a piece of pipe, the next minute she's hunched over and dropping to the ground like a sack of potatoes. Hang on. I'll start at the beginning.

So when I wake up this morning it's still pitch fucking dark since it is only 4:30 AM and it's cold as hell and the goddamn streetlight is shining right into my room on the second floor of the Steelworkers Inn. Truth be told I didn't actually go to sleep all that long ago, so I've felt better. I've felt way better. My head is throbbing like a sore muscle, my eyes are so blurry I can hardly make out the damn alarm clock so I can smash my hand down on the snooze button. I can taste the stale smoke on my breath and to top it all off I'm sure I look like I got dragged under a train for forty miles.

It's something, I'll tell you, this living on my own thing. Living in a fucking bar is basically what I'm doing. I mean, it's right there, right down the stairs. They don't shut the damn thing down until after 2:00 AM so I might as well be down there since I can't sleep with the Tom Cochrane and Air Supply screeching out of the jukebox and everybody yelling and singing and making fools of themselves.

And what else am I supposed to do? It's been three days since I've been home. I talked to Jess last night and it didn't go exactly how I planned it to. See, I decided sitting out there at the lake the day after that incident at the motel, that I needed to make some changes, some real ones, you know. Not just a new hairstyle or whatever. And there I was with Mikey, sharing a six-pack, sitting at the picnic table while the sun went down over the far side of the lake.

I guess I was feeling calm, kind of low, after what had happened the night before. How things got a little out of control. I'm not saying what I did was wrong. I stand by that. That guy needed a good scare. No, I don't regret that. He was fine when we left him all curled up like a baby on the floor with his little boo-boos. He was fine. It was more the stuff about Jess. That's what I was feeling bad about out there at the lake listening to Mikey still talking crap about Kali, a woman I knew he wanted to be with but was too fucked up to try to make it work.

And I made a decision then that I was going to suck it up and say I was sorry. Tell her I wasn't going to be screwing up like that anymore. With the girls, I mean. I guess I just went a little too far sometimes with the drinking, and it's hard to keep your head screwed on tight when you're drunk. Especially if some hot young thing comes right over and offers it up, no strings attached. I guess what I gotta do is just keep myself out of situations where that kind of shit can happen. Cut down a bit on the booze maybe, I don't know.

Anyways, after we drove back to town and Mikey dropped me off at the Inn here I gave her a call out at the farm. It rang about seventeen times. She must have had it off the hook or something. So I tried her again later. Same thing. I tried at midnight for the last time, and I have to say that pissed me off a bit because come on, it's obvious she was fucking there, where else would she have been on a school night with Lily? I knew there was no way Jessie was going to be at her mom's, even if the world was ending and her mom's was the only bomb shelter with room.

So by the next afternoon after work I guess I was a bit revved up and wondering where the hell she was. I thought about going to Lily's school to say hi, maybe meet Jess there when Lily got off, but I knew I wasn't looking too good and I'd had a few beers so I figured it maybe wasn't such a hot idea.

So when I called her again I had been stewing awhile, thinking about all the stuff that had happened, getting a little pissed off because she's probably upset about that fucking hippie and adding it to the stack of things she was already pissed off about and that my chances of coming home were going down every time someone dropped a quarter in that jukebox and played a goddamn Foreigner song.

So I headed over to the pay phone in the corner, kicking peanut shells out of the way, and I tried again. This time she finally answered, but like I said, maybe the timing wasn't too good anymore.

"Hello?" she says, real quiet and kind of defensive.

"Yeah, it's me," I say. "Where you been? I've been calling you. Where were you, staying at your mom's?" I make a point of trying to sound nice, like I care about where she was for her own sake, not because I'm pissed at her.

She doesn't say anything.

"Jess," I say. "You there?"

Nothing. I could tell then that this wasn't going to be any easy thing. That I was going to have to suck it up and say I was sorry. So I'm just taking in a breath and getting ready to spill it out, this heartfelt apology about how I want to come home and how I miss her and Lily, which I do even though I haven't talked much about that, and she comes out with, "Don't come home." She says it like a warning, which is weird. Like, why, does she have the armed guard there or something?

"What are you talking about, don't come home. Come on, Jess. I live there."

"Not anymore," she says.

What the fuck? This gets me, it really ... well, it freaks me out, if you want the truth. I knew it was bad, what I did, I knew it was, but I still thought I could get out of it. I still thought I had a chance. "Jess," I said, softer now. "Come on. I was just calling to tell you I'm sorry. About the girls and everything. I should have said that before, I know I should ... "

"Just don't come home," she interrupts. "Danny. You don't live here anymore. You don't live with me anymore. I don't want you coming out here."

Then I can feel the back of my neck getting hot, like suddenly everyone in the place is staring at me. I turn around quick, but all I see is three guys in work shirts at the bar hunched over their pints and a few people sitting at the tables eating nachos.

"What? Look ... " I'm whispering now, because even though no one is watching, I am starting to get embarrassed, like one of those idiots in the movies who has to beg and plead to get his lady to come back. Never thought that would be me. Never thought that would be me and Jess. "I should have told you before. I should have ... not gotten so pissed off about that girl's hair thing. You were right. I just didn't know what the fuck to say, Jess. Give me a little slack here. I'm not going to do that shit anymore, Jess, I'm not a total asshole here, okay?" I wish I didn't notice, but "I Want to Know What Love Is" by Foreigner is playing for the tenth fucking time that day. Somebody here is depressed and pathetic.

She doesn't say anything, and I'm thinking maybe I won her over, I don't know, but then she just says, "Get Bobby to come out for your clothes." And I think to myself, Come on. This can't be it. This can't be the end of thirteen years and a house and a kid and all those great fucking times, the skating out on the lake, the barbeques in Jess's dying garden in the summer, taking Lily for hikes in the hills. It can't be over while I'm standing in yesterday's clothes at a pay phone at the Steelworkers Inn while Lou Gramm sings about how this mountain he must climb feels like a world upon his shoulders.

"Just talk to me, Jessie," I say. I know it's my only chance. It's how we always got through, at least at the beginning. I screw up, then we talk and talk and then finally she comes around.

But I hear her take a deep breath and then she says, in this totally un-Jessie voice, this cold and calm and sharp voice that could cut through diamond, "I saw what you did to Liam. You made your choice ... you could have stayed and worked it out with me. But you left and you did that to another person, a person who hasn't done anything to you, because you were too immature to take it like a man and step up and admit what you did. You're like a child, Daniel, like a nasty little bully who torments people because he won't admit his own life is shit." Her voice is full of hate, and I can feel my guts churning, but I tell myself to stay calm and not screw it up. I try to tune her out, staring over at the wood-panelled-wall, at the big Kokanee sign blinking above the men's room door. "You know what," she says, sounding tired now. "Just don't come home."

And she slams the phone down. Right when that Foreigner dude is singing the part about how in his life there's been heartache and pain and he doesn't know if he can face it again ... its weird how that happens. How something can be going on in your life and then the next song you hear is all about it.

Anyway, so that was that. That part of the story is over. That's what I said, that's what she said, and so I went and ordered another beer and then I called up Mike and Bobby and we hung out for a while and played some darts and then I went to bed, because what the fuck else was I supposed to do? What the fuck is anyone supposed to do when their wife tells them she never wants them to come home? I wasn't going to beg. I wasn't going to get down on my knees and plead with her to forgive me for being such a bully or whatever the fuck she thinks I am, because I am who I am. I said I was sorry. I don't know what the hell else she expected me to do. So I figured I better leave her alone awhile more. She'll come around. We've been through tougher times than these and she always comes around.

So then I wake up this morning feeling like roadkill and I have to drag my sorry ass out to work and my head is like a split melon, pounding so hard I'm thinking it could start spilling out on the parking lot at AXIS. And it's a shit job, what they have us doing. It really is.

Trust me, the last thing I wanted to do was climb into a massive steel pipe and start scouring the sides and sanding off the crud, the fumes coming right through my mask making my eyes sting. The residue in there isn't fit for human exposure, I can tell you that much. I'm no environmentalist, in case you hadn't noticed, but I'm not stupid and I know when something is probably burning ulcers into my lungs.

The only reason I'm glad I was doing it is because I get paid overtime. They got these other guys coming in from out of town too, specialists with working with toxic shit, which is good, because I don't want to get exposed to anything I shouldn't, but we have our HAZMAT tickets too or we wouldn't be allowed in there. The residue, the shit that's left behind when you work with lead and zinc, it isn't exactly something you want to sprinkle on your pasta. But it's safe. The company runs tests on it before they let us in there to work and they make sure the levels are where they should be. There's no danger or anything if you keep your mask on and your gloves.

That's why it's weird when Lou suddenly drops. She's working on a piece of pipe, and then she just kind of staggers away and rips off her mask, probably to get more air. I'm watching her and I yell out, "Hey, Lou, you okay?"

And she doesn't answer. By the time I put my gear down, Dave, the occupational first aid guy on stand-by, is already over there asking her what's up. She kind of shakes her head and then she just collapses forward in slow motion. Dave catches her just in time, but like I mentioned before, Lou is no delicate ballerina. She still ends up on the floor in a heap, but at least he got her down gently.

Her eyes are closed as Dave checks her over and she just looks like she's sleeping or something, wearing her blue coveralls and her work boots, dust in her short spiky hair, her mask pulled down by her neck, the row of silver studs up her ear the only indication she's a female.

Dave calls for help on his walkie as a few other guys start hovering over her. I look over and notice Mike for the first time since Lou collapsed. It's the strangest thing, but he's just working away on a section of piping on the other side of the room like nothing has happened. It's the first time in a while that I get kind of scared, like I finally get how fucked up he might be. I mean, he might as well be whistling to himself or something, the way he's pretending that nothing's happening, like Lou is just taking a nap or something.

I walk up to him. The other guys are with Lou, so I figure she's covered. "Hey," I say, and Mike ignores me, working his steel brush into the pipe, twisting it back and forth roughly. "Are you here? Didn't you see what just happened there?"

He glances over his shoulder. "What, the dyke? She'll be fine. Probably fainted or something."

He's sweating, his hair is soaked, and his eyes are red and puffy. "You get any sleep last night?" I say. He left the bar around two, right around when I went to bed. At least I think he left the bar.

He gives me a kind of side smile. "Nah. I stayed on till they kicked me out. Guess who showed up?"

I ignore his question. "Man, you look like shit. You can't keep coming into work looking like this. They're gonna notice pretty soon. What are you taking to stay awake?"

"Jenny. 'Member good ol' Jenny? She was fine. Very fine. Don't know why I ever let her get away."

"You let her get away because she was a slut, Mikey, she was a crack whore and she was dragging you down with her. Tell me you didn't leave with her."

He shrugs again. "Nah. But I almost did. She's having trouble with her old man, but I couldn't really bring her back to Mom's place, you know?" He fits two pieces of pipe together and steps back. "I'm ready for lunch. You want Dairy Queen? I need some onion rings."

By then Johnny O, the paramedic who's also on stand-by because we're working in a confined space, which is considered more dangerous, has shown up and I could hear him call for the ambulance over his walkie. He's listening to Lou's chest and checking her eyes. "Okay," I say to Mike because really, what's the point in arguing with him or telling him what to do? I'm not his fucking mother.

Then Forrester comes in looking all hot and bothered and says, "What's going on here? Is she okay?"

Dave says, "Yeah, she seems to be. We'll have to transport her. " He looks around at us. "I'm thinking these guys should clear out of here, though. It might be something in the pipes."

Forrester shakes his head, irritated. "Nah. We tested the room. She must have the flu or something."

Dave shrugs. "Your call."

When the paramedics get there and start loading Lou onto a stretcher she kind of wakes up a little and coughs, then shields her eyes with her hand.

"How you feeling, Lou?" Johnny O asks her.

"My fucking head is killing me," she mumbles, and they wheel her out.

"So you in on the onion rings or what?" Mike asks. I can't believe he isn't paying attention to what's going on eight feet from him, but he's been like this before and I know why. I know he won't eat much too, that the drugs make it so he doesn't really want to eat. He'll order the onion rings and he'll eat two of them.

"You think we should get out of here, Mike?" I ask, watching as they get Lou around the corner and out of sight. It's occurring to me by then that maybe it could be the room. I mean, it's a possibility anyway. I was feeling a little weak myself, a little sick to my stomach, although I could have just been imagining it. Who knows?

Mike brushes his hand on his coveralls and starts to head past me. "That's what I'm saying, man. I said do you want to go to Dairy Queen ... you on fucking Pluto or what?"

"I don't mean for lunch, asshole. I mean get out of here. Maybe Lou ... "

And he just keeps walking, ignoring me. Forrester is talking to the supervisor of the project, a skinny little guy with glasses and about forty years' experience. Then Forrester says, "Okay, guys, just carry on here. We'll let you know when we hear how Lou's doing, okay? Let's get moving, we lost some time there."

Mike brushes right past him as he's talking and heads out to the hallway, and Forrester watches him go. I didn't like how he was watching him and I knew what he was thinking. Mike had to be suspended from work last year because he was considered a danger to himself and others when he repeatedly came to work loaded and sleep-deprived. He would make stupid mistakes, leave materials out in the open, trip over gear, fall down ladders. Because of the union, the best they could do was order him to get treatment, which he kind of did by going to two AA meetings and walking out on the third and then by cutting down on the booze and drugs, which was about when he met Kali and things started looking up.

But I didn't know how many more chances there were for Mikey, never mind the fact he was in the union, never mind the fact his dad worked here for thirty years before he "disappeared," never mind the fact his mother May does bookkeeping up in the office part-time. Sometimes your time is just up and that's that. But my time wasn't, my time wasn't even close to up. I pull my gloves back on and yank the mask over my nose and get back to scrubbing, the dust raining down around me like sand from the sky.

About twenty minutes later, Forrester comes back. "Hey, guys, come on now, you need to get out." He looks serious, seriously worried, his glasses low down on his nose, his hair sticking up a little where he probably had his hands in it while talking on the phone or something.

"Why, what's up?" one of the guys asks, poking his head out from a section of steel that looks like a barrel on its side connected to another barrel and then another, all held together by thick pipe.

"All you guys have to go up to Grace River General right now. Come on." He sweeps his hand around. "We missing anyone?"

"Mike," I say. "We're missing Mike Robinson. He's out for lunch."

Forrester nods. "Go find him. You all have to go up there for tests. They found something in Lou's blood. They figure it's coming from in here and it ain't good, so get up there."

Jesus. We all start gathering our gear.

"Never mind that, just go on up and get your tests done."

"Is she gonna be okay?" someone asks. "She pretty sick or what?"

"No idea. All I heard was you guys should be heading up there. Me too."

We all start filing out of the boiler room. I toss a look over my shoulder before I go, look in at all that steel and the dust on the floor, the buckets of chemical soup we use for cleaning. I could be crazy, but my stomach seems like it's feeling worse, like I could just hurl over the metal stairs and down two levels as I'm walking to the locker room.

I find Mike at the Dairy Queen, a half-eaten order of rings on the yellow table in front of him. He's digging around in his flannel shirt as I walk up. He nods at me. "Hey, man. You got a smoke? I can't seem to locate my pack. Musta left it at work. Did you see it in there?"

I don't sit. "No. I don't have your smokes. We gotta go, man. Forrester says we all have to go up to Grace General and get our levels checked. Lou's sick and they think it's something she was exposed to."

Mike pats his pockets again, looking more pissed off by the second. "Shit. I just fucking had them. Maybe they're in the truck." He stands to go, but I grab his arm.

"Hey. You in there?" I give him a little shake. "We gotta go get tested. Now."

He shakes me off, "Do me a favour, man, don't fucking touch me, okay?" He's talking loud, almost slurred. He can't be drunk. I don't smell booze on him and he wasn't gone long enough to get hammered. Unless he's been drinking all morning. "That's number one," he hisses in my face. "Number two is, I'm not going to the hospital, I'm not sick, the dyke's probably just got the flu like I said before."

"Mike. They want us up there. You should get the goddamn tests. You want to end up with lead poisoning and go postal?" We always used to joke, him and me, about how if you got too much lead they say it can make you crazy, like more aggressive and violent. That's only in extreme cases, of course. I remember us reading up on lead in the *Encyclopedia Britannica* in his mother's basement, sitting on the shag rug when we were sixteen. Just a couple years before we got jobs at AXIS.

"Fuck off, Danny. Just leave me alone. Don't you have your own shit to worry about? Hey, didn't your wife leave you or something? I seem to recall she never wants to see your face again." It's all I can do to keep from slugging him in one of those bleary eyes. "You run on home to Jessie James there, cowboy. Solve your own problems. I don't have any problems anymore." He holds his arms wide, showing me how free he is, like a giant drugged bird in a flannel shirt.

This pimple-faced kid comes up and clears his throat, looking around nervously. "Hey. Can you guys take this outside maybe? Like out to the parking lot? We have people eating here."

Mike gives him a little poke. "I was just leaving, there, little man." He picks up his cap from the table and pushes it down on his head. "Don't you worry, the riff-raff is leaving. Aren't you, Danny?"

I know it's kind of a joke, but there's menace behind it and I'm just fed up now. "You know what? You're right. I do have my own problems, man. Do whatever the fuck you want."

And I walk out, leaving him in there collecting his onion rings. He didn't respond to what I said, he didn't even seem to notice I spoke. I tell you, it isn't easy watching him like that. I know he's being a royal asshole, but he's been my friend since I was seven years old. And I don't even care that he's being an asshole, to be honest I don't have the energy to get pissed off about anything else right now. He's right. I have enough of my own shit to deal with. Let him take his pills or smoke his crack or whatever the hell he's doing. There's nothing I can do anyway.

I make it up the hill in the truck to the hospital parking lot. I slam the truck door behind me and walk toward the front doors, and I already know the doctors will find something bad. It could be stress, sure, it could be lack of sleep, it could be the fact that my life is one big jumbled-up puzzle with missing pieces right now, but one thing I can tell you for damn sure is that I don't feel right. I don't feel right at all.

Kali

I haven't had many customers at the store today, so I just tried phoning my mother a few minutes ago. She's in Varanasi working with a women's organization called the Society to Empower Women Everywhere. But she stays with her old university friends Chandra and Hugh and they live in some little apartment above a tailor and are impossible to reach. There's no answering machine and they aren't ever there; they're off volunteering at orphanages, finding blankets for street kids, holding secret meetings for women after midnight.

Anyway, even though I'm at work and I have a box of shampoo to put out and a display of essential oils to put together, I would have liked to have talked to her. I have a bad feeling, or maybe I should say the bad feeling I already had has gotten stronger. My intuition is telling me it might be time to pack up and get out of here, and she's always been the one to tell me to trust my intuition, to follow it fearlessly. She's much better at it than me, though. Part of me thinks I made the wrong decision coming here, being with Mike ... But I know she would disagree: "There's no such thing as a bad decision, Kali," she would say. "There are only hard lessons and gentle lessons. In the end, you always learn."

I remember climbing into her lap once when I was six. Those folds of cotton and velvet, the smooth, round wooden beads around her neck. I remember nuzzling against her, inhaling the rose oil she wore every day, resting my head against her shoulder, her greying hair brushing my cheek. She was working, or trying to, but no matter how stressed she was for time, no matter how many papers she had to grade, it was rare she would turn me away if I came to her. This time she patted my leg. "What is it, Kali?" she asked, still peering at a sheet of paper over her bifocals.

"Why did you name me that?" I asked.

I had been wondering this while I sat in an overstuffed, tartan-covered easy chair with my mother's orange sarong wrapped around me. I had been pretending I was an Indian princess in a beautiful sari like the pictures tacked to the red and blue walls of the apartment. Pictures from the many trips my mother had made to India, pictures of beautiful people and wonderful places I had never seen, crowded marketplaces with foreign, dangerous-looking food that might give you a tummy ache, huge temples like fairy-tale castles, a murky brown river with rickety boats lurching through waves, throngs of brightly dressed people bathing in the water. But it hadn't occurred to me until that moment while I was sitting in the chair pretending that I was about to embark on my very first elephant ride that I wasn't sure what my name meant and that it probably meant something wonderfully exciting.

"Why did I name you Kali? Because it's a strong name, love. A strong name for a strong girl." And she put the paper down, turned me a little so she could see my face.

"But what does it mean?" I asked. My friends at the Waldorf school were all talking about their names lately. "Isolde's named after a princess and River-Skye said her mom thought she was too beautiful just to be named river or sky so she named her both." To this my mother looked slightly scornful, but she tried to hide it.

"Well, that is interesting, Kali. It's interesting you're talking about the origins of your names. And Isolde is right, she was named after a princess, but a rather ill-fated one. Things didn't turn out well for old Isolde."

I was almost breathless. "Why?"

My mother laughed. "Oh, don't worry, I don't think your little Isolde will ever find herself in the position of being an Irish princess who falls in love with one man, marries another, and instigates a war between two counties."

I wrinkled my nose at the mention of falling in love. "Eww."

My mother shoved aside unruly piles of papers and stacks of toppling books from the old table she used as a desk and opened a huge, shiny picturebook on Hindu goddesses. She showed me a page with a hideous blue-faced woman with too many arms, a long, snaking tongue, murder in her eyes.

"Kali, the goddess of death and destruction," she told me, whispering it like it was some delicious secret she had been waiting to tell me.

I was horrified, tears sprang to my eyes. Surely she was joking? "You named me after a monster?"

My mother just laughed, pushed her glasses up onto her wild curls. "No, no, love," she said. "You've got it wrong. Our Kali, she's a warrior. She's the one who destroys the demons so we can all live in peace. She unearths the darkness in order to bring the light." I looked again at the picture, the bulging eyes, the sly smile. The strength. The power she had. There was no fear in her eyes, not a trace of self-consciousness. "Do you see?" my mother asked, prodding me, encouraging me to come to the right answer, the one where I wasn't afraid to take it on. This legacy of battle.

The small bell over the front door of Earth's Bounty rings and in comes Sierra. She gives me a wave over the giant bin of vegetables she's carrying.

I come out from the behind the counter. "Need a hand?"

She shakes her head and drops the bin near the cooler. "I just heard some news, Kali." She wipes her forehead with the back of her hand, her braids swinging. She looks like Rebecca from Sunnybrook Farm in her denim overalls, her pigtails. Except she has a few years on Rebecca.

"What's up?" I'm thinking maybe her suppliers just raised their prices or something. It doesn't take much to get Sierra going. She's a born fighter, unlike me. I have to work at it. But she doesn't look feisty. She looks serious and concerned.

"Up at AXIS. They had an accident of some sort. Some kind of chemical exposure." She walks over to the counter and leans against it, looking out at the street through the picture window with the painted bushels of wheat and the giant sun. She knew it was coming. She and I have talked about how it was a matter of time before something had to happen to wake people up.

"What happened?"

"A bunch of guys got exposed to something toxic during boiler maintenance. They're all up at the hospital. They had to transport a woman, Lou, I think her name is, to Vancouver. The gal I talked to figures her kidneys were failing. I don't know how bad it is. Most of the guys weren't there because of the maintenance shutdown, but still. Some were." She glances at me. She knows about Mike. He was often in here, hanging around when my shift was almost over, sniffing bars of organic soap, shaking vitamin bottles. "I don't know who was there."

Who was there. It dawns on me suddenly that I know who was there. Mike told me a couple of weeks ago that he was on the cleanup crew. He was going to be there. I suddenly feel weak. And helpless. What am I supposed to do? Go up to the hospital? I haven't seen him since that night, and I haven't heard a word from him. It was more than ten days ago now. And I know what happened with the environmentalist. Jessie told me about it. I went over there a few nights ago to talk to her and she was packing Danny's stuff into garbage bags.

And it's funny, after I heard about what he did, what both those guys did, I just sort of shut down. All that time I had spent soul searching, meditating about what I was supposed to do, how I was supposed to proceed with Mike to make him willing to communicate, it just kind of dissolved and sank into the walls of Jessie's house, into her dingy carpet and faded couch.

But now I'm on fire a little, tingling with purpose. Now I know I have to go see him, I need to know if he's okay. This is something I can help with. Maybe I can't fix us or him, maybe I can't even make myself forgive him despite all the reasons I know he did what he did. But I can try to get him healthy. If he's been poisoned I can help him detox.

Sierra's watching me. "He was up there, was he?"

I nod.

She grunts and pushes herself away from the counter and walks toward the cooler. She bends down and starts unloading giant sheafs of rainbow chard, bunches of broccoli, a bag of organic spring greens. "Go on then," she says over her shoulder. "I can manage here."

It isn't a long walk up the hill to the hospital. Only a few blocks, really, if you don't count the bridge, which I don't because I always like crossing this particular bridge with its steel grid arches and the river raging beneath it. That river runs so fast you can imagine that anything that gets pumped into it could somehow miraculously be neutralized by the sheer force and power of the water. But I'm not that naïve.

I think about the environmentalist as I walk. I haven't heard a word about him since Jessie told me what happened. She said he was heading home but that he might be back through town in a couple of weeks on his way to Nelson. She said he might pop in but that most likely she wouldn't see him again, and she seemed so forlorn ... anyway, it was just as well that he was gone. He was stirring up too many emotions and I would be worried about his safety.

It's chaos at the hospital. The ER is full of workers and family members, hardly any of whom I recognize. I see Danny slumped in a plastic orange chair near the door to the treatment rooms and go sit beside him. He looks up, his eyes rimmed with red and full of tired sadness. I try to let go of whatever personal judgments I have about his violence and aggression with the environmentalist, as well as his infidelity with Jessie, and say "Hello, Daniel. Are you all right?"

He looks surprised to see me, or that I'm talking to him, I'm not sure which. Probably both. I cross my legs under my skirt and scan the room for Mike again, but I don't see him.

"What are you doing here?" He's genuinely perplexed.

"I'm looking for Mike," I say, still scanning. I see six men in T-shirts and jeans with no boots on, which I quickly assume is in case of contamination. They probably stripped out of their coveralls and were told to remove their boots. I see a woman frantically pacing with a cell phone to her ear, another woman sitting in a chair across from me with an infant in her arms wearing only a diaper and a two-year old tugging at her shorts. She looks lost and terrified and all of twenty-one.

Daniel sits back heavily in the chair. I look down at his bare feet, strangely white and vulnerable against the grey speckled linoleum floor. "He's not here." He coughs suddenly and I immediately think of the chemicals. Did he inhale them? I'm racking my brain for remedies while I process this information about Mike.

"Where is he?" *Dandelion?* Good for the liver but not the one

I'm looking for ... wait. "Was he not there this week? Did he have the week off?"

"Nah. He was there." He looks at me sideways. I'm concerned for him. Daniel, I mean. Something is clouded over, his eyes aren't as blue as they usually are, there's a sort of veil over them that isn't fatigue or hangover. "I tried to get him to come up for testing, but he said he wouldn't. He's not acting normal. He's high, I guess. I don't know. You could try his mom's, but I doubt he's there either."

"Okay." I dig through my knitted bag for my bottle of water and unscrew the cap. I take a long sip, watching the room. The woman with the baby has risen and is standing at the admitting desk talking to a nurse who keeps shaking her head and shrugging her shoulders as if to say, *Don't ask me.* The two-year-old has started to cry, and is pulling on her mother urgently, so hard the woman stumbles a bit as she turns and navigates back to her chair. She sits again and pulls a can of Coke from her diaper bag. She opens it and hands it to the child, who accepts it happily and sits on the floor to drink it. Oh no, I think. If she thought it was bad already, the sugar and caffeine should have that child tearing around the room like a whirling dervish in about five minutes.

"Hey, have you seen Jess?" Daniel asks, as though he just thought of it. As though he hadn't been wondering that from the second he saw me come in the door.

"Yes," I say. I give Daniel my full attention now, pulling my energy away from the distraught mother, the nervous workers, the frantic wife on the phone and the overwhelmed admitting nurse. I reach over and touch his arm. His skin is hot to the touch under his T-shirt and he jumps a little. He has at least three days' growth on his chin, which I have never seen on him before, and he is truly, in my opinion, a broken soul. I will myself to have compassion, and at that moment the answer comes to me. "Milk thistle," I say and release his arm.

He looks confused, maybe wondering what on earth that could have to do with Jessie. But we both know I'm not going to play both sides, that my loyalties lie with my friend. "What?" he says.

"Milk thistle. Go to the store after this and ask Sierra for milk thistle. It's a detoxifying herb. It will help your liver process the toxins."

He raises his eyebrows. Looks me over. Probably taking in the rainbow-coloured tank top and the brown Indian cotton skirt. "Uh-huh," he says. "Sure. Thanks." His gaze flickers away and I know I've lost him. He can't imagine it's as easy as that. I guess even I know it isn't.

May's house is like the witch's house in *Hansel and Gretel*. It looks so perfect, so appealing on the outside, but it's full of black magic and trickery inside. It's in a nicer neighbourhood, two streets up from the river with a park at the end of the road. These houses were built twenty years ago, and are bigger than the tiny rows of company homes that populate the rest of the town, small squares with stamp-sized lawns. Her home is white with gables, yellow climbing roses, a slate walkway with solar-powered lanterns, double doors. I know they didn't live like this when Mike was growing up, that in fact their old house with the peeling paint and the crumbling steps was the smallest square on the block in their old neighbourhood. It wasn't until her husband left that they moved in here, and how they did it no one has been able to tell me. Maybe May secretly hid money away in a stocking under the bed the whole time she was married, who knows?

I'm sweating now, dripping actually, from the walk back down the hill. The doors seem to sway a little as I knock. May pulls them open and her preset smile dissolves, her eyes hardening to cobalt blue marbles. "He's not here," she says. She doesn't try to close the door in my face so I know she's curious as to why I'm there.

"Do you know where he is?"

She keeps her hand on the door. Her gaze flickers out across the river, which we can see across the street, and over the town. "No." Her hand drops. "He hasn't been home for several days. A company man came looking, but I told him I had no idea where he was."

She looks real for a fleeting second, she looks like how a normal mother would look if her troubled son had gone missing, but then the mask comes up again and she straightens. "I told them to try your house," she adds, barely able to keep the sneer out of her voice. "But I knew it was a long shot."

"I didn't do anything to him, May. We had an issue come up. I tried to get him to talk about it and he ran away."

She smirks. "Well, from what I hear you do a lot of talking and most of it is criticizing Michael. He's doing his best. He was, anyway. I don't know what happened to the two of you, but he's taking it pretty hard. It's setting him back. He was doing well before ... "

"May. He wasn't doing well before. He hasn't been doing well since I met him."

She raises her eyebrows. "What a coincidence."

I turn to go. What's the point? Then I stop and turn back. "You know, I could never figure out why you hated me so much. What did I do? Is it because I'm different, because I don't work at the smelter, because I have children, what?"

She looks me over and I can tell she's gathering her words carefully. She has a quality of speaking that seems as though she has rehearsed everything to get the maximum effect. It strikes me suddenly how lonely she must be as she stands like a suburban soldier in her massive doorway, framed by lattice heavy with roses. Such a big house for such a small woman.

"I don't hate you, Kali," she says. "But you don't know my son. For you it's nothing to have an affair with a local working man. A nice change from your fancy restaurants and fancy friends in the city. But you don't understand what this could do to him. To offer him some fairy-tale life with you and those girls and then have it taken away. Just let him be. You'll only make it worse with your nagging and meddling." She's watching me closely, making sure I'm really hearing what she's saying. The wind picks up and carries some loose petals across her doorstep, a few falling at her stockinged feet.

"But I didn't take anything away," I say. "He ran. And he didn't come back."

She shakes her head, looks away, back out over the town. She takes a breath. "Well, stop chasing him, Kali," she says firmly. "It's the best thing for both of you." And she steps back, gives me a slight nod, and she's gone, the door closing gently in front of me, that cavernous house swallowing her up, leaving her alone with her demons.

I back up and turn away from the house, start walking again. I pick my way slowly past houses, cut through a yard, and walk along the river. I think about my name as I go, kicking pebbles along the riverbank, watching the churning grey swell of water roll along like a gathering storm. The way she said it so firmly, like a scolding parent. A reminder of who she is versus who I am.

On my way over the bridge I think of one other place I can try. I turn right after the bridge. I consider going into 7-11 for some water, but I'm driven now, I'm determined to find him and at least try. Nobody else seems to want to. Everybody else seems to have given up. And even though it really is the last thing I want to do, that I would much rather go home and be with my girls, water my lupines, weed the potato patch, just *sit* with a cup of tea, I know this is not something I am meant to turn away from and that I will keep going until I know it's time to stop.

It's a few blocks down Main Street, and I just allow myself to feel it, feel the pavement under my sandals, the muscles in my calves working, my arms swinging, the blood humming in my veins as I pass strangers on the sidewalk, past the overflowing indigo lobelia and sunset pink petunias in the baskets under the awnings. I build up strength, because I suddenly know with utter certainty that he will be at the Steelworkers Inn and that he will be drunk.

And so it's no surprise at all when I walk in and the light is shut away with the door behind me, all the sunshine and blue skies and bursts of flowers fade away like a pleasant dream and I'm assaulted by the smell of spilled beer and stale whisky and crushed peanut shells. It's so dark that I can't focus for a moment, but soon I make out the bar and the blinking neon and the forms of men and women sitting around the small tables. A lonely figure sits at the end of the bar and I know instantly that it's Mike.

I approach him, walking right up to his stool. The bartender, stacking glasses below the counter, eyes me warily over the polished wooden bar. The lonely figure is busy doing something with his hands that I can't see through the curve of his bare elbow. An untouched bottle of Bud sits in front of him. I peer over his arm and see a pile of wood shavings and realize he's whittling something with his small Swiss Army knife.

The bartender rises from his task and points a finger at Mike. "You don't so much as scratch that bar or you're paying for it, hear me? I had about enough a your shit, Mikey."

Mike doesn't respond, just whittles away, head down, lost in his task. I sit beside him carefully. I've seen him like this before, lost in thought as he whittles away. This is something he enjoys, he often would carve little figures of animals, a tree, a boat, while we sat outside in the evenings. He once made Summer a small cat out of a chunk of firewood. It fit in the palm of her hand and she cried when she lost it in the schoolyard the next day.

"What are you making?" I ask gently.

He looks over, startled. He drops the knife onto the pile of wood shavings. Looks me up and down. Blinks as though to see if I'm really there. Then he turns back to his work and picks up the knife again. "Don't know yet," he says gruffly.

He seems tired. Exhausted, actually. I wonder if he's slept at all in the past couple of days. Although the light is dim he looks older somehow, more burdened. "Michael."

"It's shit is what it is, it's nothing," he says, suddenly slamming the small piece of wood down. He looks up at the ceiling, closes his eyes. Then he reaches for his beer. "It's just shit," he repeats.

"Can I see?" I reach over for it, but he puts his hand down on top of it before I can take it.

"What do you want? You come in here for a beer or what?" He finally really looks at me and I can see a glimpse of him in there, although I don't really like what I see.

"You need to go in for treatment. Daniel, your employers, your mother ... they're all concerned about you."

His eyes narrow slightly. "Yeah? Well, tell them I'm doing just fine. Okay? Your job is done. You can go now. Leave me to my work here." He clumsily picks up the knife again. Then he grabs the wood and shoves it at me. "You wanna see? You see that?" He's holding it in my face, too close to actually see anything but a blur.

I gently move his hand back. It's a crudely carved square with a small chimney and a door etched unevenly in the front. "A house?"

He laughs at me, pulls it back. "Yeah, a house. Good one. A house. You got it, sister. I decided I'm gonna have me my own house one day. Build it my own damn self too. I got books on it and shit. It's not so hard. I could do it." He's slurring, his words tumbling over each other.

"I'm sure you could."

He points at me with the hand holding the knife. Although it's very small, no longer than my index finger, I still get a chill when he holds it near me.

"Put that down, please." I can see it now, that I'm too late to do any real good. If he were sober, maybe I could reason with him. But not like this. He's so close to explosion, to implosion, to some sort of meltdown that I don't think I can contain.

He waves it in my face, the tiny blade glinting. Then he grins, shakes his head, and puts the knife down. I take a breath. The bartender is chatting with someone at the other end of the bar and hasn't noticed any of this.

"Mike, you need help. I'm not saying I want to help you, you don't have to have anything to do with me if you don't want to. But please, go up to the hospital."

He looks at me. Stares. Doesn't say a word. And then he leans over. "You answer me one question, there, Kali girl," he says quietly, the dangerous, angry drunk gone for a moment, replaced by a sad, dejected man. "Answer me one question, and if you answer it right, I'll go. Okay?"

A warning sounds in my mind, like an air raid siren. I know I should refuse his offer, but I'm so sure I can answer it right, I'm so sure I will know what to say.

He takes my hand clumsily, which surprises me. "Did you love me? Before?" His eyes ... they're wrong somehow, they don't look like the eyes of the man I knew. I can smell the rotten beer on his breath. Without thinking I pull back from his heavy, clutching grip, break free, and the second I do I know I've answered wrong.

He smiles sadly and raises his beer to me. A salute.

I shake my head, try to repair the damage. "Mike. Of course I did.

I still love you enough to want you to get help. I wouldn't be here if I didn't … "

But he shakes his head and makes a rude buzzer sound. "Nah. You got the answer wrong, sweetheart. And I was just fucking joking, by the way, so you don't have to look like your fucking dog died or your *plants* or something, Jesus." He laughs, a horrible, fake-sounding laugh. Then he thrusts the half-carved house at me. "Here," he says. "You have it."

I take it reluctantly, still trying to think of the words I need. I set it in front of me.

"You take that," he says. "You know why?"

"Mike … "

"*Do you know why?*" His voice is raised now, and the bartender looks over.

I look down at the small carving. I shake my head. "No. I don't know why."

"Because it's fucking nothing, that's why. Just like you. It doesn't mean a fucking thing!" He's almost shouting now, and the bartender starts walking down toward us, pointing a warning finger at Mike.

"So you might as well take it." He picks it up, hurls it across the room. "*Take it!*" he yells, and the bartender grabs him by the shoulder and I pick up my bag and back away from the bar as it all drains out of me, the fight just leaves. And it's now that I know I've done everything I can, as I look at that rage bubbling over as the bartender restrains Mike, pushes him toward a wall, yells at me to leave. I can see it flowing out of him and on to me, I see that desperation and fear and misery and I know I don't want it anymore. I can't make it pretty with flowers or cover its stench with essential oils or bring it back health and beauty with herbal teas and scented baths.

It's now that I know it's finally time to stop.

Jackson

I gotta fight to keep my eyes open as I cruise along the highway toward home. It's not far, only six miles or so from town, but it's a narrow, winding road and I've had a long day so I have to make sure I don't nod off.

I finally get to the long gravel driveway that winds up around a group of stunted pine. I worked on it myself, shovelling heaps of gravel out of the back of the pickup and getting Brooks to smooth it out with his Spider-Man beach shovel. I had to go over it again later, but he had a great old time so it was okay by me.

Home at last. Jesus. What a night. You'd think there's been a goddamn nuclear explosion or something the way the town is freaking out. AXIS finally put on this meeting at the town hall to inform everyone about what had happened. I guess a bunch of people are starting to worry they might be getting sick too. As well they should. I wonder how Danny is doing, even though I haven't seen him since that night and I haven't wanted to. From what I hear things aren't going well for him and Jess, but I haven't talked to either one of them. Anyways, he wasn't there, and Mike wasn't either, so I guess they're dealing with their own shit.

I felt for this one guy, Sumo, the big guy who runs the laundry. His real name isn't Sumo, but I guess you can figure out why he gets called that … anyway, he was saying how he was real worried because he was the one taking in all the dirty coveralls at the end of the shifts and how was he supposed to know they were covered in poison?

The weasel they sent from management just basically kept repeating what the official statement in the newspaper had said: that Axis regretted any inconvenience or discomfort the recent thallium exposure had created and that we could all be assured that measures were being taken to secure the safety of all concerned and that the risk had been contained and all involved parties were receiving the utmost in medical care and expected to fully recover ... blah blah blah. What a bunch of bullshit. I wouldn't believe one word that comes out of their mouths. The thing is, they don't seem so shocked. They don't seem so appalled, even. They say Lou, she had an underlying condition and it was just bad circumstance she happened to collapse while she was at work. But I heard from one of her cousins that they don't think she's gonna make it.

And this one woman, some young girl I don't know, standing there with her baby and her two-year-old pulling at her skirt, and her face was red as an apple and she looked so goddamn scared you could have knocked her over by breathing on her. "What about my baby?" she said, the words choking up on the way out. "My husband's in the hospital and he can hardly breathe on his own and these kids were touching him and kissing him and up against his clothes every day. What about them? Are they gonna be okay? Are they?" Young and timid as she looked I do believe if someone had handed her a gun she would have taken a shot at Scotty Hibberd when he told her even if the kids were exposed it was nothing to worry about. They could treat it. Nothing life-threatening. No, I don't think she would have thought twice about it.

Everyone should be asleep by now, but the lights are shining through the sheer living room drapes. All the lights are on, in fact. Maybe Caroline let them stay up and watch movies or something. Damn it. That's the way it works around here. She's the fun Momma and then I come in and tell everyone to go to bed.

But when I walk in I know something's not right. The TV is blaring, but it isn't the *Late Show* or *Conan O'Brien*. It's *Power Rangers*. I kick off my boots on the mat and head into the living room. Travis is sitting two feet from the TV, his back to the couch, where his mother is fast asleep, half wrapped in a green and yellow afghan. Brooks is curled up in a little ball at her feet, still in his jeans and his dirty T-shirt.

"Hey, buddy." Travis is just wearing his pyjama bottoms, his chest bare and shining in the glare from the TV. He turns and gives a wave before turning back to his show. "Hey, Dad. Watching *Power Rangers.*" He sounds like a teenager, or maybe one of my buddies. Like it hasn't occurred to him that he shouldn't be up at this hour.

"I see that, bud. I'll be right back, okay?" I walk over to the couch and lift Brooks up. He squirms and then relaxes back into deep sleep again. How long was he up before he passed out on the couch? Jesus. And how long has Caroline been out? The same old questions, and the answer is never good.

I tuck Brooks into bed and head back to the living room and flick off the TV. Travis starts hollering at me right away. I kneel down. "Hey."

He glares at me.

"I need to talk to you for a sec, okay?"

Travis doesn't say a word, looking past me to the couch where Caroline is moaning in her sleep.

"Travis, when did mom fall asleep? Was it a long time ago? Did she put you to bed and you just got up to watch some TV?" Oh, god I hope that's the case, though I'm pretty sure it isn't. "It's okay, I'm not mad, buddy, I'm just wondering, is all."

Travis shrugs. "Dunno. I guess around five or so. During *Wheel of Fortune.* I tried to wake her up."

Travis flicks the TV on and sits in front of it again. Okay. Okay. Five o'clock ... the kids probably didn't eat dinner. I suddenly feel so goddamn tired I could just crawl under the afghan next to my moaning wife and close my eyes and fall asleep with the TV blaring. But I know I can't. I go to the kitchen and see a trail of crackers from the cupboard to the small round table. The package must have split when they tried to open it. A leaning tower of crackers rests on the table, as well as two small plastic plates and the opened jar of peanut butter. A few of Caroline's empty vodka coolers bottles are sitting on the counter.

I head back to the living room and turn off the TV again. Travis doesn't even move this time; he just sits and stares at the blank screen. I pull him up by the armpits. "Come on." I lead him by the hand to the kitchen, sit him down at the table, and then start rummaging through the fridge. "Okay, bud. I'm going to make you a sandwich. You hungry?"

"I guess."

"Good, okay, I got some ... baloney." I toss the package on the counter. "And some ... no, no cheese. Baloney it is. With mustard." I pull out the bottle and turn to Travis. "Sound good?"

Travis shrugs, hugging himself. "She didn't make us dinner, Dad. I asked her to, I told her she had to 'cause Brooks was real hungry. But she didn't listen. She was just sleeping there all night."

I come over and sit across from Travis. "You did good. You shouldn't have to make your brother dinner. But you did good, taking care of him like that. Okay? Sometimes mom just ... she just gets tired, that's all."

Travis nods. "I tried to put him to bed at eight o'clock like we're supposed to, but he wouldn't go. I even tried to read him a book, but he only wanted Mom. He just lay there on the couch all night 'til he fell asleep."

I have to look away from that little face for a second. I can see that anger behind his eyes, that look that tells me it's my fault. And he's right. He's right about that. "Okay. I'm gonna make you that sandwich now."

By the time I get Travis fed and off to bed it's almost 12:30. I clean up, stacking the bottles by the back door with the rest, sweeping up the cracker crumbs and globs of peanut butter. Then I carry Caroline to bed too. She wraps her arms around me like one of her sleepy children. She hums a little under her breath, something soft and sweet, but I can't quite make out what it is.

The next morning I wake up to the sound of yelling kids and clattering dishes. I wander into the kitchen. Caroline is buttering toast, singing Elton John's "Tiny Dancer" to drown out the boys, who are fighting over a cereal box. She's wearing a huge purple bathrobe and large fuzzy slippers.

"You had more than me last time. I want the rest!" Brooks shouts, his small face red with rage.

154

"Uh-uh. I'm bigger. You're not having it." Travis's voice carries a volcanic edge that we're pretty familiar with around here. Caroline seems blissfully unaware as she sings, throwing in her imitation of a piano when she can't remember the words. I decide to nip it in the bud before Brooks gets a backhand to the face from his brother. I grab the box and hold it high above their heads as both sets of hands try to grab it. I pour out an equal amount in both bowls.

"You are such a baby." Travis mutters under his breath to Brooks, who delivers a swift kick to his brother.

"*Boys!*" I yell just loud enough to be heard.

Caroline stops singing and looks at me, her butter knife poised in mid-air. She waggles it at me before turning away again. "Well, hello there. You joining us for breakfast this morning?" Besides the fact that her eyes are a little more red than usual, she looks fresh and clean, her blonde hair washed and drying in soft curls around her face. "How'd that meeting go, darlin'? Did they make you all do a thermal scan to see how many toxic chemicals you have shooting around through your blood?" she asks as she pops more bread in the toaster.

I pour myself a coffee. "No, not really. There were some pretty worried folks there, though. Can't say as I blame them. At least I haven't been out to AXIS since the maintenance shutdown or we'd be pretty worried too."

She snorts. "Whatever. Everyone's getting so hysterical about that stuff. For god's sake. How many people are actually sick, Jackson? Like, two or three? It's not the Black Plague or anything. People have been working around this stuff forever. Your dad, my dad." She turns to me with a smile.

I take a sip, watching her. Thinking how easy it is for her to brush things aside. "It's pretty serious, Care. Lou's been sent to Vancouver. They don't know if she's gonna make it. A few other guys are in the hospital. One's on a respirator. Some have been throwing up for days."

She sits at the table with a plate of buttered toast. The boys both reach for some and she takes a piece too. "Okay, so it's a little serious," she says with a smile before biting into her toast. "You're right. At least you weren't there. Thank god for that, right?"

Yeah." I clear my throat. "So the meeting went pretty late. There were a lot of people who wanted to talk. They were wondering when AXIS will reopen, stuff like that."

"Yeah?" She takes another bite of toast. "So when will they?"

"Ow!" Brooks suddenly shrieks, and I look over and see that Silent Travis is twisting his little brother's arm in his hands as hard as he can. Brooks drops his spoon with a clang onto the table and picks up his toast crust and hurls it at his brother, who starts laughing.

"Ha ha! I gave you a burn. Look at your arm! You're such a wuss!"

Caroline swats Travis on the head, hard enough to make a dull smacking sound. "You sit down. What the hell's the matter with you? Brooks, come here, baby. Come see Momma." Brooks pushes himself away from the table and comes and buries himself in her lap, snuffling into her robe.

"Baby," Travis sulks, getting up to leave. He looks miserable, more miserable than an eight-year-old kid should look. Like he's got way too much on his mind.

His mother catches him as he goes by, pulls him close. "He's the baby, but you're my big boy. My big strong boy, right? You treat him good. He's the only little brother you've got."

Travis allows himself to be hugged, then escapes to his bedroom down the hall.

She looks over. "You were saying?"

"I was saying the meeting went late." I feel a little cold all of a sudden. I have something I need to get off my chest about last night. It's as good a chance as any. "Caroline." I try to say it gently, but I know she can hear all the things I don't say, I know she can tell I'm upset.

She shakes her head at me. "Jackson," she says quietly but firmly. "Don't. Okay? Don't start." She looks down at Brooks, his tousled head resting on her chest.

I just nod.

"So," she says brightly, "it's a beautiful day. You taking the boys somewhere special while I'm slaving away at the flower shop?"

I don't answer right away. I just watch her for a minute. Then I take another sip of coffee and sit down at the table. "Yeah," I say. "I gotta go help Mom out with her chicken coop for a while. Her hens have been getting out. The boys can give me a hand."

"Good," Caroline says softly, reaching out to stroke Brooks's soft brown hair.

After I finish wrestling with the chicken wire, which has somehow been twisted out of shape enough to let the hens out so they can peck at my mother's peonies and rose bushes, I head back inside. The boys are at the kitchen table, eating homemade cinnamon buns while my mother kneads a giant lump of brown dough on the counter.

Travis waves his bun at me. "Hey, Dad. We helped make these. You should have one. They're so awesome."

"Yeah," Brooks pipes up. "I put the raisins in. They're so awethome."

"Help yourself," my mom calls over her shoulder. "We made a big batch. Take some home for Caroline too, if you like."

I settle down at the table. The sun is shining though the big windows, and the kitchen smells like warm bread and fresh air. "Thanks, Mom. She's not big on sweets, though."

"Oh, that's right. I always forget, don't I?" My mother has a few mental blocks when it comes to Caroline.

"You cook better than Mom." Brooks says, licking the brown sugar crust on his bun.

She turns to him. ""Well, it's nice of you to say so. But your mother is a wonderful cook. She makes a mean lasagna, if I recall."

"Yeah, but sometimes she forgets to make us dinner," Travis says, his mouth full.

There's a horrible, awful silence, and I want to grab Travis and cover his mouth, drag him out the door. Anything to escape that look my mother is giving me right now, her hands stuck there in mid-air, dough oozing through her fingers.

She turns to the sink and starts scrubbing her hands. "What do you mean, dear? When you say she forgets?" She was a schoolteacher for years at the elementary school in Grace River and she speaks to both my kids like they were her prize pupils. She dries her hands on a towel and sits down at the table, looking at her grandson expectantly.

Travis shrugs, and his eyes dart over to me. I shouldn't do it, but I shake my head. *Oh god, please don't, Travis.* But it's Brooks who speaks anyway.

"She forgetted to make dinner yesterday night." He licks his finger. "She was supposed to, but she forgetted, 'cause she was sleeping on the couch."

Here we go. My mother nods like this is the most normal thing in the world. "I see. And why didn't you wake her?"

"I tried," Travis says. "I did. But she wouldn't wake up, because she was, you know." He tips an imaginary drink to his mouth, letting his tongue loll out.

I stand. "Travis ... " It comes out more like an order than I mean it to.

My mom steps in. "Boys, you go on out to the swing for a few minutes." The boys look guilty as they scramble from the table and out the door. She reaches across for my hand and I don't want to take it, but what can I do? "Jackson," she says, all sad and disappointed and god knows what else.

I don't say a word.

"Jackson, you've got a lot on your plate right now with your job and the plant. I'm not trying to make your load any heavier. But this is not the first time I've heard these stories. You know that. And I know you love her, Jackson, but there is such a thing as being too forgiving."

I don't say anything for a while, just stand there holding her hand and looking out the kitchen window to where the boys are swinging on the old tractor tire from the willow. It's hard to talk to her about this stuff, you know, because my dad, he had a bit of a problem with booze too, and how we all got through it was, we just didn't mention it. And the fact that my mom is mentioning it now with regard to Caroline, well. It doesn't seem fair somehow. I figure the same rule should apply for me. "I'll do what I can, Mom," I finally say, because it allows me room to move. "What I can" might be no more than what I'm doing already.

So we're driving home that afternoon, the boys bouncing on the seat of the truck, when I suddenly realize I just don't want to go home. It's actually kinda the last place I want to go. I just want to stay on the road for a little while. I rack my brain to think of something to do, and then I suddenly remember that conversation with Liam the environmentalist from a couple weeks ago. How he told me to go get tested in another town. I just got mine done a few weeks ago and the smelter's doctor said the levels were more or less normal. Well, why not? It would probably be a waste of time, the guy was probably just paranoid, but what the hell? I could drive the boys to Nelson; maybe we could go get a burger.

An hour later we're at the Saturday clinic in Nelson. The receptionist looks at me kind of funny when I say I'm an AXIS employee who needs a blood test.

"Don't they test you right there at the smelter? Is this about the contamination? I don't think we're dealing with that ... "

"Yes, they do test us there, absolutely. But this isn't about all that contamination stuff. I wasn't exposed to that. No, this is just a regular lead test. I just ... I missed the last one, and I happened to be here anyway, so I thought what the hell."

She looks a bit pissed, but after waiting an hour with the boys bouncing off the walls, I get in to see a doctor who puts in the order for the bloodwork.

We drive home at dusk, the orange sun lighting the hills on fire. I rub that small Band-Aid on the inside of my elbow as I drive. I feel kind of stupid, to be honest. I'm sure there was no point in driving all the way out there. Just because I was afraid to go home.

By the time I pull up to the house the boys have both fallen asleep. They'd worked themselves into such a frenzy they had nowhere to go but down. I watch them for a minute before I get out of the truck. Brooks is curled on the seat like a cat, his legs tucked under him, his seatbelt wedged into his round tummy. Travis is sprawled beside him, his legs wide, his mouth open. His hand rests on his brother's back gently, like he's reassuring him about something, even in his sleep.

Caroline doesn't have a drink that night, at least as far as I can see, and as I watch her dance around the living room with Brooks in her arms, and scrub Travis's hair in the bathtub, too late for dinner, I can feel the pressure lift off me. I start thinking maybe I overreacted again, maybe things really are okay. I start thinking maybe being home from AXIS for a while will be okay, that we can all hang out together. Maybe work on the house or something. The front porch needs the railing reinforced before one of the kids breaks his arm, and the garden could use a lot of work.

We eat popcorn and laugh our way through the cheesy parts of *Top Gun* after the boys fall asleep. Caroline curls against me under the afghan and falls asleep before the movie's over. I don't wake her up. I just hold her close, breathing her in. That soft sweet smell she has from working with flowers all day.

But Sunday, after a day of fighting kids and housework, Caroline cracks a cooler around four o'clock. She tips it at me with a smile. "Just the one, baby. Don't get all *Jackson* about it." We sit down to watch TV after the boys go to bed, and when she's on her fifth cooler and starts singing along to the commercials in her showgirl voice, standing to do the can-can, I just shake my head and tell her I'm heading to bed.

"Don't be a loser, Jackson ..." she calls down the hall. I make sure the boy's bedroom door is closed as I pass by.

Monday morning I get up and make the kids' lunches and send them out the door for the bus. It's the last week of school. Soon they'll be spending a lot more time at home. I think about that, how Caroline'll have them when I'm at work ... she's still asleep in the bedroom. The sound of the kids running around the house looking for lunch bags and notices didn't even make her stir.

The phone rings and I pick it up.

"Jackson Emery?" a young female voice says.

"That's me."

"I have your blood test results. Would you like to set up an appointment to discuss them?"

"An appointment? No ... I uh ... I live in Grace River, I didn't think I'd have to drive back there. You know what, never mind, I'm not too worried."

"Oh. Well." I can hear papers rustling, the click of a keyboard. Someone coughing in the background. "Well, we don't usually give results over the phone, but since you live in another town, it should be okay."

"Fine. Okay."

"So. Your lead levels are elevated."

Elevated doesn't sound bad. Just a little higher than normal, which I already knew. My last level had been a twenty-one, which was only really one point above what they considered safe. "Right. Yeah, I work at AXIS, so I pretty much figured."

"Well ... when I say elevated, I do mean quite high, Mr. Emery. You're sitting around forty-two right now."

Forty-two?

"So, I have to advise you to see your doctor up there. The levels won't go down until you remove yourself from the source of the contamination. He may suggest you take some time off until you start to feel better."

Feel better? Is this a joke? I'm not sick. Am I? Maybe all the tension and fatigue hasn't been because of Caroline after all ... "All right," I say. "Well. The plant is shut down right now anyway, so I guess that's good. So ... okay. Thanks a lot."

"Mr. Emery? It may take longer for the lead to decrease in your system. Please call your local doctor. You need to get those levels down. The long-term effects can be quite serious. Nervous system damage, high blood pressure, kidney problems ... "

"I know what the long-term effects are. Thank you." I hang up. Shit. Shit. Forty-two? Forty-two was crazy, Twenty-one points above what the smelter lab had told me, and I haven't even been into work for a week. Jesus. Had they been lying to me for fifteen years? To everyone? I wander through the house to the back door, open it, and take deep gulps of spring air. I feel out of control all of a sudden, dizzy. Jesus. I almost wish I hadn't done the test, I wish I didn't even know.

Caroline wanders in wearing her purple bathrobe. She pours herself a coffee and sits at the table. "Hey there," she says brightly. She takes a sip, watching me over the rim of her mug.

I don't answer.

"Who was that?"

"Clinic," I say, still stunned. Still trying to figure out what the hell ...

She looks confused.

"I got my bloodwork done in Nelson." Her eyebrows raise. "I just got the results. I'm at forty-two."

"But you just got tested. You were only a twenty something."

"I know. Caroline, they've been lying. Like that environmentalist guy said. AXIS must have been lying to us."

She looks skeptical. "Whatever, Jackson. Don't be so dramatic. There must be some mistake. I'm sure your levels are fine. They must have done the test wrong."

I shake my head. "How do you do it wrong? There's either lead in your blood or there isn't. And I haven't even been there for a week. If anything the levels should be down. I have ... doesn't this worry you? I could have gotten really sick if I hadn't found out. If my levels were three points higher I would have to do chelation therapy."

She dismisses this with a wave. "I don't even believe it. Why would I be worried about it? And chelation therapy ... big deal. My dad did it twice. It's just medicine, Jackson. It doesn't kill you."

I get quiet for a moment, thinking about this. I watch her sip her coffee and look casually out the kitchen window at the hills. "You don't believe it?"

She shakes her head. "Nope." She smiles.

I don't smile back. "So just because you don't want to believe there's a problem, there just isn't one?" I'm walking on thin ice now, ice I've helped keep frozen, I admit it. I can feel it start to crack underneath me now.

She sits back in her chair. "What are we talking about here, Jackson? Paranoid hippies? Or is this really all about me and what a terrible person I am. Again."

I'm not even sure what I'm talking about, to tell you the truth. I'm not sure I want to go here. But I do anyway. "Something could have happened to the boys Friday night, Caroline. Something bad. And you would have been too drunk to do anything. What if there was a fire? Or ... "

I watch her face flicker from cold indifference to hardened steel. "A fire? Oh, please, Jackson. I just ... I was just lying down on the couch and I fell asleep watching TV, is that a crime? The kids could have woken me up if they needed me. They could have woken me up."

"They tried."

Her expression flips again, to indignant rage. She sets her mug down with a bang. "Jesus, Jackson, I had a few coolers. I thought we were talking about AXIS, anyway."

I can feel the anger building up, I know I can't stop this now, that it's beyond me. I take a deep breath and breathe slowly into my coffee, trying to stay calm.

She laughs. "Oh, that's it, honey, breathe in the good, breathe out the bad. You know, you're such a wimp. You really are. Whatever you have to say, just say it, don't sit there like a ... "

"Shut up." I say it real quiet and it shocks her into silence. "This isn't about me."

She rolls her eyes. "Oh, no, it never is. It's about the children," she says in a warbling voice. "How I'm ruining their lives by having a few drinks after dinner. How will they ever survive?"

"A few ... a few drinks? You passed out at five o'clock on Friday. You didn't even *feed* them dinner!"

She blinks, obviously taken aback by this information. She didn't even know, she doesn't remember. And then I get it, just like that. A lightning strike, a lightbulb, whatever, I just finally get it. It's like I turned over a rock and let everything that was black and horrible and ugly come scrabbling out, and now here they were moving around on the surface of things. Impossible to ignore. "I'm taking the kids," I say. "We're going out to the cabin for a few days."

She raises her eyebrows. "Give me a break. Don't even joke about that."

I stand. "No joke. I'm picking them up after school. You can stay here. We'll go out there. Kids'll love it. I'm not working anyway and it will give you time to think things through." The plan doesn't sound bad as the words leave my mouth.

Caroline just stares at me, her mouth opens wide. "You must be fucking joking me. You're not serious. Jackson. You find out there's a bit of lead in your blood and suddenly you want to take off on me? You're acting like a crazy person. You don't have the guts to walk out that door. And you sure as hell aren't taking my kids anywhere." She's like a caged animal, her legs curled up under her bathrobe as she hugs her knees, her eyes snapping, her teeth bared.

"A bit of lead? A *bit* of fucking lead?" I've got to get out of here; I'm going to lose my mind. "This is happening, Caroline, stop trying to tell me it isn't. Stop trying to tell me that you're not a drunk. Stop telling me there's no fucking lead in my blood!" I start to walk past her. "I'll see you when you get your shit together."

She grabs my sleeve as I go by, holds on tight. "Jackson. Okay, I'll stop. I don't think I have to, I don't. But I will. For you." I try to peel her hand away from my sleeve, but she holds on. I want to believe her, but I can see something behind those tear-filled eyes, a resentment she can't disguise.

So I shake her hand off, my heart thumping in my chest. "You need help." Those three little words I never thought I'd say. The words that make you want to curl your lip up even though they're true.

"Help," she spits. "You're the one who needs help if you try to take those kids away, Jackson. I swear to god." She shakes her head in disbelief. "You won't do it. I know you. You're a coward. A scared little baby." She rises now, pushing me away. Her face turns red with rage, her eyes like slits. I've never seen her look so ugly. I brush past her and head for the door. Only a few steps and then I'm out.

"You hear me?" She runs after me. "You're pathetic." Shove. I block her small hands, backing out the door. Five steps down the porch and another twenty to the truck if I'm lucky. "You're so pathetic, Jackson. Don't think I'll take you back." I walk outside. Will myself to keep walking.

"I won't take you back," she screams from the porch. "I won't."

Twenty-six steps later I make it to the truck, climb in and squeal out of the driveway. I tell myself not to but I look in the rear-view mirror, watch her all the way to the highway. How she just stands there getting smaller and smaller,

I drive on, and it's the will of god that no one happens to be in my way because I wouldn't even see them coming. I'm still watching her. Jesus. My throat feels like it's tearing open I want to scream so bad. But I still leave her there, that crazy purple robe moving around her in the wind like useless butterfly wings.

Jessie

*I*t's hot today. We haven't had a moment's peace from the heat, not for weeks now. The yard is a grey crispy thing that I don't even bother watering. I don't see the point. It's just me and Lily now and neither of us could care less how green the grass is. What I do care about are my beets, which I'm yanking up while I sit out here on a dead patch of grass by my garden. They're pretty small. In fact, I might be pulling them up too early, but oh well. They are the only thing that's grown this year, except for the wrinkled-up cucumber I found under some wilted leaves. Lily probably wouldn't even eat it, even though she eats cucumbers whole like big green Popsicles.

But for some reason I planted a lot of beets, and for some reason they lived, despite the fact that I forgot about them for the most part. Especially lately. Lately I've been working every available shift at Nick's, and I think he even put me on some that he didn't need me for. You never know what I might need ... the truck fixed, new shoes for Lily ... but I'm not asking Daniel for anything right now because that would mean I would actually have to talk to him, which I've been doing a pretty good job of not doing. And he hasn't dropped a bag of money on the door in the last week, so I figure for now it's pretty much up to me.

"Mom!" Lily shouts down at me from the porch. She's standing with her arms folded, a big mean scowl on her face. She's done school now, god help me, and the last couple of days have been interesting, let me tell you. This is not a child who likes to be ignored while her mother picks beets and contemplates the universe.

"What's up, Lily?" I pull out another beet. I like that little give, that popping when it separates from the ground. I shake off the dirt and lay it on the pile beside me.

"I'm HOT!" She stamps down the stairs and over to me, arms still folded. Her face is streaked with dust from playing on the driveway. She was kicking a soccer ball around, but it looks like she did a face-plant somewhere along the way. Her cheeks are flushed pink and her hair is stuck to her forehead with sweat. She does look hot, I'll give her that.

"So go run through the sprinkler." I yank another beet. You know, I'm pretty sure I planted other things in this bed too, now that I think of it. I'm pretty sure Kali gave me some green onion seeds and some old mouldy-looking potatoes, which were supposed to grow into plants and then make baby potatoes ... but all I see is a big mess of green and purple beet leaves lying sideways on the dry earth like they're all too tired and thirsty to bother standing up straight.

I should call Kali and ask her what the hell happened to the rest of the things I planted, but she's probably at work. She's like me, just trying to work as much as she can. She acts like she's taking this whole Mike thing in stride, like it's just his "path of destruction" or whatever, and that she's heading down a different path now and all that jazz, but come on, I know she's probably holed up in her place every night staring off into space while she drinks her tea.

Lily has plunked beside me and is playing with a beet. "No. I wanna go the lake."

I return to my pulling. "Can't. I'm too busy today."

I watch her sideways as she slices through the beet with her thumbnail, the juice seeping out onto her hand. I reach over and grab her arm. "Stop that." It comes out a little meaner than I meant it to, it's just for some reason these beets, the sole survivors of my hard work, they mean something to me. I don't want fingernail cuts in them.

She tosses the beet down and stands, staring me down. Then she reaches over and gives me a little shove with two hands, not hard enough to push me over, but hard enough to let me know she means business. I pull her hands away and see that she's left two smears of beet juice on my shirt.

"You're too busy all the time," she says. "I want my dad to come home. I saw him. I saw him at 7-11 in his truck when I was driving with Gran. So he isn't away, anyway. So I guess you just *lied*!"

I don't have the heart to give her shit for pushing me, or even to correct her. Her little face suddenly explodes into tears and I pull her over, dirty hands and all. She wails into my hair. "Why isn't he home?"

And now I just feel like the lowest scum on earth. I should explain something here. About how I let Lily in on the whole Daniel thing. What I did was, the day after what happened out at the motel, when I picked her up from my mom's place, I just told her that daddy was gone for a while for work. I've been so confused and so worried about myself and what I was going to do, and where we're going to move, because this is Daniel's grandmother's house, not mine, and how I was going to make enough to get by and should I get a lawyer, and do I really want to go to court and me me me and the whole time Lily's been sitting on the couch watching TV and eating bowls of ice cream for breakfast and I just figured she'd be okay, because she always is.

"You saw him?" I brush her sticky hair from her face. "Did you say hi?"

She shakes her head. "He didn't even see me. I waved at him a hundred times and he didn't see me at all. He didn't even look." And she covers her face with her hands and turns away from me, running like a little drunk, weaving in and out of overgrown flower beds and finally stumbling up the porch steps and into the house.

Well, hell. I can see that trying not to think too much isn't going to be the solution. I can see that this child needs to see her father, even if he's the last person on earth I want to see right now.

I drop my little shovel. Look over at the pile of wilted beets. There must be forty of them. I don't know what I was thinking ... obviously I just sprinkled seeds everywhere and didn't think too much about what might actually grow.

I head into the house trailing clumps of dirt and bits of dried grass behind me. I don't bother taking off my shoes and if you could see the state of my house you would understand why. I haul Lily out from under her bed, walk her to the bathroom, tell her to take off her shorts and T-shirt, and stand her under a cool shower. Then I pull off my own clothes, which, by the way, look like I was in an accident and almost bled to death on account of Lily's beet juice shove, and hop in with her. By the end of the shower she's singing a song about a mother duck who loses all her babies and they all come quacking home at the end. It's a pretty happy song, after you figure out that the ducklings didn't get eaten by a crocodile or something, so I sing along as I lather my hair.

When we get out of the shower I tell Lily to put on some clean clothes as she's about to pull on her stained shorts again.

"Why?"

I wrap myself in a towel and head to my dresser for a clean T-shirt. "We're going out." I find one with no holes in it and a big picture of a cartoon sun from when I was a camp counsellor at Sunshine Ridge horse camp the summer I was sixteen. It still fits, and I pull it on.

Lily drops the shorts and looks at me suspiciously. "Where?" She's probably thinking grocery shopping, which she hates more than making her bed. She usually spends the entire time trailing me and saying, "Can we get that? Can we get that? Can we get that?" and wailing when I tell her we're not buying marshmallow puff cereal or a bag of jujubes or a family pack of Oreo-flavoured pudding.

I pull on my cut-offs, which surprisingly are still clean enough. I pat her head on my way out the bedroom door. "To find your dad."

Down in the kitchen I have a momentary lapse of confidence. I sit down hard at the table, looking at the scraps from me and Lily's breakfast, the bits of rubbery fried egg that somehow made it all the way over to my half-empty cup of cold coffee, the cream congealing in a ring around the inside of the cup. Gross.

I think another minute, mostly about what I want to say when and if I actually do see Daniel. I mean, the last time I talked to him was when I told him not to come back. Ever. And then there's all the shit that's happening at AXIS. I hear stuff every day at Nick's, mostly from Sunny, who knows how to keep her ear to the ground, and I know exactly who's sick and who isn't. I even know the exact lead count in Daniel's blood, for god's sake, I could sit here right now and tell you the results of every test he had done up at the hospital. I could tell you that Mike never got tested at all, that he's disappeared somewhere since the incident, and that nobody's seen him since Kali found him at the bar six days ago.

And I can even tell you the top three rumours about where he is— number one, he's gone to Vancouver to do some boozing and hang out with the hookers on the downtown eastside; two, he's gone to Castlegar to look for work, although hardly anyone believes that one; and three, he's in a drugged-out stupor on the floor of Rusty the town dealer's place over on the other side of the river. Take your pick. Any way you choose, things aren't looking up for old Mikey. He's made it through worse, though.

Anyway, back to Daniel. So I may not have personally given him a call and asked him how everything was going and how he was feeling, but at least I bothered asking Sunny and some guys about him, at least I have real feelings and compassion, which is more than I can say for him—that scene at the motel being my biggest supporting argument.

It doesn't matter. I know where I stand. The tricky part is how I'm going to fit him back into my life for Lily, when I've already ripped him out as neatly as a scratchy label from a new pair of jeans. I guess I'm going to have to sew him back in, and I'm telling you right now it's not going to look a thing like it did before.

I settle Lily in the front of the truck with me, and to avoid having to answer any tough questions like "why did you lie to me and tell me my father went away when actually you kicked him out of the house," I crank up the AC/DC. Lily immediately covers her ears. "I HATE THIS SONG," she shouts. I hit fast forward on the tape to make her stop shouting and she stares at me with her eyes all narrow. "You always play that song. I hate it and you know I hate it and you play it all the time anyways."

I try to keep my eyes on the road and will myself not to swerve into the grove of pines on the left by the river on purpose. I take a deep breath, then reach over and unroll the window to let in the breeze. I suddenly want my mother, my casserole-making, Pop-Tart-buying, *National Enquirer*-reading mother, and even though I've been avoiding her, even though I haven't even called her to tell her what's happening and I've refused to answer her calls or respond to her messages where she threatens to come out to the farmhouse, and where she says "Jessie, you need to sort this out with your man. He's living at the goddamn bar and eating god knows what and he's out of work, for god's sake … " Despite all of that, she's still my mom, and I still want her to tell me it's all going to work out somehow.

I hit play again, ignoring what Lily said about me always playing the song she hates, partly because she's right. I just figure it's hard work being a grown-up and I should get to listen to "Hell's Bells" when I damn well feel like it.

"You Shook Me All Night Long" screeches out of the speakers and Lily bobs her head to it. This one is her favourite. Usually I sing along, but I'm not in the mood, still thinking about Mom's Irish cream-flavoured coffee in a chipped teacup, the sound of the golf channel coming from the living room where my dad is sitting doing a crossword from one of those *100 EZ Puzzles* books.

Lily lowers her window and lets her hand ride the breeze, hollering along to the words. I know, I know. Not appropriate for a six-year-old. Well, none of us are perfect. By now that should be pretty freaking clear.

I know where he's staying, everybody does, and I know he's there most of the time because there's still no work and there might not be for a while from what I hear. It's strange driving down Main Street and seeing so many people on a Tuesday afternoon. There's guys walking along with coffee, guys and their wives and kids going into Sortino's Pasta House for lunch, young guys crowded around the entrance to the Steelworkers having a smoke. I pull into the parking lot beside the Inn. Well, at least the shutdown is bringing everyone together. Not anyone I know personally, but still. At least some people are benefiting from it.

I hop down from the truck and go around to Lily's side to open the door for her. She holds my arm and steps down. "Hey, there's Uncle Bobby." She skips toward the entrance to the bar, waving and calling out, "Hey, Uncle Bobby!"

Sure enough, there's Bobby standing with that group of guys. He takes a drag of his cigarette and squints at us through the sun as I walk over. His black shirt is stuck to his round belly with sweat and he's wearing his black leather biker vest even though it's about 102 degrees.

He lets the smoke out and wanders over, crouching down to see Lily at her level. "Hey there, jellybean. What's shakin"?" He stubs out the smoke with the heel of his boot and hold out his arms for a hug. Lily sits primly on his meaty thigh as he tries to balance so he doesn't topple over.

"What's up, Bobby?" I'm scanning the street for any sign of my husband, but I don't see him and I'm relieved. I'm relieved for every minute I get before I have to see him.

Bobby stands, still holding Lily, who now perches on his hip like some weird little princess in the frilly Easter dress her grandma bought her last year. She looks like she's surveying the peasants as she rides her elephant—no offence to Bobby—through the streets of Grace River. She reaches over and pets his bearded face with her little white hand. "You seen my daddy? We're looking for him."

"That right?" he looks at me with a big question in his eyes. I nod, just once, a short answer. I'm not in the mood for any big conversations about the state of my marriage and I'm sure as hell not in the mood to talk it all over with one of Danny's best friends. Don't get me wrong, "Uncle Bobby" is real nice guy to have at a barbeque and he never drinks so much that he gets obnoxious, and honestly, he's my second favourite of Danny's friends after Jackson of course. What the hell is going on around here? I mean, these are people I used to see every couple of days and now I feel like they're strangers.

"Yeah," I say. "Is he here? I need to talk to him."

Bobby nods, gives Lily a smile. "Yup, I just saw your daddy having a little refreshment in there. It's a hot day, so he needed to cool off."

I roll my eyes, but Lily beams. "Yeah, we were hot too. We had a shower. That's why I'm so clean." She juts her chin forward, showing Bobby her face, and he laughs and then sets her down.

"Well, should I go in and get him for you?" he asks me. I chew my lip. Right. Lily can't go in there. Shit. Well, maybe it would be better if I went in on my own first. The group of guys at the door suddenly disperses, taking their cloud of smoke and their swearing and their too-loud laughter and then it's just me, Bobby, and Lily on the street. There aren't even any cars. For a second you could hear a pin drop on the hot asphalt.

"Maybe I should go in first," I say. "Would you watch her?"

Bobby nods. "Sure thing. Maybe me and the Bean here will go sit on the bench there by the 7-11 for a minute. What do you say?" He ruffles Lily's hair, but he's watching me, maybe trying to figure out if he should be helping me or warning his buddy that all hell is about to break loose. Lily stamps a little sandalled foot. "Well, I wanna see him! I came to see him too!"

I need to do something. And Lily can't go in that bar. I make a choice. "Okay. I'll be back with him in two minutes. You stay out here. Find some shade, okay?" Lily glares at me, and Bobby puts his hand on her back and leads her away.

I head into the bar, which is almost empty except for a few guys here and there. I wave at the bartender. "Hey there, Jim. You seen Danny?"

Jimmy looks up from wiping the bar and just stares for a minute. But then he snaps out of it. "Sure thing, Jess. I think he's up in his room." He looks unsure about whether to say where that is, but I just keep looking at him like I'm waiting and he finally coughs it up. "Number eight. Left at the top of the stairs."

The hallway smells like piss, excuse my French. But it does. And it probably does because somebody was too drunk to make it to the bathroom. It's pretty gross up here. Funny, all these years and I've never had a reason to walk up that dark staircase with the paint peeling off the stairs and gouges taken out of the drywall on the way up. Somebody up there must be looking out for me.

Number eight is halfway down the hall. It must have a lovely view of the bank across the street. I knock three times, my heart pounding in my throat. I wait, then I hear heavy footsteps and then the door swings back into the room. Daniel just stands there looking at me for a minute, and I figure this is a good time to scratch the mosquito bite on my elbow. I inspect it by turning my arm around, something that always creeped my friends out. They said I looked like a circus freak or something. Sure enough, the bite has gotten infected and huge, shining like a red traffic light on my arm.

"Do you want to come in?" he finally says.

I shrug. "Actually, I'm here because of Lily. She's out there with Bobby. She wants to see you."

"Yeah?" He turns and glances toward the window. "She's out there? She wants to see me?" He sounds surprised. Happy. Hopeful.

"Yeah, she wants to see you." I stress the "she" so he gets the message. "I guess it's okay, as long as you don't take off with her or anything. We have to get used to this visitation thing sometime, right?"

He looks confused. "Visitation?" He shakes his head. "Jesus Christ, Jess. Come on." There's something pleading in his voice and he gives me one of those sideways smiles, the one that really worked in high school, the one that makes that dimple pop out on his right cheek, the one that makes those little lines appear by the side of his eyes now that he's older. The one that doesn't work worth a shit on me anymore.

I scratch the bite again. "Yeah, visitation. I mean, I know we have to figure it all out with lawyers and stuff, but I don't think Lily can wait that long. So we can sort it out for now."

He nods. Then he opens the door wider. "Come in for a sec. Just while I get my shoes on."

I look back at the piss-stained hallway. I think about coming in, just for a minute. He's looking at me like, *Come on, don't be crazy. You can be civil for two minutes, right?* But I can't. "I'll meet you downstairs." I say. I start walking, tossing back over my shoulder, "You know, you should clean the clothes and shit off your floor if you want Lily to be visiting you. And throw your goddamn empties away."

He doesn't answer. I'm sure that would have made him hot under the collar, but he manages to restrain himself.

Down on the street I can feel all my energy drain out, melt out of me into the pavement. My legs are shaking, I can hardly cross the street to where Bobby and Lily are sitting under an awning on a bench, Lily with a giant freezie, Bobby with a 7-11 coffee. I sit beside Lily, reach for her freezie. She gives it up without a fight and I take a big slurp of it. "You guys making out okay?"

"Yup. Did you know Uncle Bobby got a new motorcycle? He said he would let me ride with him."

I brush hair from my forehead, lean back. Close my eyes. "Is that right?" I'm barely listening as she goes on about how it's purple and silver and how it goes super fast.

Then I hear a shout from across the street. "Hey! Lily Bean!" Daniel is jogging over to us. He sweeps her up in his arms and she pats his back like a mother pats her baby.

He sets her down and she's beaming, red freezie juice staining her mouth like she just ate a small animal for lunch. "Daddy," she says, satisfied, giving him another pat on his shoulder. She looks at me with something close to mistrust, a look I don't like. She knows I've been lying to her, she thinks I've been hiding him away or something.

Daniel looks up at me from where he's crouching on the sidewalk, down at Lily's level. "Well," he says. "What should we do?"

How the hell should I know? It's not like I'm used to this kind of thing. Bobby stands up and says, "Well, why don't we head on over to Nick's for some lunch or something. You hungry there, Lily?"

She nods furiously. "A milkshake, right, Dad? A whole one, I don't want to share with you and Mom." She beams over at me, grabs one of Daniel's hands.

"Sure thing. Absolutely," he says.

I'm trapped. I do not want to go to Nick's and I do not want to let them go there alone. So what the hell am I supposed to do? I can't take being the mean mom anymore, though. Lily already doesn't trust me. I know I have to suck it up and go.

We walk the three blocks or so, Daniel and Lily walking hand in hand, Bobby beside Daniel and me trailing a few steps behind. Oh god, it's torture, I swear. What was I thinking? I should have worked out some kind of supervised visits with his mom or something. I'll have to do that. I'll do that for next time.

Nick's is pretty empty. Most of the regular guys are off fishing or camping or hanging out with their families. Nick isn't there, which would have been a consolation, and Sunny isn't working either. I order a black coffee from Glory and sit back.

The food arrives and I still haven't said a word, although Daniel keeps looking up at me while he's talking to Lily, probably wanting me to say something. But I don't, I just sit there and drink coffee and stare out the window while Lily chirps and sings and shows off for her dad and he laps it up like a lovesick dog.

Bobby lights a smoke and taps the table with his lighter. He clears his throat. "So you hear about Jackson and Caroline?"

I don't stop looking out that window, watching a rig try to park straight in one of the oversized spots beside the diner. JT, I think. He does this route every two weeks or so. Delivers frozen meat to the big grocery stores. He once left me a box of frozen chicken breasts as a tip.

"Yup," I finally say, thinking for a sec about Jackson out there at the lake by himself with the boys. Maybe I should go out there and visit him. See how he's doing. "So he told her to get clean?"

Bobby nods. "Something like that. Said she wasn't good for the boys like that. I guess she did party pretty hard."

I glance over at Danny, and he glances back, then steals a fry from Lily's plate. "So he just up and left, eh?" I raise my eyebrows at Daniel, which makes him smile again. This is getting too familiar, too much like some kind of private joke, so I look away again.

"Sure did. He'll be back, though?"

"What? Why? Why do you think that?"

Daniel laughs now. "Come on, Jess. Jackson loves her. He loves her more than any other girl he ever knew. You think he's gonna just live out there by himself? His whole life had been with her, taking care of her and shit ... "

"Daddy!" Lily flicks Daniel on the forehead. "No swearing." They have a deal, those two, that she gets to flick him every time he swears. I'm surprised he never had a permanent bruise there.

He laughs. "Sorry ... taking care of her and *stuff*, I meant. Anyway, he keeps her in line. It was like a goddamn full-time job for him." Lily giggles and reaches over and flicks him again, and this time I can see a lightning flash of irritation that disappears as soon as it comes. He ruffles Lily's hair.

"My point is," he says. "What the hell else is he supposed to do?" Lily ignores this one, serenely slurping her milkshake.

He and Bobby smile at each other. He's pleased with himself about his relationship expertise, I guess. If they had beer, they would be clinking bottles right now.

I blow some stray hair out of my eyes. "Oh, he'll find something, Danny. It sounds like a pretty pathetic fucking job to me."

The smile fades a little. He reaches for another fry. Lily is staring at me, surprised that I used the f-word, but she knows better than to try flicking me.

"We'll see," he says, tipping his head at me. A bet of some sort.

I nod, look for Glory for the bill. "Yes, we will," I say. "You know, it's time Lily and me got going."

He looks a little panicked. "Well ... when will I see her again?"

Tears are starting, squeezing out of the corners of Lily's eyes. I can tell we're close to critical meltdown here.

"Soon," I say soothingly, meant for Lily. "Real soon. It's all going to be okay." I realize as I say it that it has to be. That this hostility and crap I'm putting out, it's not going to fly if I want Lily to be happy.

As we get up to go I realize I'm suddenly very tired. I want to crawl into my bed in that sunny bedroom in the farmhouse that doesn't belong to me. I know if I play my cards right Lily and I could stay there. I know as I watch him swing Lily up on his shoulders and gallop out to the parking lot that Daniel will do right by us. He was the one who screwed up, after all. I'm starting to see a picture of how it will be. Me with Lily during the week, Daniel taking her on weekends in some little rental house he gets near town. He can walk Lily to the park. Take her swimming. Stuff he never did much when we were together. And I would get a couple days off a week, except when I'm working. How bad could it be? It'll be okay. It's all gonna be okay. Right?

Daniel

oday was another day of waiting. Man, I feel like that's all I do, like I'm some old retired guy like my dad, just strolling around downtown and saying hello to people all fucking day long. Except I'm not as friendly as my dad, so I do a little strolling and then I usually just head back in and have a beer at the Steelworkers.

My dad, he used to go nuts too. Once he told me that after being retired for four days he just marched right back up the hill with his metal lunchbox and his ham and mayo sandwich and a Thermos full of instant coffee and he told them he was coming back to work. He said they just laughed like he was telling them a good joke and they patted him on the back and told him to go home and enjoy the sunshine. He said it was the first time in forty-six years that he came close to punching out his superiors. He said he wanted to, he wanted to wipe those condescending smirks off those snot-nosed kids' faces, but he didn't. He just turned around and headed for home. He told me as he crossed the AXIS Memorial Bridge he hurled his lunch box, the same one he'd had since I was a baby, off the bridge. He didn't even watch when it hit the water like a cannonball.

And anyways, I don't exactly have a lawn to mow or a garden to weed anyway, do I? If I was home, if Jess would let me come home, I got a list of things in my head I could be working on right now. I been thinking that there's no reason we couldn't have chickens like Jess wanted a couple years back. It was one of her schemes, you know, like when she made those deck chairs or wanted to start raising chickens for the eggs and selling them to the same neighbours she'd been hoping would buy her deck chairs. But I said no, chickens were a pain in the ass. And they are.

But it's true we have a chicken coop out there, because Grandma and

Grandpa used to have them, though they raised them for meat and not eggs. But that coop would need a complete overhaul and to tell you the truth I never had much energy for it. But now if I was out there I think I would do it. I'd clear it all out, get rid of the junk that's collected in the old coop, the old oil pans and the bales of rusting wire, the old paint cans and the empty flower pots and the bits and pieces of useless old tools. I'd clean it out while Jess was at work. I'd put up new chicken wire and then I'd go buy a dozen or so chicks and there you have it. A dream come true for old Jess.

But no, I'm stuck in this dark hole-in-the-wall of a room. I've already done my little morning walk, I've already gone and gotten my 7-11 coffee and grabbed a paper and read about how AXIS is still closed until further notice but how everything is getting all cleaned up and everything is expected to return to normal ASAP. I've called Bobby to see if he wanted to go for breakfast, but I got no answer. I even tried Mike, because I figured Jesus, as a friend I guess it's my duty not to give up on the guy, even though most everybody else has. But May said she hadn't heard from him in going on a week. Since the shutdown. Vancouver, I figure. More drugs, more women, nobody there who knows who you are, nobody who works with you or who you're related to. Sounds good, in a way. A few days of anonymity. Most times when he comes back from those little trips he's a little worse for wear, though.

So now it's just me all alone in this room and I have to say I'm feeling a bit sorry for myself. I am. I'm sitting here thinking, Well goddam. Daniel McAllister. What the hell has happened here? Thirty-three years old, your wife has left you, for the time being at least, you got some elevated toxins swimming around in your blood like fat leeches, sucking out the good stuff and leaving you tired and pissed off. Mike's on a bender, Jackson's fucked off with his kids and left his wife, and even if he hadn't he was starting to really piss me off with all that righteous crap ... And Sunny, who won't talk to me of course, being Jess's best friend. If I come into Nick's she tosses me a look of cool jagged steel and gets Glory to serve me even if I'm in her section. And that Caroline's probably drunk somewhere.

Anyway, I don't like sitting here thinking so much. I don't like thinking about the chicken coop and Jessie, or Lily playing out in the yard, stripping all her Barbies and dumping them in the rain barrel for a swim and then forgetting about them until I have to fish them out like they were some sad group of drowned beauty queens. I'd rather not think about how I might get to see her every few days if Jess feels like it, or think about lawyers, or the friends I don't have anymore. Like I said, I'm feeling pretty sorry for myself.

So around noon I figure I better get away from the stale smoke smell of my room and that fake-wood panelling and the pink peeling walls and go eat something. I wander down to Apollo's, the Greek joint on the corner. It gets a pretty good lunch crowd, especially now that half the town is on vacation, and they have a roast lamb special that'll knock your socks off. I'm getting sick of Nick's burgers every day. He doesn't have a problem with grease and he doesn't feel he needs to try to drain it off before he serves his food.

So in I go, find a table by the door, order from Margaret, the owner's wife, and I sit there and drum the table. I ordered a beer, which will help. I see a few guys from work, plus a friend of my Aunt Josephine's having lunch with a bunch of the hospital volunteers, and Johnny O sitting with his partner, both of 'em wearing their paramedic uniforms. I can hear his walkie squawking, so he must be on duty. He catches my eye and gives me a wave, his fork full of moussaka. I wave back just as Margaret brings me my beer.

Halfway through my lonely little lunch there Johnny O stops by the table on his way out. He motions his partner along and then sits for a second. "How's it hangin' there, Danny?" He's a good guy, Johnny, he is, but I'm not in the mood for those manly back-patting sympathy parties right now. I just want to eat my lamb, finish my beer, order another one. Go back to my room and watch baseball or trout fishing or something.

"I'm doing okay. Just waiting like the rest of the goddamn town."

Johnny nods. He's heard that before, probably a few times since breakfast. "So you back out at the farm, or ... " His walkie squawks and he reaches down over his big belly to turn the volume down.

"Nah." I take a swig of beer. Then I give him a little wink. "Not yet, man."

He smiles. "Yeah, I hear you. In the doghouse, eh?" What the hell would he know? He has a wife he's been with since high school too and they have about four kids. They don't hang out with our crowd, those guys. They're the churchgoing, Sunday-picnics-at-the-park-by-the-river-with-the-Italian-grandparents crowd. His wife is this little thing who cooks him three meals a day and embroiders covers for the Sunday-school books. We don't exactly have a lot in common. Still, I guess it's okay to have someone to talk to for a change.

But then his partner, Cal, I think his name is, runs in and smacks his shoulder. "Johnny, we gotta go. We got a call. Let's go."

Johnny pushes his chair back and gets up. "Where at?"

Cal glances over my way real quick, and something about that look makes the hairs on the back of my neck stand at attention. Johnny heads toward the door and then I hear Cal say "cottage on old Mission Road" and then Johnny looks back at me too and then I hear Cal say "gunfire" before the door closes behind them and by then I'm already out of my chair. I'm out of my chair and running out of that restaurant leaving my half-drunk beer and my gristly lamb bone and I'm running to my truck down the street behind the Steelworkers Inn and I'm starting it up just as their siren wails past me heading for old Mission Road. Kali's place.

Kali

I'm folding napkins because I can think of nothing else to do. They are the cheap kind, the ones that come wrapped in crinkly plastic. They are stacked, two towers of white squares, on the table that will be used for the buffet. May wanted the wake here at the family home. If she could have, she would have kept the body too, tucked him into his childhood bed and closed the door. She would have pretended he was just sleeping. She could have kept it up for years.

All of Grace River's finest ladies are in the kitchen unwrapping meaty casseroles, platters of pretty sandwiches. Most likely, they are talking about me. May can't control herself. Even at the funeral she had been wailing, "Why?" as she sobbed onto Annabelle McAllister's flowered rayon shoulders while I stood not two feet away. "Why didn't she call, Annabelle, why?" This is what she focuses on, although we both know it makes no difference. I understand that she has to have someone to blame. I'm the perfect one because she never liked me in the first place.

I fold the cheap paper into rectangles, though some fleeting part of me wants to shape them into origami cranes, twist and wring them in my hands until they form something beautiful. Set them free in a flock of crepe paper, fluttering out the open window into the spring air.

The murmuring from the kitchen stops and May appears, chin out, bravely carrying a bowl full of melon balls and setting it on the table. She says nothing. She still can't speak to me. She has not attempted conversation since the hospital, after the doctors told her there was no chance. Even then, all she could bring herself to do was whisper as she walked by me and Daniel in a daze, shock aging her ten years, etching her already lined face with deep valleys. "It's your fault," she had said quietly, tapping me thoughtfully with her finger as she passed. It wasn't said with any real force or malice, but I know she meant it.

"How are you, May?" I ask her now, folding, folding, stacking my napkins into perfect piles. I see her hands are trembling as she pulls the plastic off the fruit bowl and I think, *Skullcap, valerian root, nettle.* Despite the war zone of our relationship, I would brew these herbs into tea right now if I thought she would drink it. But she's never been interested in my teas, or the tinctures or salves. Mike said she had called me "a bit witchy, don't you think?" I just laughed. I considered it a compliment.

May sighs now, a long, warbling sort of breath. "Surviving," she says coolly, avoiding my eyes. "I suppose I have to get used to the idea that I won't be seeing his smiling face when he comes through that door." She indicates the front of the house with a sweep of her black-clad arm. Her words carry the scent of blame, and also the stench of a lie. Mike rarely smiled lately.

I pat the last napkin. "Well," I say, "give it time." I walk into the kitchen without looking at her. I have committed myself to staying for the reception, to greeting and hugging Mike's relatives and friends, to having to ... explain. And also I can't bear it on my own, I can't bear to go back to our little ramshackle home, to my gardens and those kitchen curtains. The way I watched them drift in the breeze. Those curtains won't give me peace.

In the kitchen bodies part for me, propelled by some unseen force. I walk to the sink and turn on the taps to wash my hands. I can see though the window that Daniel is slumped in a lawn chair smoking, Jackson and Caroline are sitting on the porch steps beside him, along with some other guys from the plant that I don't know. They don't look like they're speaking. What is there to say? It strikes me suddenly how little I fit in now. How uncomfortable I would be walking out there and sitting down with those people. I feel a heavy pat on my back. The warmth tingles through my thin dress.

"Kali. My dear. How are you holding up?" the voice whispers in my ear. "Don't you worry. She'll realize it wasn't your fault. I mean, we all adore you. And those kids." I look up now, Annabelle's face inches from my own, her perfume assaulting my senses ... overripe roses, the tang of fermented crushed petals. "We all know you were the best thing that ever happened to Mike."

"How can you say that?" I'm curious. It makes no sense. Obviously this isn't true, obviously I am in fact one in a long series of other worst things that ever happened to Mike. I think of the woven bag I left in the front room. In it is a small brown paper bag of borage leaves that I chew in times of panic, in tidal waves of grief. I crave it now, desperately, like a junkie. All I want is to go sit on the cold bathroom floor and place a single leaf on my tongue, close my eyes.

Annabelle looks taken aback. "Well. We all know Mike was a little ... rough around the edges. You smoothed him out, you and your kids and your little house and your gardens and herbs." *Erbs.* Her cheeks hang in jowls, truly she is so fat all I can think of are her poor kidneys, her liver. *Chickweed, dandelion, fennel ...*

"I guess you could say I smoothed him flat," I tell Annabelle. I almost laugh.

She looks at me, horrified. "Well," she finally says. "I know it must have been very traumatic for you." *Tro-matic.* She stands there still, because she wants more information. Annabelle is a shark, she inhales any information tossed in her path, rips it apart, and chews it up until it becomes a thing you couldn't recognize.

"Yes," I say. "It was."

I survive the reception by working. I offer platters of tiny meatballs harpooned with toothpicks, I dish out gelatinous trifle to children who have been scolded into sombre moods, I wash mountains of dishes. Nobody touches my wild green salad with homegrown sunflower sprouts and small edible violets. People don't think they should be able to eat a thing so natural and raw. It scares them with its honesty.

I collect my bag and jacket and approach the couch that May has retired to, lounging diva-like on the overstuffed cushions. Her hanky is pressed to her cheek as she stares out the living room window to the neatly clipped lawn and the small pond. She is flanked by her formidable sisters, both of whom watch me warily as I approach, a hint of warning glittering in their cool eyes.

"May." I kneel down to her level, my long skirt tangling under my legs. "I have to go get the children." I let Jessie take them home with her when she left an hour ago. They were overwhelmed with confusion about the whole thing, weren't sure how sad to be about a man they didn't know well ... I wish I could have left them with their dad for longer, but he had been on his way to Calgary for a business trip when he dropped them off yesterday.

May sniffles. "Oh, the children. Of course." She pats her dry eyes. I think we both know that despite her feelings toward me, my children are now the closest thing she ever had to real grandchildren.

I pat her knee and get up. The sisters nod their goodbyes and place hands on May's shoulders as though to protect her from the further blow, the reminder I have given her of what she's lost. As though she could ever forget.

I drive through the sleepy streets of Grace River and cross the bridge near Memorial Arena, where Mike had played hockey. I went to a game once, like the other girlfriends and wives, though I didn't enjoy it. Violence doesn't sit well with me, even in a controlled environment.

I pass AXIS. Its long arms reach out and hug the small town, but I'm not deceived. Twilight has set in, and on a normal night AXIS would be lit up bright as a Christmas tree, but now it sits like a sleeping black spider. And although I have seen the suffering caused to almost every family in town because of the chemical exposure and the subsequent shutdown, still some tiny part of me is grateful that at least for now there is no silent toxic rain of lead particles seeping into the soil, into the river, into the walls of the houses.

I'm on the outskirts of town now, heading down the dirt road past dry hills blooming with teal green sage. I turn down a long driveway toward Jessie's, where my children will be waiting. I park and walk to the front door. Jessie has let her garden go, leaving it to the weeds and the birds.

"Momma!" a voice cries, muffled through the window. I see my two girls, their faces pressed to glass, deforming their perfect features into those of grotesque circus children. I wave at them and come in without knocking.

However excited their greeting was, they don't come to see me, and I hear the television in the living room, which explains why. I find Jessie in the kitchen, sitting at the table and drinking a glass of wine. She has the local paper spread out on the table in front of her and she's still in her sundress from the funeral. She looks up guiltily.

"Hey," she says. "Sorry. I know you don't like TV. It's just Summer and Lily kept fighting over the Barbies."

"It doesn't matter." I sit down heavily.

"Do you want some wine? Or, no, tea maybe? I think I have some mint."

"No," I say. "I'd better get home."

Jessie takes a sip of wine. Her hands are shaking slightly, and she looks thin and wrung out with sadness. I remind myself that whatever grief I feel, Jessie knew Mike almost her whole life. They may not have been close, but they were connected. I wonder how many times he had sat at that very table with Daniel, drinking beer, coffee, talking hockey.

"Was it because of AXIS?" Jessie asks. "Do you think? I mean, did that make it worse? I just … I just don't understand how … "

"What do you mean?" I ask gently.

"I looked up thallium poisoning online. And I talked to my dad about it too. If it's left untreated it can lead to psychosis … you know. Mental problems."

I nod. I had researched this as well. "It's impossible to say, Jessie. Maybe. Who knows? There were so many things." I breathe deeply, trying to maintain my calm.

She nods. "He was doing so much better, Kali," she says, her voice breaking. "We all thought he would have ended up in jail or dead or something if he hadn't met you … " She pauses, realizing her mistake.

I shake my head. "I didn't take away the root problems. Just maybe some of the symptoms." May was one of his roots, twined like a woody wisteria vine around his ankles, showy and wispy and delicate on the surface yet bringing him down inch by inch.

The girls come barrelling in now, all dirty T-shirts and bare legs. "We're hungry," they sing in that warning singsong. Kieran's face is smudged with jam, Summer has a blue aura around her lips that can only be from Freezies or Kool-Aid, forbidden treats around our house.

I stand. "Let's go."

Jessie reaches out and takes my hand. "Kali. You know it wasn't your fault, right? You do know that?"

I squeeze her hand. "Actually, Jessie, it kind of was."

My blame lies in believing I could fix him, that somehow I could take those terrible things that shaped his childhood and transform them into something he could live with. My blame lies in finally realizing I couldn't, in giving him hope and then taking it away.

I bring the children home, hot and sticky and whining. We pull up to the house just as the moon rises in a silver crescent over the hills. I walk briskly to the door, to get it over with. It has been three days and still I can't get used to being here. I probably never will. I only thank god the girls were at their father's.

I feed them toast, scrub faces, pull pyjamas over heads, and tuck them into their wooden bunk beds. Summer hugs me tightly around the neck until I gasp for air.

"When is he coming back?" she asks sleepily. She means Mike. Summer is too young to know the difference between Mike being gone and Mike being dead. It's all the same to her.

The only solace I can keep is that they were never truly close, Mike and my girls. He tried, as best he could. He wanted it so badly, to be a good man. But sometimes wanting it just isn't enough. Sometimes the thing you've been looking for your entire life eludes you right until the end, hiding behind corners, teasing you, calling to you in the wind as though it were alive and real. As though you ever really had a chance.

Kieran is curled away from me, snoring already. She is probably still in shock. I have been dissolving remedies under their tongues three times a day. Ignatia for grief, arnica for shock. Last night after their dad dropped them off I rubbed lavender oil into their temples while they slept, to calm them and give them good dreams. I didn't even try it myself. I knew it wouldn't work. I knew nothing could keep those dreams away.

I walk into my tiny kitchen and sit at my table. There are flowers, long dead, sitting in the centre in a blue glass vase. Shasta daisies, Nootka rose, electric blue delphinium. My window is open and the curtains sway gently in the night breeze.

I reach over and pull the curtains aside. Stare at the blackness. I know out there somewhere is my garden, lush and full of life. I know it must need watering, and I consider this. I finally get up, walk to the door, and pull on black gumboots over bare feet. I go out into the night.

The trilling shriek of crickets greets me, and a dog howls from the neighbour's property as I hunt around the side of the house for the tap attached to my sprinkler. I find it and turn it on, listen for the faint shushing of rain-like showers on the garden beds. Then I lean against the house, watch the garden appear hazily before my eyes, the dark shapes of the corn patch, the crawling vines of squash, the leafy mounds of lemon balm.

I hear May, she haunts me through the night sky like I know she will for years to come. *Why didn't she call, Annabelle?* She meant the police, of course. Or an ambulance. Anyone but her. I never had a chance to explain that it happened so fast. That there I was in the kitchen peeling apples, and suddenly his truck was barrelling down the driveway. He stood out there on the lawn raving, swearing, crying, yelling things I couldn't understand. All I could think was, *Too much damage. It had to start somewhere, and it wasn't here,* and I was tired of dealing with it myself. So I called May, I called her and told her to get over here and fix it before it was too late. As we argued, I watched those kitchen curtains swaying softly, the pattern of tiny bluebells rippling in the wind. I didn't realize, you see.

"Oh," I said to May when I finally looked back at him and saw the shotgun. "Oh no." And May started screaming in my ear, asking me what it was, what was happening. I hung up and watched him through my kitchen window. He just stood there, calm now, looking at me with that gun in his hand, not five feet from where I'm standing now. And I did call, I did. It's just that by the time I picked up that phone again and dialed 911 I could see him raise the gun to his head and I knew I was calling the people who couldn't do a damn thing, that this was the kind of emergency that happens after too many other things have already gone wrong. He died right there, near the purple blooms of echinacea. The hard rocks around my garden catching his fall.

part four

Jackson

It's late and I'm downstairs watching the sports highlights on CBC news. I only get the one fuzzy channel out here at the lake, plus the TV is about the size of a small microwave, so I can't see much except for the bright green baseball fields and a bunch of players running in different directions.

Earlier, when I was watching the news, they had this story about some little town in Arkansas that had a tornado come through it and rip most of the houses from their foundations, toss trees around, knock down fences. They showed the elementary school, how it just collapsed like some giant kid came along and stomped on it.

It's funny how a storm can sweep through somewhere like that, and everybody hears about it on the news and some people even send money and teddy bears for the kids or whatever and then by the next week it's like it never happened. But not to the people who still live there, not for the ones whose trailers were flattened into a pile of useless tin or whose boats were flooded when they crashed along the rocks. For them, they'll be repairing the damage for a long time. But for most people it was just like a blip on the radar and then it disappeared.

I'm getting tired of the fuzzy baseball highlights, since I never liked the game much anyways, so I get up and flick off the TV. As soon as I do it gets real quiet. The kind of quiet you can only get out at a lake.

The kids are asleep in the loft upstairs. The downstairs has this big open room with a table my dad made himself out of pine trees he felled on the property, the sofa bed with the orange cushion, the pine TV stand my dad made, and an old ripped-up recliner. There's a couple of small bedrooms with fake-wood panelling and that's about it, besides the sink and the old fridge that clunks and dies every once in a while, and a two-burner stove that needs a good cleaning.

I head over to the fridge, trying to keep quiet, and I grab myself a beer, then head out to the front porch. Out here you start to notice the sounds creeping out of the night, like the croaking frogs, the splash of a fish, the lonely loon calls. I settle into one of the lawn chairs and set my beer on the porch railing. It's something out here. There isn't another soul in sight. It's July long weekend coming up and soon the families will come out and camp, the high school kids'll be out here every chance they get.

Makes me think of my dad a lot more when I'm out here. Going out in the fourteen-foot aluminum and fishing for trout, fetching him beers from the shallows of the lake where he'd tied the bottles together and left them to keep cool—those were the days before the fridge. Out here he hardly ever got mad, he hardly ever called me useless or smacked my hands across the dinner table or flicked bottle caps at me to get my attention.

Anyway, I guess I should mention that Caroline, well, she's upstairs too, in the bed in the little loft with the window wide open. My bed. The one I've been sleeping in since I left our house.

Thing is, I figure we've had our own storm pass through here and what happens in these kind of natural disasters is that you turn to the ones you love and maybe for a little while all the wrongs they've done you are temporarily forgotten. I'm not saying I'm going to ditch Caroline to the wayside again after it all settles down again. At least, I don't think I will. No. It's just that after Mikey died things changed for me, the way I saw things got scrambled up a bit.

There we were, all of us at the funeral together and then at the wake, sitting out on May's veranda there and I was just looking around at all these people I'd known all my life and thinking how we were like a bunch of strangers. How we really didn't know each other at all anymore. Or maybe it was actually the other way around. That we did know each other now. That all those little things you try to ignore about people, all those bad habits or cruel words or things they did that they shouldn't have, you try to brush aside. And now all of those things were up on the surface. And some of them I could live with and some I couldn't.

Not that I was thinking about Caroline then. No, at the time I was thinking more about Daniel, actually. Watching him sit there all pale and sick-looking, draining his beer and reaching for another from the patio table. Thinking about how him and Mike, they'd been closer than him and me, for a long time. I was thinking how in some ways Danny was still a kid, still looking for thrills, still trying to see what he could get away with, what he could talk himself out of, and I figure somewhere along the road I just got tired of it. It just wore me out.

And I was thinking about that night out at Black Rock. That boy who died. The fact that Danny did that, he was responsible for that whether he was a kid himself or not. Most people, they would have a thing like that happen and maybe they would change their ways. Maybe they would stop bullying and being a prick and drinking all the time and cheating on their wives, but Danny never did. It occurred to me out on May's porch that maybe I was waiting for him to be a better person all those years. Maybe I could see it in him and I was just hoping it would come out. But I figure he must be a bit like Black Rock himself. There might be something valuable in there, there might be something good, but you'd have to blow the whole mess sky high to find out for sure.

It's not pretty, but it's just the truth. And then all those people at the funeral getting up and talking about Mike and how he was such a good guy and he'd give you the shirt off his back and I had been sitting there thinking, *Who are they talking about, here?* Just because a person is dead, it doesn't make him a saint. All you had to do was look over at Kali sitting there with her girls and see how all her happiness had been pricked out of her like air from a balloon and you wondered when it would ever fill up again and I was mad as hell at Mike for what he did. Mad as hell for all those chances he had, all those years he just didn't get his shit together.

I don't know. I guess I sound like an asshole. I guess I sound like I'm judging these guys or something, but maybe I am. Maybe if I had been judging them more, speaking up more, some of this stuff wouldn't have happened.

And then Caroline sidles up and sits beside me. The first thing I notice is she's drinking lemonade, although I guess it could've had vodka in it or something. And I was about to tell her that anything she had to say she better go ahead and say through her lawyer until we sorted out all the custody crap, but what comes out of her mouth is, "I been going to AA, Jackson."

And I look over at her and I can see this realness that hasn't been there in a long time. She's not drunk and she's not hungover. "Yeah?" I try not to seem too interested, just sit there watching Jessie as she fusses with Lily's wild curls on the porch swing. Sunny's sitting beside her on a lawn chair, her head on Big Bobby's shoulder. Jess has a cigarette burning in an ashtray by her feet, but I haven't seen her take a drag since she lit it. And even though she's working on Lily's hair, combing it out with her fingers, her eyes are a million light years away from anything that might be happening on that porch.

Caroline keeps talking. "Yeah. I've been to eight meetings so far. Lorraine ... that's my sponsor ... she says I need to start working on the steps with her. You know, one on one. She says when I do I'll probably start to realize what a mess my life is and I probably won't like it much, but that's when I can start making the big changes."

"Uh-huh." I watch as Lily gets free and heads down the steps to the backyard, where my boys and some other kids are whipping a frisbee at each other.

Caroline leans in and all I smell on her breath is sugary lemon. "But one thing I figured out already is that I want to try again, Jackson, I want another shot." She's talking quietly, evenly, and I can tell she's trying to stay in control, probably because of all the people out there, but she doesn't need to worry because as far as I can see not a single one is paying any attention to her. They have their own worries.

"I need to be with those boys. I'm not going to end up like Mikey, Jackson, I swear." She reaches out and puts her hand on my arms and I don't move it away. "In fact, when I heard that he was high when he did this," her voice lowers to a whisper, "when I heard he'd been drinking for days and he was high on coke and god knows what else, that's when I picked up the phone. That's when I knew I had to stop. That's what they call hitting bottom. In the program, I mean. I guess Mikey's bottom worked for me too."

I wanted to believe her. And I knew that maybe I shouldn't. But I could feel her warm hand on my arm, that hand as small as a girl's, and I could feel this little tremble in it and I knew she was scared, she was terrified I would say no. I just looked at her and I said, "So what's step one?"

And she smiled and said, "Admitting I am powerless over alcohol and that my life has become unmanageable."

I nodded. Squeezed her hand. "Well," I said. "That's a good start, anyways."

And that's all you can hope for. A good start. A fresh start. As for me, well, I figured out pretty quick that I'm not going back to that house that we lived in. No, that whole life we were living there has to change. I mean, if you're the kind of thing that hides under rocks and that rock gets lifted, how do you stay there? It was only a hiding place. It wasn't where you were meant to be.

After the wake was over they all started to wander away. Kali came out to the porch and just gave us a wave and not much else before taking off and I wondered for a second if I would see her again. Jessie and Lily had left earlier with Kali's girls. It's funny ... when I hugged Jessie goodbye I felt this terrible guilt come up for all those times I knew what Danny was doing and I never said a word to her. And I just whispered in her ear that I was sorry. I know she probably thought I meant about Mikey, but still. At least I said it.

And then Bobby took off with Danny to go get a beer at Laredo's for old times' sake. They asked me if I wanted to come, but I knew they didn't really want me to and I knew I sure as hell didn't want to either.

And so when everyone was gone but me and Caroline and the kids whipping the frisbee into May's peonies, I told Caroline. I told her if she wanted to come back that we had to make a new life. I told her I wasn't going back to my job because that was another rock I'd been hiding under for too long and now that I saw what else was under there it just wasn't the place for me. I told her I wanted to sell the house. I told her I wanted to move. Not far, because my mother is still here, and

Jessie and Lily and Sunny and Bobby, and the rest of my friends and family. But far enough.

She came out here to the cabin that first night, this scared fragile thing, and though I knew it wouldn't last because I know who she is and I know that spunk and sass and hot-headedness will be back whether she's drinking or not, I couldn't help but have a glimmer of satisfaction that for once I was the one calling the shots. We were in *my* family's cabin. I'd been taking care of the boys on my own, making their meals, driving them around, taking them out on the boat. I could do it all myself, I always could and so I didn't need her. I brought her back because I wanted to.

And so she swam with those boys and they laughed for the first time in a while and she tucked them in and sang them pretty much all the songs off of Elton John's *Love Songs*. I sat out here with a beer watching the fish jump in the twilight, watching the ripples they left when they went back under. I could hear her whisky-soft voice through the open window as she sang "Don't Let the Sun Go Down on Me" twice. I figure the boys were long asleep by the time she got to that one. I guess she was just singing it to herself. Or to me.

And now here we are, a couple days later and four more AA meetings under her belt. And sure, she's let a snide comment slip here and there about some folks in her meetings being losers, and she's even told me one night how she just wished she could have one beer and how it wouldn't kill her, for god's sake. But she didn't. She drank root beer with the boys and played checkers with them on the table my father built instead.

I'm just thinking of going in and crawling into bed when I suddenly remember that this afternoon when she drove out here after work she had the *Kootenay Blaze*, a weekly newspaper for the whole region from here to Nelson. She brought it up to the porch where I was tying some flies to the boys' fishing rods so we could go out on the boat before dinner. "Hey, there's something in here you might want to see," she said. I just nodded at her and kept on tying flies. I figured it was a wedding announcement for some old high school friend or something, so I let it go. I actually forgot about it until now.

I head back inside and take it off the kitchen counter where I left it when I made some dinner earlier. She'd folded the pages over and circled something in the classifieds with a dark pen.

I take it back outside with me and settle back into my chair, lighting a match and starting the Coleman lantern. The frogs are having a party out here on the lake, and it's suddenly so deafening I wonder if it will wake the boys. I hold up the paper. I have to squint a little to see it, but I can make out the words:

Home Business 4 Sale, Creston area.
Mechanic's shop on acreage with small house.
Good local clientele. Home needs work, but lots of potential.

Well, how about that. I sit back. Reach for my beer and take a swig. How about that. And I know right then and there that I want it. I know I might not be able to get it, I know I might call tomorrow and find out it's gone already or find out there's things wrong with it ... but it's the first time since figuring out all the things I didn't want that I finally know what I do want. And hey, I even know I tried it before and I know that I failed. But what the hell. Maybe it's time to try again.

Kali

I’ve sent the girls with Bio-dad. He came right away when I called
him. I should have called him earlier, but I guess I couldn't even think
straight. I just had to get through those few days, the funeral … Anyway,
he was here within an hour, though it's an hour and a half to his ten-acre
property on the outskirts of Nelson. I thought at first I should go too,
that I should just go and lie in the Mexican hammock that he has tied
between two gnarled pear trees and sink deeper into this fog, this haze
of half-memories and the far-off numbed hint of pain, like a tooth
that continues to throb even after the dentist has frozen it. But I knew
it would be a distraction, with Bio-dad plying me with vegetable curries
and bread he baked on a flat rock outside in the sun, or the connection-
seeking best intentions of the meandering hippies who populate his
land, living in yurts, trailers, sleeping under the stars.

I don't need distraction. I need the opposite of distraction. I need
focus. Clarity. That's why I've sent the girls away. I found that I somehow
couldn't function, I couldn't think, because despite the tragedy, despite the
life altering, the girls still wanted their toast and honey in the morning,
they still wanted the *Arabian Nights* stories read to them at bedtime, they
still wanted to be hugged and kissed and patted and told it's going to
be okay. And I did that at first, but then I found I couldn't. Probably
when I realized I was going to have to Do Something. Whatever that
Something might be.

What I've learned in my two days alone is that it's obvious I can't
stay at the cottage. The night haunting of my garden hasn't disappeared
as I sit trembling in my bed, listening to crickets, frogs, the terrible
screaming ghost cries of a coyote pack. I try to meditate, I take my
own herbs, I drink my own teas, I light candles and place them in the

four directions, I play Buddhist chanting on my stereo, and still I only see that morning. I only see the gun, hear that crack like the sky was splitting open, then the terrible, sudden silence. And I still see the way the sun shone down, illuminating the beauty all around the gruesome figure crushing my flowers, some faceless body who was no longer anyone I had known, no one I could recognize. And then that sound, that high wail like a thousand Celtic women keening for their dead. I looked around to see who it was before realizing it was me.

How can I stay somewhere that still has a phantom stain that like Lady Macbeth I will never erase? I spread fresh earth over the garden beds to cover the blood, but it had soaked in long before, the plants indifferent to the source of this new richness, this seeping of minerals into their roots.

And so I realized this morning as I lay in my messy bed, piles of clothes strewn around me, the blankets bunched, my favourite pillow nowhere to be found, that what I need is to go home, which is somewhere I haven't been for years, since before I had children even. All the moving, all the different businesses, the organic bakery, the short-lived travelling crepe stand at music festivals, the jewellery making. All this running away, this trying to find my true self. All the havoc this coming and leaving has created in the lives of those around me.

I want to go home now. To my mother. *She's* home, her surroundings don't matter. She's home wherever she is, Uganda, London, East Vancouver ... she's where I can go to lick my wounds. I can't pretend anymore to be worthy of this name she's given me, this warrior Hindu goddess who doesn't shy away from the darkness, who stares it in the face and takes it down. I've stared it in the face. Now I want my mother.

She's in Varanasi. I tracked her down at her friend's place above the tailor when I got out of bed. When Chandra answered the phone my relief was so enormous, so engulfing, that I couldn't speak for an entire minute and just listened to Chandra crackling though the lines in her perky British accent. "Is anybody there? Hello? Who's calling, please?"

"It's me, Chandra," I finally blurted out. "It's Kali."

"Kali, of course! How are you, darling? Your mother's just come in from a lovely dip in the river and she's just rinsing off. You must remember, dear, how dreadfully muddy the water is here. It's like having a mud wrap and a swim at the same time! Of course, you can't mind all the pollution and garbage floating around either, can you?"

I just listened to her singsong, closed my eyes hard and pictured her at her ramshackle kitchen table overlooking the street, two blocks up from the Ganges, the holiest river in the world. The river where pilgrims come to wash away their sins, where locals come to purify themselves, where they float their dead on wooden rafts and light them on fire, send them off into the next world in a haze of smoke and flame.

I was a teenager when I was there last, sixteen years old and in my last year at the alternative high school I attended in East Vancouver. My mother had made contact with Chandra and Hugh through some university friends and knew they were overseeing an orphanage near the banks of the Ganges. Too perfect, my mother thought, as we had been planning a "working holiday" and had been considering volunteering in India. Too perfect that they had an opening for volunteers, and of course not at all coincidence that it happened to be so close to the very river my mother had devoted three years of study to in university. Not a coincidence, of course, because all things were meant to be.

And so we spent a month bathing babies with questionable water, applying ointment to infected wounds. I sat in a stone courtyard and played with the children with a bright beach ball I had brought from home, blown up to their wide-eyed amazement into something colourful and fun. At that point I was only just considering going to university and studying political science, an idea that sprouted into fruition several years later and then died like an undernourished plant when I met my husband and had Kieran after two years at school.

But then I was all innocence and strength and filled with a fierce purpose: to serve others as my mother did, to push boundaries, to do what others thought irrational, even dangerous. I remember some of my friends' mothers saying, "India? But isn't it dirty? There are lots of diseases there. Have you had your shots?" And me flipping back my long hair and proudly telling them my mother didn't believe in shots.

I met wonderful people, both westerners and Indians, I learned to love tea, I spent four days on a thin mattress on the floor moaning after a bad yogurt drink from a street vendor. I fell for a young university student from Calcutta doing a paper on pilgrims to Varanasi and we spent two weeks wandering together in my spare time though elegant temples, confronted on the streets by the ravages of poverty and illness and then dining in the evenings with the educated upper class who were friends of the Brits my mother and I were staying with. Even at sixteen I was aware of the irony.

And though my mother and even Chandra and Hugh despaired at the fact that we sat up in our room on proper chairs at a table laden with enough food to feed ten more people, even though they did everything in their lives to balance out this injustice, I didn't. I sat slyly watching the candlelight flicker across the chocolate-smooth skin of my sweet summer romance and secretly wished we had a car, wished we were back in Canada and could do the things my friends were doing with their boyfriends, like go for a drive through Stanley Park, watch art house double bills at the Hollywood Theatre, walk hand in hand along Kits beach, something that would be considered scandalous here. Beyond my scattered moments of selflessness maybe I have always been a selfish creature at heart.

Anyway, this morning I finally convinced Chandra that I did need to speak to my mother right away. She went looking for her and moments later I heard a breathless "Kali, what is it? What's happened?"

"Something ... just the worst thing. Something terrible. Mom."

I heard the sharp intake of breath, even through the crackling lines. "The girls ... "

"No, no. Not that. It's Mike."

There was a pause, where I'm sure she was composing herself, and then possibly racking her brain. "Mike?"

"Mike. The man I was with. The man who worked at the smelter."

"Oh yes."

She didn't ask me what had happened because she knew I would tell her when I could get the words out. She had never met him, of course. She had been away for five years now. The last time I saw her was when she flew to Vancouver to spend a month with me after Summer was born. She had tried to get along with my husband, but it had ended badly, with him calling her a hypocrite do-gooder who chose to live half a world away from her grandchildren and her replying that it was better to be the kind of grandmother who prayed for the betterment of all humanity every morning at sunrise than to be a dictator who ordered his three-year-old to pick up every single piece of the dried macaroni she had accidentally knocked from the counter or be sent for a time-out.

"He's gone. He died. I killed him." The words came out before I could wind them back in, before I could hold them back like I had been for the past week. "I mean, I didn't kill him, I didn't actually kill him, but he died here, in my garden. He killed himself. And it was my fault."

There was a long pause in which I could hear faint murmuring, a soft chant of some sort as my mother processed this information the best way she knew how, probably evoking the help of some Hindu god or goddess as I counted the beats of my heart in my throat, the steady thumping. "I'm very sorry that your friend has passed on," she finally said evenly. "Now I want you to really think about what you just said. This is not the sort of thing to say lightly, to claim responsibility for another human being taking his own life."

"Oh, come on, Mom!" I burst out. "It happened to me and if I want to say it was my fault, if I really believe on some level that it would never have happened if it weren't for me, then just let me. It's the truth. There is no other way of seeing it. It wasn't my *karma* to have him die in my garden."

"Maybe it was his."

"No. I just don't believe it. I've been trying to, I've been trying really hard, but I just can't."

"It will take time. But you'll remember who you are. You'll realize it was his time. You're traumatized right now. Do you have a support network there?"

I thought of poor Jessie and her crumbling marriage, I thought of Mike's other friends worrying for their jobs, terrified their jobs might be making them sick. I think of Jessie, Sierra, Bio-dad and his meandering hippies. I could reach out to any of them, but none of them feel like home, none of them can provide any real answers.

"No," I said.

There was another pause. "Then you should come here. To me. I'll find the money. Just come."

"To Varanasi?" I pretended like I hadn't even considered it until now, but of course I had. I looked around my scattered kitchen, the piles of dishes, the loose herbs spilled across counters, piles of overdue library books on the table, the girls' shoes and sandals kicked off and left where they landed. I thought about what I would be leaving behind, both good and bad. I wondered if I would come back if I left. I wondered if I would even have stayed so long if it weren't for Mike. "When?" I asked.

And I'm no fool. I know this time will be different, that I won't be so young and vibrant and full of life. I will be worn and used and filled with the sadnesses and heaviness of the world. I won't have a young suitor who is beguiled by my forwardness escort me to the hidden treasures of the town. I won't be caring for a room full of sickly abandoned children, because I have two of my own to nurse back to health.

But some things might be the same. Perhaps I can still take some time to sit on the banks of the Ganges and watch the bright unwinding fabrics as the women unravel their saris to wash in the brown waters. I can still listen to the shouting of children, the coarse voices of men, the teeming bodies splashing and chanting, offering their watery devotion up to the heavens.

I can sip chai and ponder my existence, and when I'm ready, walk in, keep walking until the dark water laps my waist. Stand, as the women do, and wash my sins away in that river so filled, so brimming with the prayers of a million longing souls. And perhaps the smell of a funeral pyre will sting my nose, the ash brushing my cheeks and settling like fine silver dust in my hair. My new life beginning as another ends.

Daniel

I didn't mean for it to happen. Nobody, not one goddamn person who knows me would say that I ever woulda done something like that on purpose. I'm not a bad guy, here. Sometimes things just get out of control, and let me tell you something, the one who comes out looking like the asshole isn't always the one to blame. You have to look back, like, I don't know, half an hour or so, or three years, or ten years, or whatever to get the whole story.

I know I've done my fair share of stupid shit. I know I've done things that maybe I regret. But I'm not a bad guy. That's why I'm here in the pitch-black standing in the fucking dry grass in a field full of sleeping cows. That's why I need to climb this godforsaken rock.

I unbuckle my belt and slide the plastic ring of what's left of my six-pack onto it, then do it back up again. I need my hands free, but there's no way I'm going up there without my beer.

If you want the truth, I never did climb Black Rock. It's funny in these small towns, how rumours get spread and it's like a train rushing through the place, too fast to stop it. Not that I tried. That night people think I climbed it, about a month before that kid died, we were all pretty drunk and people were partying pretty hard and not paying much attention. I went around the side to find an easier way, a part of the rock with more chunks that stuck out or something, but no such luck. And it was dark as hell, not much of a moon.

So I just started climbing and after about three feet I landed on my ass in the sage and I was so drunk on rum and Coke I just lay back against the gravel and the prickly grass and I stared up at the sky. I must have passed out for a bit because next thing I knew Bobby was shaking me and asking me if I was okay. I guess he figured I fell or something.

And I told him I was just fine and he asked me if I climbed it and I said hell yes. And he must have been making out with some chick in his Trans Am because he never asked me why I didn't call him from the top, and neither did anyone else.

And so here I am, because you know what? I coulda done it. A lot of other guys did. That's what I told that kid before he fell—a lot of other guys did it, so why couldn't he? And I guess some part of me feels bad because maybe other guys did but I never did and who was I to force some stupid kid up there? It doesn't matter now. I know I'm just talking shit. Point is, I'm going. Here I am. Standing at the bottom looking up. And it's high, sure, but I can see lots of places I might be able to hold on to, and there's that flat platform on the top once I work my way up. Plus, the moon is so big it looks like it's touching the hills and it's shining like one of those glow-in-the-dark planets Lily has stuck to her ceiling.

So this is it. I take a breath. I find an outcropping about six feet up and I grab on and pull my boots up to a small ledge. I reach up again and take another step. Slowly, bit by bit, I make it about halfway before I start sweating, start thinking how it could hurt if I fell now. How it could kill me. And every foot I go, I make a point not to think about what I did. Not with the kid, but the other thing. I make a point just to climb. I tell myself, Danny, if there's one goddamn thing in your life you're going to do right it's climb this fucking rock. Period.

I have to stop for a minute as I get closer to the top, because I'm having trouble getting my breath and I feel so dizzy I'm thinking I might pass out and then I'd be done for sure. It's then, while I'm resting, that I get a good picture of Jessie standing in the kitchen back there and I feel it like a punch to the gut because like I said I didn't mean for it to happen. And I have to breathe real slow and tell myself just to climb and stop thinking. But then as I reach up again and feel the cool surface of the rock for somewhere else to grab I wonder if maybe she'll call the cops. I mean, I doubt she will. It was an accident. It was definitely not something I meant to happen, which makes it an accident, right?

And while I'm thinking all this I suddenly feel this flat shelf above my head and I know I'm there, I've made it. Hauling myself over onto the top is even harder than the climbing, maybe because my arms are so tired they're shaking like I'm having a seizure, and also I have to be careful of the beer banging against my leg, because I don't want to crush it against the rock on my way over.

I just lie there for a sec, taking deep breaths, pressing my face into the cool rock. Then I flip myself over and sit up. Unbuckle the beer and set it beside me. Look around. I can see the lights of Grace River off to the left and then a few little pinpricks here and there where people are still sitting up in their living rooms watching TV. And then there's the shadow of the river moving along through town and the dark bumps of the hills and that's about it. Nothing you couldn't see from the steep part of the road on your way out of town. But I guess it's quiet. I guess it's peaceful, even. Although that's not why anyone I knew ever climbed the damn thing. It was supposed to be all about the danger. But it doesn't feel so dangerous anymore now that I'm up here. That kid, he could have made it. Just bad fucking luck, that's all.

Speaking of which ... I dig my smokes out of my shirt pocket and light one up. Take a long, slow drag and watch those lights flickering over in town. I guess you could say I screwed things up pretty bad. I guess you could say I let my emotions get the best of me or however they say that. Here it is: I figured things weren't so bad. I figured that Jess and I, well, it was just a matter of time. That she had some cooling off to do. And then when Mikey ... well, she was nice to me at the funeral, giving me hugs and everything. I kind of thought it was almost like old times for a bit there.

But then this morning I go out there to the house to get my golf clubs and say hello and to tell the truth I could have used a friend to talk to and she had said if I needed to talk about Mikey to come on out for coffee sometime. So I did. I figured it was a good time. And then I'm driving along the road toward the house and I see that fucking hippie's van pulling out of the driveway. Out of *my* driveway. And I think, Now keep calm, Danny, there's probably a good reason, but I can feel myself getting worked up because what the hell reason could there be?

He pulls out of the driveway before I get to it or I would have blocked him off and asked him a few friendly questions, and he takes off in the opposite direction at a good clip, dust flying up around his van. I don't get a good look at him. All I see is his arm resting on the windowsill. Looking relaxed. Not a care in the world. Fucking town's going down in flames, Mikey's … well, anyway … and he's looking like he doesn't have a goddamn care in the world.

So yes, I'm pretty pissed by the time I park the truck by the shed and head up to the house and up the stairs and across the porch. And I'm thinking that maybe there was a lot more going on here than all the bad things I did, that maybe there's a whole other reason this marriage is falling apart, and he just drove down the fucking road with his arm out the window … And no, I don't knock, and yes, I slam the door behind me when I come in the house and I yell her name instead of saying, *Jess, honey, I just dropped by for tea*. Because I want some answers.

And so she calls me from the kitchen and there she is with her big canning pot on the stove and she's got jars lined up along the counters, some empty and some full of what looks like beets and the way she looks at me over her shoulder like I'm the last man on god's green earth she wants standing in her kitchen as she stirs her finger in the pot full of water makes any doubt I had about the nature of their little relationship pretty much disappear.

And all I can say is, "What the fuck?" And she says, "Hello to you too" and she starts to arrange her jars a bit and I say, "What the fuck was he doing here?" And she shakes her head and looks out the window and she doesn't say anything and it drives me crazy because I know that look, that look that tells me, *Daniel, she's thinking about a lot of goddamn things and you my friend are not one of them.* And I just lose it, thinking about her and that guy, because I just know something happened, I'm sure of it, and this whole time I've been going through all this shit with work and Mikey and she tried to blame me for everything and look at her. Refusing to talk to me, staring out the goddamn window. So I charge over there and I grab her arm and I say, "Hey!" because I just want her to fucking talk to me, notice me, and she pulls her arm away and says, "Don't you touch me" and gives me this disgusted look, like I'm the lowest scum on the earth. And that's where things went bad, that's where that one step, the arm grabbing, it turned to something worse.

It turned into me grabbing her shoulders and pushing her back against the counter and yelling at her and calling her names that I will not repeat here and then the jars started smashing and spilling their red liquid all over the floor around our feet and when I finally snapped out of it and saw how dead her eyes were, how they had gone from scared to dead, I just pushed her away and backed off. And I could tell she was okay, because nothing I did could have really hurt her, but when I left her standing there in her jeans and her summer camp T-shirt soaked through with beet juice, and those smashed jars and the pool of red on the floor and all over the counters I couldn't deny the fact that it looked pretty bad, that it looked like something worse than what it was.

And now here I am wondering what's next. Will she call the cops? I don't know. She didn't say another word to me, just stood there looking down at herself, pulling her shirt away from her skin. Like I said, she wasn't hurt or anything. Once she cleaned up the mess nobody would even be able to tell anything happened.

But I guess my chances are pretty much shot now as far as moving back there goes. What pissed me off the most was she didn't say anything. She didn't tell me. She didn't tell me what I wanted to know about her and that guy. All I wanted were some answers. Then maybe we coulda got past it, I don't know. And yeah, I figure I'm entitled to be pissed off seeing some guy I felt it was necessary to give a little wake-up call to a couple weeks ago pulling out of my wife's fucking driveway.

Anyway, I guess it's official now. No wife, no job, no best friend. I wonder why I don't just want to jump off this rock altogether. But I don't. I guess some things are still worth living for. There's Lily. Even though I may have screwed things up pretty bad there with Jess, Lily's still my kid. She belongs to me too. And AXIS will open up again soon. It's just a matter of time. It's the only thing that's a sure thing in this town, the only thing worth depending on. Worth waiting for.

I reach for a beer, snap it off the plastic. I pop the top and hold it high into the night sky. This one's for you, Mikey, I think. And then I take a long sip, staring out there into the dark. Thinking how hard it was to get up here. Wondering how the hell I'm ever going to get down.

Jessie

We went camping once, me and Daniel, before we had Lily. We followed the Grace River south, past the border, all the way down to where it flows out into the Pacific in this cute little town in Oregon. I remember tracing the shape of that river as we drove along the winding highway through southern BC to the mountains of northern Washington. I watched it go from calm and silvery to rushing green and stormy on the outskirts of Spokane. I wanted to remember what it looked like, to somehow have it printed in my mind. I wasn't sure why. I just wanted to see how it changed as we drove along. How everything about it changed, but it was still the same old river.

I was thinking about that this morning on my way to my mom's to get Lily. After Daniel. After what happened. I wasn't thinking about what happened, I was thinking about the river as I drove along toward town closer to where the heart of the damage was. According to Liam, anyway. See, he had come out to the farmhouse before Daniel came along. He came because he was making another trip out Nelson way and he was driving though town and he wanted to check on me, see if I was okay. He said he had wanted to tell me something before he left and he hadn't gotten around to it. He wanted me to know that it wasn't a hopeless cause. That's what he said while he stood on my porch. I had beet juice on my hands and splattered across my T-shirt from pouring the beets into the jars, but I was still happy to see him, even though I knew it was another goodbye.

Anyway, he meant the river. He said just because some parts of it were toxic and even deadly and could make people sick, that it didn't mean that there weren't parts that were still clean and pure and good. And that was why he did what he did, because there was still hope. And the heart of the damage, he said, was close to these towns like Grace River, where there were too many people who didn't want to think about it or change it or care about it. If you go north, he said, to the source, it's still pretty clean and healthy. He told me not to underestimate the power of rivers. Or the power of people to do what's right. And then he hugged me, beet juice and all, and left.

And then Daniel came. And when *he* was gone I left the farmhouse just how it was. I didn't clean up the pools of red or sweep the pieces of glass. I stripped off my jeans and T-shirt and I left them on the floor too. I knew no amount of scrubbing would ever get those stains out. Then I went upstairs and had a shower. I made a pile of clean T-shirts, my cutoffs, two pairs of jeans and some underwear and carried them into Lily's room where I made a pile of her clothes too. I also grabbed her unicorn from the bed and a couple of her Angelina Ballerina books and her Silver Cloud Barbie with the diamond studs in her ears and her hair chopped off and coloured with a pink felt.

I put all these things in a plastic bag from the hardware store and I walked out the door. It was strange, because I wasn't shaky, I wasn't freaking out. I wasn't sad. I didn't look back when I walked out the door, I didn't even glance over at the kitchen and what was left in it. I didn't think. I didn't wonder. I didn't wish. Nothing. I just left.

I left the door wide open when I walked out and then I got in the truck and pulled out. I didn't look back at my garden, I didn't look back at Lily's bike lying in the driveway. I didn't think about all of Lily's toys or my picture albums or the scrapbook I made of Lily's first two years or my horse riding trophies or my prom dress hanging in the closet smelling like mothballs. I didn't think of all that until later.

And then I drove along the river, like I said, window down, churning up dust and pebbles as I went. I drove past Kali's house and I didn't wonder how she was. I drove along toward town and when I saw the old acreage with the mechanic's shop that Jackson tried to run once, I didn't think much about him either.

I thought about putting on music, but I was afraid to fill my head with anything else. I was waiting to start thinking about things.

I drove through downtown, past the Steelworkers Inn, past AXIS

Memorial Arena, over the bridge to my mom and dad's. I parked in front of their house and I walked up their perfect little walkway and when I got to the bottom of their steps I stood there a minute looking at my mother's garden gnomes, at this one in particular that I could tell she'd painted and fixed up because she'd drawn a big pink smile on its little plastic lips that hadn't been there before, I could tell that the paint was over the lines of what had been a more sombre expression. And I reached my bare foot over and I kicked it. Hard. It fell against the bottom concrete step and tumbled backward into her patch of black-eyed Susans, staring at me the whole time. Then I walked up the steps and opened the door and went in and called for Lily. She came running from the kitchen, where I guess they were finishing up a late breakfast judging from the chocolate syrup smeared across her cheek.

My mother came in after her, a platter of bacon in her hand, a look of total confusion on her face. "Aren't you supposed to be at work, honey?" she asked.

I picked Lily up, set her on my hip. "Yup. I took the day off." Lily was silent, rigid against my hip. She could sense there was something wrong.

My mother shifted the bacon to the other hand. "Well, why don't you join us?" she asked, still looking like maybe she should call the psych ward and tell them to stand by for further instructions. My dad hollered from the kitchen, "Come on in. Your mother made Belgian waffles."

But I backed toward the door, keeping a smile plastered on my face, probably looking a lot like that garden gnome I'd kicked over into the flowers. I shook my head. "No. I'm taking Lily on a little trip." As I said it a plan formed. I mean, I knew I was going somewhere. I knew I wasn't staying at my parents' or anything. I just hadn't figured out exactly where I was going yet. But now I had an idea.

"A trip?" Now she had that warning sound in her voice, like when I was a kid. That, *Oh, I'm just repeating what you said, but really I'm about to tell you that it ain't gonna happen.*

My father appeared in the doorway, his Blue Jays coffee mug in hand. "Where to, Jess?"

I looked at Lily and she looked at me back, the first hint of a smile on her chocolately lips. And then I felt it all coming back to me. The thoughts. The realness. My self. And I felt like shit, I won't kid you, I felt confused and strange and afraid, and I could suddenly even feel a throbbing in my left shoulder where Daniel had grabbed me hard and pushed me. But I knew I was doing the right thing. Whatever it was. "We're going away. Camping. Just me and Lily."

"Yay." Lily clapped. "Can we have marshmallows?"

I nodded, still thinking through what I'd just said. I set her down and she headed for the door and started to put on her sandals.

"Camping?" My mother's eyebrows couldn't have been raised much higher without becoming part of her hairline. She set the bacon down on the coffee table and folded her arms. "You're not making any sense."

"No?" I chewed on my lip, eyed the door. I just needed to get through it. For some reason it seemed impossible, but I just had to do it. The smell of sugary pork and grease and vanilla and syrup wafted through the room, which was already starting to gather heat from outside.

"No," she said firmly. "You have a job. You have responsibilities. Especially now." She looked pointedly at Lily, then at me.

"Mom, do you remember when I was fifteen and I wanted to go to that 1950s dance? I stayed up so late the night before tearing apart one of your old dresses and trying to get it to fit me properly?"

She looked confused but recovered quickly. "Sure I do. That dress was in tatters by the time you were done with it."

"Right." I could see that Dad was watching me closely while he sipped his coffee, his glasses nudging the rim of the mug and knocking them off centre. "Well, what I remember about that is that the next day I found out that they had changed the theme to Hawaiian Luau. And I'd already been working on the dress, and I'd gotten some old shiny shoes from the thrift store and I'd bought some of those bobby sock things. And so I was pissed off. I was mad that they changed it. Remember?"

She sighed heavily and glanced over at my dad, wanting him to hop on board with the whole psych ward thing, probably. But he just had another sip.

"And you said to me ... do you remember what you said?"

Lily rose from her place by the door and was now wandering over to

Hornet, my parents' yellow-and-black-striped cat, who was sitting under the coffee table eyeing the bacon and swishing his tail.

My mother held her hands up as though to say, *Enlighten me.*

"You said that I wasn't on the planning committee for the dance. You said that I never made decisions, or if I did that I never stuck to them, and so how could I be mad at the dance committee for changing their minds? You said if I had pitched in and helped plan the dance I would have a say in whether they changed their minds or not but that people who don't want to take responsibility don't get to complain when others make decisions for them ... you went on and on, Mom, for a fucking hour, I swear, and all I wanted was to wear that stupid dress I had stayed up making and it didn't even fit me properly. Do you seriously not remember this?"

And I knew I was mad, I could feel the heat of it rise up in my chest, but I also knew it wasn't her I was mad at and so I tried to get control. All three of them were watching me silently, my mother probably shocked by the fact that I just swore at her.

"Well," I said. "I guess what I'm saying is that you're right. I've never taken much of a stand for anything, so I don't have much right to complain. And I'm not. I'm not going to complain about my job anymore, or about my messy house. About Daniel." His name on my tongue tasted like poison. I wanted a drink of water to wash it away.

She tilted her head. "Well, what *are* you going to do?" She might as well have added "Missy" at the end of it.

"I'm going camping,"

Lily raised her arms in a silent "Yay," but she seemed to know that she shouldn't say it out loud. She tried to pet Hornet, but he swiped at her and jumped up on the coffee table to try to get some bacon. My mother moved fast and scooped up the platter before he could reach his paw out.

"Jessie, I can't for the life of me figure out what camping has to do with anything."

I shrugged. "Camping is fun. And I've never done it on my own. With Lily, I mean. I've never done anything on my own. Not ever." I looked over at Dad and felt tears pricking my eyes, I could feel this desperation for him to understand, for someone to understand me. He walked over and set his mug on the coffee table. Then he nodded at me. Looked at Mom. Nodded some more.

"Well, sure. Camping is fun. You're damn right. Now … do you need anything for your little expedition?""

I exhaled. Thought about that for a minute. Smiled. "Actually … "

And now here I am, on the street outside my parents' house. I have loaded their old tent from the 1980s into the back of the truck along with two sleeping bags and a couple of blue camping foamies from the basement. My mother has grudgingly packed a cooler full of pop and Wonder Bread and peanut butter sandwiches and a pack of hot dogs and buns and a Tupperware container full of Oreo cookies.

My dad brings me a propane lantern and a waterproof box with matches and first aid stuff, which I wouldn't have thought of. He places them carefully beside the sleeping bags and pulls the corner of the orange tarp he's lent me over it and tucks it underneath. My mother is emerging from the house with an armful of what look like sweaters.

My dad gives me a friendly pat on the shoulder. "So where do you figure you're headed on your adventure, Jess?"

And I love him so much at that moment for not asking me all the things he must be dying to know. Not asking me about Daniel, which I'm sure he suspects has something to do with why I'm leaving. Not asking me about Mike, or my job, or when I'm coming back or if I'm coming back or where I'll go next. Because he knows I can't answer any of it. All I can do is take the first step. The whole trip isn't mapped out for me yet.

"I think we'll head north," I say.

"North, eh? How far do you figure?"

"I guess we'll follow the river up there. I guess we'll stop when it starts … I hear it's real pretty up there. "

He nods. "That's what I hear." Squints up at the turquoise sky. "Well. Make sure you two keep warm and dry at night."

"I will."

They stand on the curb to wave us away and after I've hugged them both and ignored my mother's questions of "When are you coming back" and "What about work" and told them both I love them I pull away from that house and I watch them as they wave, my mother looking worried and disappointed and my father looking proud and pleased. I look over at Lily, how she's twisted her whole body to try to see them, waving frantically. Then she flips around on her seat and points to the stereo. "Music!"

I crank up the AC/DC and we're on our way.

We pass AXIS, quiet and grey and sad-looking without all the cars and trucks parked in the lot, without those giant funnels of smoke pouring out of it. In about a mile I'll turn left onto Highway 13 and follow the river north.

As we head out of town and I listen to Lily sing along to "Back in Black" and feel the sun warming my face through the window I think back to that trip with Daniel all those years ago. How we headed in the opposite direction to the one I'm going in now.

And I think of how we camped in our little tent on the banks of the river and we lay in our sleeping bags at night and listened to the sound of water moving over rock, the shushing lullaby. How in the mornings I would crawl out of the damp tent and stretch and wander down to the riverbed. Most mornings I would jump into the river in my underwear and shriek when the cold water shocked me awake. Daniel never came in with me. He would sit in the entrance to the tent smoking a cigarette and shaking his head at me or else just keep on sleeping until I woke him up and told him we should get a move on.

I remember when we finally got to the end of the road. How we stood at the edge of the Pacific Ocean in that little town in Oregon and watched the river disappear into it. How all that beauty, or all that sickness and poison, depending on how you looked at it, just flowed along until it turned into something else entirely. Something bigger. Something more powerful. Something good.

Acknowledgements

I couldn't have written this book without the encouragement and sharp eye of Betty Keller, whose dedication to helping writers focus and realize their dreams continues to amaze me.

Much appreciation to those who read the first draft of *Grace River* and offered their critiques and suggestions: Ghislaine, Sherry, Dana, Lizette, Gael, Sarah, and my wonderful aunts, Chris, Mary Lou, and Kate. Thanks to my parents, Janice and David, to Garrett and all my friends and family for their support, and to past and present writing group members, particularly Kim, Diane, Jim E., Vici, Jan, Carol, Steve, Jim S., Eugene, and Joan. Also to Clara and Rashmi for checking the India sections. A special thanks to my children, Teagan and Jake, for putting up with their dreamy, distracted mother. You are much loved.

Finally, I would like to mention those family members who passed away during the writing of this book: grandmothers Carolyn Knight Hendry and Elsie Stevens, grandfather Clifford Stevens, aunt Chris Palmer and great-aunts Jeanne (Mickey) Gifford and Mary Haggart. Their love and strength held me up and helped push me forward. They will all be greatly missed and remembered for the gifts they brought to my life and to the lives of everyone who knew them.

REBECCA HENDRY was born in Ottawa and grew up in Brockville, Vancouver, Peterborough, Montreal, and Yellowknife before settling on the Sunshine Coast at age eleven. She writes regularly for *Just Business Magazine,* and her fiction writing has appeared in the *Windsor Review, Dalhousie Review, Artistry, Wascana Review, Event, paperplates,* and *Room of One's Own.* Rebecca's short story "The Woman Across the Way" was longlisted for the 2005 Writers' Union of Canada short prose competition, and her short story "Jesse Beautiful" was nominated for the 2003 Journey Prize. Rebecca's interests include music, art, alternative medicine, travel, and movies. She has worked in film, theatre, and on music videos, and has taught creative writing to children. Rebecca lives in Roberts Creek, British Columbia.